SIMPLY
INSATIABLE

Books by Kate Pearce

SIMPLY SEXUAL

SIMPLY SINFUL

SIMPLY SHAMELESS

SIMPLY WICKED

SIMPLY INSATIABLE

Published by Kensington Publishing Corp.

SIMPLY INSATIABLE

KATE PEARCE

APHRODISIA

KENSINGTON BOOKS

http://www.kensingtonbooks.com

APHRODISIA BOOKS are published by

Kensington Publishing Corp.
119 West 40th Street
New York, NY 10018

Copyright © 2010 by Kate Pearce

All Kensington Titles, Imprints, and Distributed Lines are available at special quantity discounts for bulk purchases for sales promotions, premiums, fund-raising, and educational or institutional use.

Special book excerpts or customized printings can also be created to fit specific needs. For details, write or phone the office of the Kensington special sales manager: Kensington Publishing Corp., 119 West 40th Street, New York, NY 10018, attn: Special Sales Department, Phone: 1-800-221-2647.

Aphrodisia and the A logo Reg. U.S. Pat & TM Off.

ISBN-13: 978-0-7582-4138-2
ISBN-10: 0-7582-4138-0

First Kensington Trade Paperback Printing: May 2010

10 9 8 7 6 5 4 3 2 1

Printed in the United States of America

This book is dedicated to the people who make things happen in my literary world. My agent, Deidre Knight, and all the wonderful folks at The Knight Agency. And John Scognamiglio, my editor at Kensington, who never even blinks when I tell him what I'd like to write next. Thank you both.

1

London 1819

He'd made a fool of himself.

Over a man.

Lord Minshom raised the bottle at his elbow, drank deeply, then carefully set it down again. He licked the brandy from his lips and tasted his own defeat and humiliation at the hands of that upstart, Lord Anthony Sokorvsky. A man who'd had the nerve to walk away from him—from *him*!

All of London was whispering about how his former sex slave had forsaken him for a woman. Minshom smiled bitterly in the direction of the fire and exhaled, feeling the tug of recently healed bone. At their last meeting, Sokorvsky had punched him so hard he'd ended up unconscious at the bottom of the stairs with two cracked ribs. Luckily, Robert had been there to drag him away before Sokorvsky and his nauseating lady love had descended the stairs to gloat over him.

Minshom picked up the bottle again and drank until there was nothing left. And it wasn't as if he was "in love" with Sokorvsky. He didn't love anyone, didn't believe he was capable of it anymore. All his sexual encounters were exercises in power, opportunities to show that he was still at his peak and able to subdue or seduce anyone he wanted.

Yet Sokorvsky had found the balls to walk away from him. And for the first time in his life, despite his threats, Minshom had given up the pursuit and allowed his former lover to follow his heart. He grimaced at his own saccharine choice of words. Was he slipping? Was he losing his touch?

"My lord?"

He turned his head toward the door of the oak-paneled study, blinked at the blurred outline of his valet and occasional secretary, Robert Brown.

"What?"

Robert came farther into the room. His dark red hair glinted in the meager candlelight, the only spot of color against his pale skin and somber black attire.

"Would you like to retire for the night, sir?"

Minshom held out the brandy bottle. "Get me another one of these."

Unlike most of his staff, Robert held his ground and didn't even duck.

"I'll get you more brandy if you take it up to bed with you, how's that?"

"Go to hell."

"I'm already there, sir; I've lived with you for far too long. You'll have to think of something else to threaten me with."

Minshom raised an eyebrow and threw the bottle toward the marble fireplace, where it shattered into a million glittering fragments and almost put the fire out. "Get me my brandy, damn you."

Robert sighed. "I'll go and get someone to clean that up, sir. I wouldn't want you cutting yourself."

"Leave it."

Robert hesitated, his brown eyes fixed on Minshom's. He

was in his early thirties, had come to Minshom Abbey as a stable boy and had stayed with his master ever since.

"Sir . . ."

"Come here and kneel down." Minshom pointed to the rug in front of him.

"Are you sure you don't want to go upstairs? Anyone could come in."

"And see you sucking my cock? I'm sure they've all seen that before."

Robert looked resigned, but he did as he was told and came to kneel in front of Minshom. He eyed Minshom's groin.

"After the amount you've had to drink, I'm not sure I'll be able to get a rise out of you, sir."

"You'd better try hard then, hadn't you?"

Robert sighed again and undid the buttons of Minshom's placket, pushed aside his underclothes to reveal his half-erect cock. Minshom reached forward to slide his hand into Robert's thick pelt of auburn hair.

"Make it fast and hard; make me come."

He closed his eyes as Robert's warm mouth closed over his shaft and began to suck and pump his flesh. He hadn't been back to the pleasure house since his injury. The discovery that Sokorvsky's woman was Madame Helene's daughter hadn't helped either. Would he ever go back there? Was it time to move on?

Coward.

He could almost hear his father saying it, the way his lip would curl, the sting of the beating he would no doubt get for his impudence in begging for the punishment to end. He dug his fingers deeper into Robert's hair, heard his valet draw in a hurried breath and suck faster. Perhaps he hadn't completely lost his ability to make men sexually serve him after all. But then he and Robert had always been simpatico.

A slight commotion in the hallway below registered through his drunken arousal. He wasn't expecting guests and had told his damned butler to deny anyone who inquired. He had no desire to see the glee in his so-called friends' eyes as they recounted yet more gossip about Sokorvsky and his new love. To be fair, he'd liked Marguerite Lockwood, had felt an unexpected stir of interest in his loins despite his refusal to fuck women. She'd reminded him of someone . . .

The disturbance was getting louder, rising up the stairs, coming closer. The agitated sound of his butler's voice and the clearer high tones of a woman. What in damnation was going on? Robert stopped sucking and tried to raise his head. Minshom shoved him back down again.

"I didn't tell you to stop."

He didn't bother to turn his head as the door flew open and his butler started apologizing.

"I'm sorry, sir, she refused to leave and . . ."

And sure enough, his vision was filled with an apparition from the darkest recesses of his personal hell.

"Good evening, Robert, good evening, Minshom."

Minshom kept one restraining hand on Robert's head. He used the other to wave the butler away and waited until the door shut behind him before addressing his visitor.

"What the hell are you doing here?"

"Visiting you?"

"I didn't give you permission to do that."

She raised her eyebrows and took off her bonnet, holding it at her side by its wide blue ribbons. Her long brown hair was neatly parted in the center and drawn back into two coiled braids over her ears. At first glance, she still looked far too young to be anyone's wife, let alone his.

"I don't believe I need your permission to visit my own house."

"It's my house. Don't you remember? When you married me, everything you brought with you became mine."

"How could I forget? You've always been very good at making me feel like a possession."

He met her clear hazel eyes and smiled. "And yet, here you are. Where you are not wanted."

She sighed. "Can we stop this? I need to talk to you."

He glanced down at Robert. "I'm busy. Make an appointment with my secretary and get out of my house."

She regarded him for another long moment and then turned on her heel. "Fine, I'm going to bed. I'll see you in the morning when you are sober."

He closed his eyes as the door closed behind her, waited for the front door to slam as well and heard nothing. Dammit, where was the woman going? He sat forward and hissed as his now-flaccid cock caught on Robert's teeth.

"Sir . . ."

"What?"

He glared down at his valet who was busy wiping his hand over his mouth.

"Was that her ladyship, sir?"

"Yes."

"Did you finally send for her?"

"Of course not!"

Minshom shoved his seat back and stood up, waited for the room to readjust itself to his unbalanced drunken gaze. Where the hell had Jane gone? Surely she hadn't had the audacity to stay and bed down here for the night? He'd made it quite clear he wanted her off his property. Minshom started for the door, almost tripping over Robert in his haste.

The marble stairway was dark, and Minshom paused to listen. A door closed upstairs and he set off again, following the faint trail of lavender-scented soap Jane always left behind her.

He was aware of Robert tracking him, but at least his valet had the sense not to speak.

Minshom passed the door into his own suite and kept going down the hall. A faint light gleamed under the door of the room next to his. He entered without knocking and found his wife kneeling in front of the fireplace, encouraging a wisp of smoke to ignite the kindling.

"I told you to get out."

She rose slowly to her feet and faced him, her expression as mulish as he suspected his was.

"I am not going anywhere."

"Despite your age, you haven't put on that much weight." He allowed his lascivious gaze to flow over her, let her see it, resent it, waited for her to blush. "I wager I could still pick you up and toss you out myself."

"I'm sure you could, if you wanted to cause yet more scandal."

"You think I'm afraid of scandal?" He smiled. "My whole life is a scandal."

"I know. I might live in the countryside, but I do read the London newspapers and the gossip columns." She unbuttoned her drab pelisse and laid it over the back of a chair, meeting his gaze unflinchingly. "And I don't think you have done anything to be particularly proud of."

"And you think I care about your opinion?"

"Probably not, but there it is, all the same."

He moved toward the chair, picked up her discarded coat and held it out to her. "Put this back on. I wouldn't want you to catch a chill on your journey back to Minshom Abbey."

She ignored him and continued to unpack her small valise, taking out a long white nightgown and her hairbrush. He stared at the back of her head and realized that Robert had slipped into the room behind him. Jane was right. Did he really want more scandal? He was already out of favor with the *ton*.

Throwing his wife out into the street would certainly make matters worse.

But then, if he was already convicted, why not add to his infamy? He took a step toward Jane, then hesitated as she started to take down her long dark hair. God, he remembered watching her do this a thousand times, the anticipation building in his loins as she readied herself for bed, for him . . .

"Stop doing that."

She looked over her shoulder at him, her hands still busy in her hair.

"I can hardly sleep with all these pins sticking in me, can I?"

He throttled down his frustration and the unexpected surge of interest from his cock, knew he couldn't bear to watch her disrobe. He'd forgotten how clever she could be. Was this battle worth fighting while he was drunk and still incapacitated from his cracked ribs? In truth, he was in no state to follow through on his threats. Perhaps he should follow Wellington's example, make a strategic retreat and face her on the morrow.

"Are you sure I can't convince you to leave?"

"I'm staying." She walked toward him, and he tensed until she presented him with her back. "Can you undo my buttons and loosen my laces, please, Blaize?"

He recoiled from her as if she were a raddled old whore. When was the last time someone had called him by his given name? Dammit, he couldn't remember, never allowed anyone to get that close to him anymore, even Robert.

"I'm no serving maid. Do it yourself."

"But I can't reach."

"I don't care." He set his jaw and snapped his fingers at Robert. "Come here and help my wife, not that she deserves it."

He walked around to face her, received the benefit of the warm smile she meant for Robert, and headed for the door.

"I'll bid you good night, then."

She opened her eyes wide. "You're leaving?"

"What did you expect? Did you imagine I'd be so delighted to see you that I'd drag you straight into bed and fuck you?"

Her expression stilled. "No, hardly that. Good night, then."

He inclined his head a glacial inch and walked out, heard her start to chat with Robert and Robert's warm laughter in return. They'd always gotten along well and he'd been selfishly glad of it in the early years of his marriage. It was only a few feet back to his bedchamber, but it felt like a mile. He glanced back at Jane's door and scowled. Robert had better be quick about unlacing her, or he would feel the edge of his master's temper. How dare she turn up and act as if she had a right to be here?

He flung open his door, steadied himself against the frame and stared at his large four-poster bed. But, devil take it, she did have a right. She was, after all, his legally wedded wife.

"Are you all right, my lady?"

As her stays and gown were loosened, Jane gripped the front of her bodice to stop it from falling down and turned to Robert.

"Yes, thank you for your help."

His smile was warm, his slight Welsh accent as soft as butter. Despite her knowing he was Blaize's lover, they'd always had a good relationship.

"You're welcome." He hesitated, one eye on the door her husband had just slammed behind him. "Is there anything else I can do for you?"

"Not tonight, although I would appreciate it if you could arrange for one of the maids to help me get dressed in the morning." She brushed at her crumpled skirt. "I suppose the rest of my baggage is still in the hall, so I'll have to make do with this gown until I can unpack properly. I wouldn't want to face Lord Minshom in my nightgown."

"Neither would I." Robert bowed. "If it helps, I'm glad you

are here. The master has gotten himself into a devilishly difficult situation."

"I gathered that from your letters." She sighed. "I doubt
he'll let me help him, though."

"He probably won't, my lady, but we can hope. Give me
your gown and I'll have it pressed and freshened for you. I'll
also arrange for a maid to attend you in the morning." He hesitated by the door. "Sleep well, and I pray I'll see you tomor-
row."

"Why, are you worried I might not survive the night?"

Robert grinned. "I don't think his lordship has quite sunk to
those depths, ma'am, but maybe you should lock the door into
his suite, just in case."

Jane waited until he left and sank down into the nearest
chair. Her knees were still shaking, her breathing as ragged as
her thoughts. Blaize's study had stunk of brandy, and glass had
littered the fireplace. Was that how he lived now? In a permanent drunken stupor, not caring if anyone saw him use Robert
to satisfy his unnatural sexual appetite?

But perhaps having caught him at such a disadvantage had
worked in her favor. He'd backed down and allowed her to
stay at least for one night. When she'd first seen the cool detached rage in his pale blue eyes, she'd wanted to run away,
wanted to forget her stupid notion of making peace with him.

But giving in was never the best way to deal with her husband. He pounced on any show of weakness with the speed
and ferocity of a starving cat. It was her lack of fear that had
first won his interest and brought about their marriage ten
years previously. Jane bit her lip. Not that that had proved to be
much of a success . . .

On the long journey to London from Cheshire, she'd spent
many hours wondering how Blaize would look, if the depravi-
ties of his lifestyle would be reflected on his countenance. To

her dismay, he was as fascinating as ever. His gaze colder, perhaps, the pure line of his jaw and high cheekbones more sharply defined, but hardly the debauched drunkard portrayed in the satirical cartoons in the newspapers.

She got up and hurried to check that the door between the two suites was indeed locked. The thought of waking up with Blaize's hands around her throat wasn't pleasant. She returned to the fire, made sure it wasn't smoking and stepped out of her gown and stays. Her suite of rooms didn't look as neglected and unused as she'd assumed. They'd even been redecorated in soft shades of blue and lavender, her favorite colors. But then knowing Blaize's sexual appetite, they probably hadn't remained empty for long . . .

Her nightgown felt cold against her skin, and she crouched down beside the fire to warm her hands. There was no water to wash in and nothing to slake her thirst. She certainly wasn't prepared to draw attention to her presence in the house by requesting anything. She was here, and she was not going to leave until she and Blaize had explored what needed to be said.

She shivered despite the building heat. Knowing her cynical, malicious, enthralling husband, she didn't expect her task to be quick or easy at all.

2

"Thank you, Robert."

"For what, my lord?"

"For this, of course." Minshom gestured at the coffee pot and dry toast Robert had set on his desk. His study had been cleaned and there was no trace of the broken glass or the tang of spilled brandy to mar its chilly perfection.

"As I'm expecting my dear wife to come and accost me, the coffee will at least allow me to face her with some of my wits about me."

Robert snorted and Minshom scowled at him. "You find this situation amusing?"

"Of course not, my lord. Why would I? It's not as if you are afraid of her ladyship or anything."

"She doesn't scare me."

"No, my lord." Robert slowly raised his eyebrows before pouring Minshom a fresh cup of coffee. "That's not why you are desperate for her to quit your house. You're just concerned about her having to live amongst such sinful debauchery."

"No, I simply want her gone."

"Yet she is still here. Her ladyship was always very tenacious, sir."

"She was. Her family didn't want her to marry me because she was so young, and yet she wore them down." He flashed a smile at Robert. "She probably regrets that impulse now."

"Her ladyship has never struck me as impulsive. As far as I remember it, sir, she married you because she was in love with you."

Minshom put down his coffee cup and met Robert's gaze. "You are impertinent."

Robert shrugged. "Probably." He bowed low and opened the door into the hallway. "I believe her ladyship is just finishing her breakfast. Shall I ask her to attend you here?"

"I suppose so."

Minshom sat back in his chair and contemplated the pile of documents awaiting his attention. He really didn't have time to bother with his wife. Despite his reputation as a lascivious rake, he had significantly increased his family's fortunes over the past ten years. Apart from Robert, he employed no secretary. After his father's incompetent bumbling, he didn't trust anyone to do the job as well as he could, so the burden fell on him and him alone.

He scowled at the inkwell. Jane should be grateful that he never questioned the household accounts she dutifully sent him via his land steward at Minshom Abbey. She should certainly be grateful enough to leave him alone.

"Good morning, my lord."

He looked up and found her in front of him. Her plain blue traveling gown looked fresh as if she hadn't sat in it for hours during the previous day's journey. She'd always been like that, neat as a pin—except in his bed.

"Good morning, wife."

She sat down, even though he hadn't offered her a seat or

stood up to acknowledge her presence. He pretended to fix the nib of his pen and ignored her completely.

She delicately cleared her throat. "Would you like me to come back later?"

"I'd like you to leave. I told you that last night."

"Why?"

He looked at her then. "I believe you know the answer. You were the one who told me to get out of your sight and your life forever."

She sighed. "Blaize, that was seven years ago. Can we not move on?"

"Really? Seven years? Is that all?"

"It feels like a lifetime to me."

She held his gaze and he wanted to look away from the memories that surged between them, their shared past, their anguish . . .

"Why are you here, Jane?"

"To see you, to try to start again."

"And if I don't want to 'start again'? What then? I am quite happy with my current existence."

"But I am not happy with mine."

He got up, walked across to the window and presented her with his back.

"You have more than most women in this country will ever have—a beautiful home, enough money to waste on fripperies and ample food in your belly."

"And I am grateful for all those things, but . . ."

He swung around to face her. "Not grateful enough, apparently, because here you are, annoying me."

She didn't flinch at his sarcastic tone, actually dared to raise her chin at him.

"I only want what most women want: a husband, a family."

His gut clenched. "You have a husband."

"Whom I never see."

"And whose fault is that? As I already said, you were the one who wanted me gone."

"I was distraught. I was not myself, I . . ."

"I don't care, Jane." He walked back over and stared down into her eyes, hoped she recognized the complete indifference in his gaze. "I'm not interested in rehashing the past. I'm content with my life as it is, without you in it."

She stared at him for a long moment, as if searching for the truth on his face.

"You're very good at hiding what you feel, Blaize, you always have been."

"I'm not hiding anything. I am truly content."

"Being portrayed as a drunken pervert in the scandal sheets?"

He almost smiled. "I don't read that kind of filth, my dear. Perhaps you shouldn't either."

She opened her reticule, drew out a bundle of letters. "Even if I didn't read about you in the newspapers, I have plenty of correspondents to keep me informed of your latest scandal."

He raised his eyebrows. "Spying on me, Jane? I'm surprised at you."

"I have no need to spy. Your peers are more than happy to provide me with all the excruciating details of your private life whether I want them or not."

He circled her, trailed his fingertips along the gilded rim of the chair and almost touched the soft downy hairs at the back of her exposed neck. She shivered as his breath hissed out.

"So you rushed here to defend me?"

"Hardly." She sighed. "I just wanted to talk to you."

He left her side, returned to sit behind his desk.

"And now we've talked and I've told you to go away. Shall I order your carriage for this afternoon?"

She sat up straight. "I'm not going until you talk to me properly, Blaize."

He gripped his pen so hard his fingers hurt. God, she was infuriating, that calm voice, that complete disregard for his wishes.

"I have nothing to say to you that hasn't already been said."

"I doubt that. People change. *I've* changed—why can't you?"

He returned her smile with interest. "Because I don't want to and I don't regret anything?"

"You've always been stubborn." Jane got up and smoothed out her skirts. "While I *am* here, I intend to visit my old friends and get some new gowns made." She started for the door, paused before she opened it. "Which modiste would you recommend?"

"How the hell would I know? And you're not staying, Jane."

He realized he was talking to himself and an open doorway. Damn her! Where had she learned such composure? In the early days of their marriage he was certain she'd been far more amenable. What had happened to her?

He covered his face with his hands and groaned. Hell, even he knew that. She'd changed after he'd destroyed their marriage. It was ironic that her newfound courage was all his doing. He went and closed the door, took the opportunity to pace the carpet, hands clasped behind his back.

Perhaps if he kept out of her way and allowed her this small victory, this "visit," she'd leave without delving into their shared past again. He stared out of the window into the wintry street below. Damnation, what was the matter with him? He'd allowed Sokorvsky to best him and now he was bowing down to Jane?

He let out his breath, watched it condense on the window pane. Surely there was a better way to ensure that Jane wanted to go home with all the speed she could muster? He smiled slowly as an idea occurred to him. A glimpse into the hellish world he inhabited would probably be enough to send her away screaming, forever.

Jane found her way to the pretty little sitting room at the back of the house her mother had used as her primary domain. To her surprise it hadn't been altered at all. It still retained the faded yellow silk wall coverings, white paneling and lace-draped windows. With a sigh of relief, she rang the bell and then sat down in one of the comfortable wing chairs by the fireplace.

"Yes, my lady?"

She smiled at her old friend, Broadman, the butler Minshom had inherited from her parents when they'd given them the house as a wedding gift. She was somewhat surprised that her husband had kept him on.

"Good morning, Broadman. In future, can you make sure a fire is lit in this room every morning and a tea tray available at ten?"

The butler didn't quite meet her eyes. "Begging your pardon, my lady, but I'll have to check with his lordship, to see if that is acceptable."

"Of course, or ask Mr. Brown. I'm sure he'll be more agreeable."

"Are you staying then, my lady? Not that it is any of my business, of course." The butler bent to light the fire and then wiped his hands on his handkerchief.

"For a while." Jane smiled with more confidence than she felt. "At least until his lordship throws me out."

The butler nodded gravely. "Ah, well seeing as he hurt his ribs not so long ago, I can understand him not wanting to exert himself."

Jane blinked at the answer. She'd meant her comment as a joke. "Lord Minshom hurt his ribs?"

"Indeed he did. I'm not sure how, my lady, but his lordship was laid up for a couple of weeks, and right grouchy about he was too. I almost felt sorry for poor Mr. Brown having to deal with him."

Jane chuckled. "So do I. His lordship is not an easy man at the best of times."

"Really."

Jane covered her mouth with her hand and looked over Broadman's shoulder right into the face of her husband, who leaned negligently against the door frame, blue eyes frosty, his mouth a hard line.

"My lord, I didn't see you there!" The butler took a hasty step away from Jane toward the door and then stopped.

"Obviously, or you wouldn't have been indulging my wife's passion for gossip."

"Mr. Broadman and I are old friends, and he was hardly gossiping. I am your wife, after all."

Jane tried to keep her tone light, while wondering what on earth had prompted Blaize to come after her. She nodded at the obviously terrified butler.

"Please bring me some tea and some fresh ink, if you have any. I doubt the inkwell in the desk here is usable after all this time."

"Yes, my lady. Excuse me, my lord."

Jane waited as Broadman inched past her husband, who immediately shut the door behind him.

"Can I help you with something, my lord?" She gestured at the chair opposite hers. "Would you care for some tea when it arrives?"

"No, thank you."

His expression of distaste made her want to smile. He'd never shared her passion for tea, preferring coffee or the stronger lure of alcohol. He took two paces toward her and then stopped.

"If you insist on staying, *I* insist you come out with me to my favorite brothel so that you can see how happy I am with my life and how little I miss or need you."

She fought not to wince at such a blunt statement of disinterest and found the courage to smile instead.

"And if I agree, you will attend some balls and events with me in return, yes?"

"I didn't say that."

She held his gaze. "Yet it seems only fair."

"Since when has 'fair' ever been a measure between us?"

God, that hurt. He insisted that what had happened between them had no relevance to his present way of life, but he couldn't resist bringing up her mistakes at every opportunity. Perhaps it was time to acknowledge that, to try to get through to him again.

"You're right. I wasn't fair to you. I wasn't fair at all."

His expression froze. "Dammit, don't you dare apologize to me. That wasn't what I meant at all."

"But . . ."

He headed for the door and slammed it shut behind him.

Jane sighed. He was proving far more difficult to deal with than she had anticipated. It was as if he'd encased his softer emotions in a hard shell. If she hadn't known him better, she would've believed he was completely callous. But she'd seen him at his worst before, seen him despair and yet still find the strength to offer her comfort, which she'd spurned.

With renewed purpose she opened her mother's old desk and took out some writing paper. It was time to reconnect with her friends and find out the true state of affairs, whether Blaize liked it or not.

3

"Jane, my dear, how are you?"

Jane allowed herself to be drawn into a crushing hug by her much taller companion and kissed the powdered, scented cheek closest to her. She hoped her rain-dampened clothes didn't offend. She'd decided to brave the blustery weather and walk the short distance from Hanover Square to Crescent Place.

"Emily, you look so well."

Her friend laughed and pretended to pout, drew Jane toward a chaise longue designed in the Egyptian style. The large sunny drawing room was decorated in fashionable homage to the current craze for Egyptian artifacts. Yellow silk hung on the walls and a variety of fantastical golden objects graced the mantelpiece and the furniture.

"I look well enough for a woman with three children. You, however, still look like a blushing virginal debutante. Are you *sure* Minshom was capable of consummating your marriage?"

Emily gasped and clapped her hand to her mouth. Jane hurried over to remove Emily's fingers from her lips.

"It's all right, Emily. I know you were joking."

Emily sighed and returned the pressure on her hand. "Goodness. Jane, I'm sorry, that was quite uncalled for. It appears that living in London has sharpened my wits beyond what might be considered amusing."

Jane sat back and took a good look at Emily, admired the saffron yellow of her silk gown and the pale blonde curls framing her face. Despite her modest upbringing, Emily had done very well for herself and married the heir to an earldom. From what Jane could see, she hadn't let her new rank change her easy and friendly ways.

Jane smiled brightly. "How *is* George, and how are your children—in good health I hope?"

"They are all well. The children are in the countryside with my parents, and George and I are enjoying ourselves in Town without having to worry about them all." Emily sighed. "Not that I don't miss them terribly, mind, but it is nice to be away from them."

"I can imagine." Jane looked fondly at her best friend. She couldn't imagine ever wanting to leave a child, but perhaps that was just her, and she knew Emily was truly fond of her brood.

Emily poured them both some tea and sat down, her inquisitive brown eyes fixed expectantly on Jane.

"So what brought you to London? Did Minshom finally come to his senses and ask for you?"

"No, I came by myself. He was as surprised to see me as you are."

"But not quite so thrilled, I'll wager. I don't think most of the *ton* even knows he is married." Emily rolled her eyes. "The recent scandal about him and Anthony Sokorvsky has been the talk of the town for weeks."

Jane set her teacup to one side. "That's one of the reasons I came to see you first, Emily. I knew you'd have the best gossip."

"I always do, don't I?" Emily laughed, "Even at school I

was always the first to know which teachers were leaving, who was having an affair with whom, who had inherited a fortune."

She sat forward. "Well, as I told you in my letters, your husband had a 'relationship' with Anthony Sokorvsky for quite a while, but, recently, Sokorvsky ended it and went off with a woman. It was quite a surprise to everyone. Minshom bragged that he'd have Sokorvsky on his knees begging to be taken back, but it didn't happen, and now some people are laughing at Minshom and I suspect he doesn't like that at all."

"I suspect you are right."

Emily refilled Jane's cup and then her own. "And there are new rumors that he and Sokorvsky actually *fought*! That part is a little unclear, but it is true that your husband retired to his bed for two weeks after his last encounter with Sokorvsky at a house party."

Jane nodded. "It might also explain why Minshom didn't follow through with his threat to personally eject me from his house last night."

"He threatened to throw you out?" Emily's eyes widened and her mouth opened. "That man deserves to be thrashed. I can't imagine why you stay married to him."

"Because I don't have the necessary family connections, money or power to blacken his reputation and petition for a divorce?"

Emily shuddered. "And you wouldn't want to be divorced, darling. No woman wants that stigma."

"So you think that living apart from him is the perfect solution for me?"

"I don't know." Emily frowned. "It seems unfair that Minshom gets to cavort around London behaving abominably while you are stuck moldering in the countryside."

Jane suppressed a smile. "I hardly 'molder,' Emily. There is plenty to do in a house as big as Minshom Abbey, and I have some wonderful friends."

"You've always had a gift for making friends, Jane, but, re-member, I've met most of these acquaintances of yours and they are not *quite* in the same class as your peers here."

"But I hardly know anyone in London," Jane protested. "I didn't have a Season, like you—I married Minshom instead."

"And more fool you." Emily leaned forward to add hot water to the teapot. "You should have insisted on having both."

Jane shrugged. "In truth, my father tried to use the lure of a Season to stop me from marrying Minshom. He offered to give me the most lavish come-out he could afford if I'd put off mak-ing a decision about tying the knot."

"He was right to do so. You should've pretended to agree with him and then had both. Or you might have met a better man in London and told Minshom the engagement was off." Emily sighed dramatically. "Lord, I wish you'd never met that man, and at my eighteenth birthday party of all places! I'll never forgive my brother for inviting him."

"Can you imagine how Minshom would've reacted if I'd done that to him?" Jane's smile died. "And, in truth, I was so in love with him by then that I couldn't have abandoned him if I'd tried."

Emily's teacup rattled into its saucer. "You were too young to make that choice and he was too old for you."

"I was seventeen, Emily. You were only two years older than me when you wed George, and George is ten years older than Minshom!"

"George was already settled and looking for a wife. Min-shom was in his mid-twenties, far too young for a man like him to settle down, if you ask my opinion. I always felt Minshom never really came to terms with his need to marry you."

Jane sat back and considered her friend. Despite Emily's sunny exterior, she was very intuitive about people and their behavior.

"I can't argue with you about that. I think he married me despite himself." She sighed as the memories crowded around her. "It was if he was always looking for a reason to leave me. And, of course, as soon as I gave him one, he was off."

"I'm sorry, Jane. As I said, the man deserves to be horse-whipped." Emily reached across and patted Jane's knee. "Now, really, what are you going to do about him?"

"I'm going to have to make him listen to me and then discuss how we mean to go on. I realized I was tired of waiting for him to come back to me and tired of living my life in limbo."

"I can understand that. After what you went through, it must've been hard to move on."

"It was almost impossible." Unable to meet her friend's sympathetic gaze, Jane stared down at the busily patterned rug under her feet. "I hated everyone; shut everyone out of my life, even you. How long was it before I allowed you to call on me again? At least a year, if not more." Jane swallowed hard. "Thank you for keeping faith with me."

"Jane, you are my oldest friend; of course I'd keep after you." Emily's tone softened. "And, in truth, you didn't invite me that first time. I just turned up at your house and refused to leave."

"I'd forgotten that." Jane managed a smile. "I couldn't let you stand on the front steps all night, could I?"

"Not unless you wanted me to contract a chill, and just think of the scandal if I died on your doorstep!"

Jane met Emily's gaze and relaxed. At least here she had an ally, a friend who knew her and loved her despite herself.

"I need your help again, Emily."

"What can I do? Send George around to have a little chat with Minshom about his responsibilities?"

Jane shuddered at the thought of exposing the oh-so-amiable George to the lash of Minshom's tongue and uncertain temper. "Oh no, that won't be necessary. I was thinking of something else entirely."

"I'm sure George will be delighted to hear that." Emily winked. "Not that he knew I was proposing to send him into the lion's den, as it were. What *can* I do for you?"

"Firstly, I would like to go out in society, and seeing as I can't rely on Minshom to take me anywhere except back home, I'm hoping you'll allow me to follow in your illustrious wake. And secondly, I want some new gowns. Can you help me with that?"

"Of course I'll take you out with me." Emily clapped her hands together and laughed. "You wish to dazzle Minshom with your new look? Force him to his knees and make him fall in love with you all over again?"

"That would be nice, but the gowns are primarily for me. I think I deserve them for putting up with Minshom for ten years, don't you?"

"Absolutely." Emily rose and pulled Jane up too. "I'll get my bonnet and pelisse and we'll go to Madame Wallace's. She'll love you."

"I'm sure she will when she sees how many gowns I intend to buy."

Emily paused in the doorway. "I've just thought of something. Do you remember David, George's youngest brother?"

"Of course, he's a captain in the Royal Navy, isn't he? Where is he based now?"

"Since the war ended he's been stuck on half-pay in an office here at the Admiralty in London." Emily grimaced. "I think he misses the sea. But he might be able to help you find out more about Minshom and Sokorvsky. He went to school with your husband and is known to be a friend of Sokorvsky and his family. I'm sure he'd be happy to talk to you."

Jane picked up her serviceable blue bonnet and put it on. "Do you really think he'll know anything? He always seemed so quiet and well behaved, it's hard to imagine him keeping company with anyone like Minshom."

"David is an interesting man and I know he'll want to talk to you." Emily hesitated. "I'm not sure if you know this, but he was once involved with Minshom."

"David was?"

"Perhaps I shouldn't have suggested him after all. I don't want to hurt you by bringing up the subject of your husband's legion of lovers."

"It's all right. I know what Minshom is like. I'm just surprised that David allowed himself to be taken in."

"You were taken in."

"I know, but I was in love."

"And what makes you think David wasn't? You know how persuasive Minshom can be when he wants something."

She followed Emily out onto the landing and watched her go up to her bedroom with an airy promise that she would be quick. Jane then started down the stairs to await her friend in the hall. Emily was right about Minshom. He could be incredibly charismatic when he wanted to, and hard to resist. Perhaps she and David had more in common than she realized. And what about Anthony Sokorvsky? What was it about him that had finally made Minshom create such a scandal?

"My lady?"

Jane thanked the footman who helped her into her pelisse and sat down to wait for Emily in the cold emptiness of the ground-floor entrance hall. Knowing her fashionable friend, it might take a while, but it wasn't as if she didn't have plenty to think about.

She hadn't agreed to Blaize's suggestion that she go out with him to his favorite brothel, had countered with a suggestion of her own and he'd stormed out. Should she accept his challenge and find out whether all the gossip was true? It might help her come to a decision about what to do next. Perhaps her dreams of reconciliation needed to be crushed and a new, starker reality faced.

She curled her fingers inside her soft kid gloves until the tips of her fingers touched her palm. Just because she had changed didn't mean Blaize had too. In truth, the changes she had seen in him so far had only increased her anxiety about her chances of success.

She stared blankly at the dim, unrecognizable landscape painting over the white marble mantelpiece. But what was worse? Staying home, hiding from her true self, afraid to face what must be done, or taking a stand and negotiating for a new future? She'd once defied her entire family to marry Minshom. Where had that fire gone? If she wanted him back, she'd have to risk his ire, his contempt, his indifference. She'd have to risk everything . . .

"Are you ready, Jane?"

She looked up and saw Emily coming down the stairs toward her wearing a short brown spencer jacket over her yellow dress and a dashing French bonnet with dyed ostrich feathers.

"Did Madame Wallace make that jacket for you?"

"She did. Do you like it?"

"Very much." Longingly, Jane eyed the height of the feathers. "What about the bonnet?"

"Now *that* was made by Julianne DeFleur, who just happens to have a shop on the same street as madame. Isn't that convenient?"

"Indeed it is." Jane smiled broadly at her friend and prepared to forget about Minshom for a while and simply enjoy herself. "Shall we go?"

"I'm already looking forward to it. Spending someone else's money is always a pleasure, especially when it's Minshom's."

Emily nodded at the butler who opened the door for them and they stepped into the watery sunlight. Jane tried to picture her husband's face as the bills started to roll in. She had no doubt that he'd feel obliged to talk to her then.

4

_____

"What the devil is going on?"

Minshom glared at Robert, who was adding another set of tradesmen's bills to the stack already in front of him.

"I assume her ladyship is doing some shopping."

"*Some* shopping? She appears to be buying up half of London and she's only been here a week." He glanced impatiently back at the door. "Where is she—is she here?"

"I believe she was just about to go out with Lady Millhaven. Would you like me to check, sir?"

"Don't 'check'—tell her to come right in here and explain herself."

Robert bowed. "I'll certainly ask her if she is able to accommodate you, my lord, but I hardly think it is my place to threaten her."

Minshom scowled. "Don't worry, I'll take care of that part. You just go and fetch her."

He waited, fingers drumming on his desk until he heard light footsteps in the hall beyond.

"You wanted to see me, my lord?"

He barely glanced at her but still caught the scent of lavender soap. "Sit down."

"When you issue commands in that tone of voice, I think I'd prefer to stand. It makes escaping so much easier."

He picked up a handful of the bills and waved them at her. "What are these?"

She moved closer to his desk, her expression full of calm interest. "They appear to be bills."

"They are bills, madam—your bills. When did I give you permission to bankrupt me?"

"You didn't. And these are only for hats, dresses and necessities. You can hardly expect me to walk around London in my old country fashions, can you?"

"I don't expect you to do anything except go home."

She continued to stare at him and then stroked the bodice of her gown.

"Don't you like this dress?"

He stared at her fingers, which had moved dangerously close to cupping her breast. In truth, she did look different, more fashionable, more mature, more desirable . . . He quashed down that thought and frowned.

"Why the devil should I care about your appearance? It's not as if I want to look at you."

Her hand slid lower over the filmy blue muslin, curved over her hip and flat stomach, and came back to rest between her breasts.

"It's made of jaconet muslin with a navy blue sarsenet slip beneath. It's the first of the gowns I have received from Madame Wallace and I'm very pleased with it."

The blue complemented her hazel eyes, drew his attention to them despite himself.

"So?"

She smiled and he resisted the desire to smile back. She wasn't a beauty; all her attraction was in the animation of her face, the warmth of her smile, the pure enjoyment of life in her eyes. He met far more beautiful women than her every day on the street, yet he couldn't help responding to the invitation in her smile, the depths of sexual heat he knew it concealed. He scowled.

"Pack up everything that arrives and send it straight back and I'll make sure to cancel all your accounts."

"There's no need to do that."

"There is. Perhaps if you bothered to pay attention to the financial affairs of our family, you might realize we can't afford such luxuries."

Jane raised her eyebrows at him. "I spend one morning a week with your land agent, Mr. Smith, going over the books. I know *exactly* how well the family is doing and how hard you have worked to restore the estate." Her gaze skimmed his dark brown coat and cream waistcoat. "And having paid attention to the books, I haven't noticed you skimping on your attire or your expenditures." She held out her hand. "If you don't wish to pay my bills, just give them to me and I'll take care of them myself."

As she reached forward, he slammed his palm down over the pile of paper. "How do you expect to do that? Even in that scanty see-through gown I doubt you'll make much money prostituting yourself."

"This gown isn't scanty and I don't need to earn money lying on my back!"

Ah, now she was angry, now he had the opportunity to make her regret drawing the full force of his attention on her. "Then how do you propose to pay your bills? I suppose you could always kill me and marry a richer man."

"That idea hadn't occurred to me, but thank you for the suggestion." She raised her chin. "I have money. I'm quite capable of paying for my own gowns."

"Money I gave you? The pin money I pay you every quarter? That is scarcely going to pay for one of the gowns you've ordered."

"I've hardly touched that money in the last seven years, so it is hardly a pittance, and I've been quite successful with my own financial investments. Ask Mr. Smith. He is quite proud of me."

"You've been investing in what exactly?"

She shrugged. "There's no need to look so skeptical. I've invested in the same things you have: consols, canals, shipping cargoes. Mr. Smith has acted as my agent, seeing as there are some ridiculous rules about women not being capable of transacting business."

He sat back so that he could study her flushed face. It was never wise to underestimate Jane. Beneath that mild, pleasant exterior beat the heart of a tenacious warrior. He would do well not to forget that in future.

"But it is still my money. And as far as I remember, what's yours is mine and what's mine I keep. Isn't that how marriage works?"

"I believe it is." She regarded him steadily for a long moment. "I'm not taking a single thing back, Blaize. Either allow me to pay the bills or pay them yourself. If marriage truly is about you owning me, and all my money is yours, then those debts are your responsibility, whether you use my money to pay them off or your own."

"I don't believe it works like that. *I* decide which bills to pay, not you. Everything will be returned and your account canceled." He held her gaze. "And seeing as you intended to use the allowance *I* gave you to pay your debts, some might say you did earn that money on your back after all."

She drew in a ragged breath. "Sometimes I don't like you at all, Blaize."

"Good. Perhaps you should remember that and go home."

She turned on her heel and left his study. He frowned after her. It wasn't like Jane to give up so easily. Had he really frightened her off or had she gone to find a pistol to shoot him with as he had suggested? He kept his seat, strained to hear her returning, sat back and pretended to be examining some correspondence when she reentered.

"Here you are." He tried not to flinch as she dropped a leather bag on his desk with a thump. "My money."

He stared at the leather sack, watched as she upended it and sovereigns poured all over his desk. Some rolled to the edge and down to the floor below.

"If I was supposed to earn this on my back, I owe *you*, don't I? You haven't been near my bed for seven years. I'd hate to take something I didn't deserve."

Minshom said nothing, just focused on the coins and her left hand that she'd planted on his desk. Her fingers were ringless. He studied the faint indentations on two of her fingers.

"Where are the rings I bought you?"

She snatched her hand away from under his nose. "Do you think I've pawned them?"

"Perhaps."

"They are upstairs in my jewelry box. Would you like me to fetch it so you can rummage through and check your property is all there?" She headed for the door, looked back at him and curtsied. "I'm going out now. Perhaps I'll see you at dinner."

Minshom stared at the bills and the money scattered over his desk. If she thought he was going to change his mind, she was mistaken. Her foolish attempt to shame him into giving her what she wanted was doomed. He had no reason to be guilty at all.

He started to gather up the money, calculating as he went, surprised at the quantity of coin his wife had amassed. Once the coins were all safely in their bag, he took out his ledger, found a clean page and entered the amount on the first line with Jane's name alongside it.

He watched the ink dry, aware of an unusual sense of unease, as if someone had prodded his long dormant conscience. He jammed his pen back into the inkwell and slammed the book shut. Damnation, he *was* within his rights to take her money. Apart from the pitiful amount settled on her by her family in the marriage settlement, legally everything else she had belonged to him.

And he had to get rid of her. She'd been here for more than a week and she unsettled him with her inability to listen to reason, to bow to his will like everyone else did, to *leave*. In truth, he was almost obliged to use any ammunition he could to get her to leave him in peace.

No doubt she'd be back when she realized he wasn't going to change his mind. He deposited the coins in a drawer and locked it. And when she came back, perhaps he could use the lure of a new wardrobe to finally send her packing.

"He is insufferable!" Jane fumed as she sat opposite Emily in the luxurious Millhaven carriage.

"And he is also right. Legally he owns you."

"I know!" Jane tried to smile. "But it doesn't make it any easier to live with his ridiculously old-fashioned notions."

"So what did you do when he refused to let you pay the bills with your money?"

"I went and got the money, dumped it on his desk and told him he was welcome to it."

Emily's brows wrinkled. "Do you think that was wise? Now you have nothing."

"He suggested that by giving me pin money, I was no better than any prostitute."

"He didn't!"

"Well, not in those exact words, but that was what he implied. I told him that if that was the case, I owed *him* a refund anyway, and then I left before I picked up the poker and brained him."

Jane met Emily's gaze and her lips twitched. Within a moment they were both laughing uncontrollably.

"Oh, Jane, I know it isn't really funny, but I wish I'd seen Minshom's face when you did that."

"He didn't look particularly happy but he quickly masked it." Jane sighed and cast a glance down at her beautiful new dress. "I don't know what he'll do now, but I'm going to have to send the clothes back."

"Stuff and nonsense. The gown you have on is a present from me and so is the pale blue satin ball gown."

"I can't take those from you."

Emily glared at her. "Yes you can, and doesn't Minshom pay you a dress allowance as well?"

"He does, it was included in the original marriage settlement, and hasn't been increased for years. Living in the countryside meant that I didn't need any particularly grand clothes."

"Then I have an even better solution. I'll deal directly with Madame Wallace and you can send me your allowance and gradually pay off the debt to me."

"Emily, you don't have to do that."

"I jolly well do. I'm not having my best friend reduced to walking around in rags, and I'll be more than delighted to impede Minshom in any way I can." She held out her hand. "Are we in agreement?"

Reluctantly Jane shook the proffered hand. "I almost looked forward to walking around London in my country clothes and seeing how Minshom handled the gossip. Despite all evidence to the contrary, he's quite proud of his family name."

Emily's smile widened. "Then you should do exactly that and see what happens. Most of your clothes won't be ready for a week or so, which gives you the perfect opportunity to play the poor downtrodden wife in public."

Jane nodded at her best friend. Minshom might think he

owned her, but as women had learned for themselves, there was more than one way to gain power in a marriage.

At dinner that night, Jane wore her oldest gown, a faded patterned pink muslin from several years ago, which she wore at home to do the dirtier tasks associated with living on a large country estate. She took her seat at the bottom of the long table, nodded cordially at Robert, who was standing by the door, and looked expectantly at the empty seat at the head of the table.

"Is Lord Minshom joining us?"

"I believe he is, my lady. I helped him dress for dinner." Robert hesitated and looked hopefully at the door. "Would you like me to go and see if he is coming?"

"There's no need to chase me like a mother hen, Robert. I'm here."

Jane pasted on a bland smile as her husband strolled into the room and across to his seat. He wore a tight-fitting blue coat and black waistcoat with white pantaloons. Mentally Jane calculated how much it must cost to have a coat tailored so perfectly to a man's form, reckoned it would be far more than the cost of a dress. Despite her inner fuming, she continued to smile.

"Good evening, my lord."

Minshom turned to her, his expression guarded.

"Are you still here? I thought you'd finally decided to go home in a huff."

"Oh no," she said sweetly. "I'm having far too much fun to ever contemplate leaving." She looked across at Robert who was edging toward the door. "Robert, Lady Millhaven took me to Somerset House today to see an exhibition of the most interesting landscape pictures."

"Really, my lady?"

"Are you sure she didn't take you shopping?" Minshom asked, his mouth curling in apparent distaste.

"Oh no, my lord. I have no money to shop. I have no money at all." She opened her eyes wide at him. "I am totally dependent on the good will of my husband."

"As you should be."

Oh, she wanted to hurt him so badly. "As I should be."

His pale blue eyes narrowed. "I'm not convinced by this sudden wifely devotion, Jane, and I'm not going to change my mind."

"I understand that, my lord." She turned her attention back to Robert, who looked distinctly uneasy. "Do you like art, Robert?"

"Not particularly, my lady. Most of the time it seems a great fuss about nothing. I like a picture to look like what it's supposed to be, not some watered-down blurry version of it."

"Then you would probably prefer the work of Mr. John Constable to that of Mr. Turner. He depicts ordinary scenes from farming and village life. One of his paintings was in the gallery today and I believe he has just been elected an associate of the Royal Academy."

Minshom cleared his throat and Jane paused to look at him. "When you've finished trying to educate my valet, perhaps we could eat?"

"Of course, my lord. Isn't Robert going to join us?"

"Robert?"

"I understood that he ate with you before my arrival. I would hate to disrupt your routine."

"No you damn well wouldn't. You positively thrive on it," he grumbled.

Robert bowed. "It's all right, my lady, I'm quite happy to eat in the kitchen."

"Leave him alone, Jane, and eat your dinner." Minshom gestured at the footmen to remove the covers from the dishes. "You can all go—we'll serve ourselves."

Jane waited until the staff filed out and shut the door behind them. She surveyed the dishes set before her and slowly inhaled. Minshom's cook was from France and it showed. She wondered how Minshom remained so slender when faced with such delights on a daily basis. She wanted to sample everything, savor every single taste and flavor.

"You are licking your lips in a decidedly salacious manner, Jane."

"I'm trying to decide what I should eat first. Your cook is very talented."

"He should be. He costs me enough."

Jane stood up to ladle some soup from the imposing china tureen in the center of the table. She took her time, aware of Blaize's gaze fixed on the loose bodice of her old gown, the lush display of her breasts as they fought to escape the thin fabric.

"Would you care for some soup, Blaize?"

He took his time returning his gaze to her face.

"No, thank you."

"Are you sure?" She held up her bowl, leaned farther forward to blow on the soup's surface. "It smells delicious."

"I'm sure, thank you."

She smiled and sat back down, concentrated on eating her soup, on the freshness of leeks and cream against her tongue and the tang of parsley and pepper.

"I wish you wouldn't do that."

"Do what?"

"Make that sound when you are enjoying your food."

"I make a noise?"

"You do. It's somewhere between a purr and a moan."

She held his gaze. "And that offends you?"

"No, but it reminds me of the sounds you make when I make you come."

"You can remember that far back?"

"Of course."

"I remember the first time you used your fingers and mouth on me. It was so shocking, and not what I had expected at all, and yet so . . . addictive."

He shrugged. "That's the purpose of sex, isn't it? To make our baser selves forget caution and simply mate."

Jane licked the rim of her spoon and studied her husband. He was so calm, so seemingly untroubled by his determination to reduce love and passion to their most primitive and unsentimental level. It was almost a pleasure to pick at him.

"Is that why you prefer men? Because they don't expect anything more than sex from you?"

"I don't prefer men."

"Gossip says otherwise."

His blue eyes narrowed. "And I told you what I think of gossip."

She finished her soup and put down her spoon, searched the delights in front of her for something else to taste.

"Have you thought any more on my offer?"

She looked up at him, hand poised over a dish of chicken in cream sauce. "Which offer?"

"Don't be obtuse. I've only made one."

"Ah, the offer to take me to your favorite brothel so that I can see for myself the depths of depravity you have embraced."

"To be fair, it's not exactly a brothel. It's a private pleasure house for both men and women run by a very astute Frenchwoman named Madame Helene Delornay."

"Women can buy sexual partners too?"

He smiled. "You have no money, remember? So you can't buy anything. And it doesn't work like that. Members pay a yearly fee to enjoy all the amenities available for as little or as long as they wish."

"And you intend to take me there?"

"If you accept my offer."

"They will let me in?"

"As my guest, yes."

"Then I think I would like to go."

"Good. Now perhaps we can finish our dinner without you moaning or threatening to unleash your breasts in the soup?"

Jane smiled at his irritated tone, wondered if she had aroused him and whether he would admit it if she asked. "Of course, my lord. Whatever you say, my lord."

5

"You're not going out with me, dressed like that."

"What's wrong with my gown?" Jane asked, hoping her expression showed only general wifely interest rather than the delight she felt. Half an hour had passed since Blaize had told her to go upstairs and get ready for their outing. So far all she'd done was brush her bangs and pinch her cheeks to add color.

Now he'd appeared through the door connecting their suites and he was frowning at her. He'd changed into a black coat and waistcoat embroidered with golden thread and skintight satin pantaloons. He snapped his fingers at her.

"You know what's wrong with it. It's a rag. Take it off and put on that blue dress you were wearing earlier today."

She blinked at him. "But you told me to send that one back."

He took three steps into her room and glared down at her. "You must have something else."

She walked across to the clothes press and opened the lid with a flourish. "This is all I have. You are welcome to pick a different one if you wish." She pursed her lips. "I think there might be an evening gown in there somewhere that I had made about five years ago."

She straightened up and jumped when she realized he was right behind her.

"You are not wearing any of those ridiculously outmoded gowns."

She stared into his eyes, aware that her breathing was as labored as his. He thrust his hand out and grabbed the front of her bodice. With one savage pull he ripped it open, exposing her corset and the swell of her breasts. She kept her hands fisted by her sides.

"Now do you understand that you are not wearing this?"

"You would prefer me to go naked?"

His icy blue eyes assessed her from head to foot. "Perhaps, but I have a better idea." He turned his head and shouted. "Robert!"

Jane remained still, too aware of the closeness of her husband and the dark sexual energy vibrating through him to dare to move or to make sense of his commands.

"Yes, my lord?"

She heard Robert's voice as he emerged from the dressing room that linked their suites but couldn't see him beyond Blaize's chest.

"Go and find a set of men's clothing that will fit my wife. There should be some in my suite, or lend her something of yours."

"Yes, my lord."

Jane waited until Robert disappeared again. "You want me to dress like a man?"

"Why not?"

"Because I have too many curves to look convincing?"

"You don't need to convince anyone but me." Blaize flicked the filmy muslin now trailing from her ruined bodice and walked back to the door. "Now take off this abomination and call your maid to help you get dressed again."

"I don't have a maid. I have Lizzie from the kitchen."

He paused long enough for her to see the impatience on his face. "Then call her. I'll expect you down in the hall in ten minutes."

Minshom checked his pocket watch again and continued his restless pacing around the perimeter of the hall. Where was Jane? Had she changed her mind? Had his deliberate roughness finally gotten through to her and made her bolt? God, he hoped so. When he ripped her gown he'd wanted to explore further, to shove his hand inside her corset and find her breasts, to bring them to his mouth and suckle her nipples to hard, aching points.

Even though she must have realized the danger, she hadn't backed down from him. The quality of her silence, the obvious tightening of her nipples and shortness of breath hadn't helped discourage him either. But then she'd always enjoyed sex, thrived on his excesses, encouraged them even, so her reaction to him wasn't a complete surprise. She'd been a revelation when he met her at seventeen and now she had only matured, her sexual appetites no doubt stimulated and explored by other men.

His gut tightened as he contemplated Jane coming in another man's embrace. It was an image that unsettled him more than he had anticipated. Where the hell was she? Robert emerged from the servant's staircase, Minshom's hat and cloak in his hands.

"Here you are, my lord."

Minshom stared at his valet. "Go and get your things. I want you to come with me."

"To the pleasure house, my lord?" Robert's smile disappeared.

"Yes, what of it?"

"Nothing, sir, it's just that I haven't been there for a while."

"You can ask permission to wait in the kitchen. When my wife decides she's seen enough and wants to go home, you can take her in the carriage and come back for me later."

"Yes, my lord."

Minshom glanced sharply at Robert. "What's the matter? Are you annoyed because I won't let you go and indulge yourself at the pleasure house? You're my property, Robert, don't forget that."

"I know that, sir."

Robert's face assumed the wooden look Minshom hated. But he hardly had time to discuss his valet's problems now; he had far more important things to deal with. Getting rid of Jane had to be his priority—if she ever got herself down those stairs. He looked up again, saw her appear on the first-floor landing, her body covered with a long voluminous cloak, her head bare.

"Ah, finally, there you are. Now come on."

She reached the bottom of the stairs and stared up at him.

"I don't look anything like a man."

"As I said, it hardly matters. No one will be looking at you. They'll all be too busy having sex." He pointed his finger at her face. "And you will remain quiet and not draw attention to yourself."

She touched her hair and drew his gaze to the single braid down her back. "Should I cut this? It's far too long to be fashionable anyway."

He frowned. "Leave it."

"Is that an order, my lord and master?"

God, he'd like to master her, have her at his feet, begging to be fucked, to be filled with his cum . . .

Unnerved by his unruly thoughts, he scowled at her. "Do what you want with it. I don't care."

He turned on his heel, beckoned to Robert and headed out

to his carriage. It wasn't far to Madame's house in Mayfair, but the night air was chilly and since the recent food riots, the streets weren't as safe as they had been. He didn't bother to wait and help Jane into the carriage. Dammit, she was dressed as a man, and she could get in by herself. Robert, of course, had other ideas, and being far more chivalrous than his employer, proffered Jane a helping hand.

Minshom didn't speak to either of them on the journey. He was too busy wondering what his reception at the pleasure house would be like. Would he be barred because of his involvement with Helene's daughter and her lover? He wasn't sure. Madame was, after all, a superb businesswoman and he hadn't hurt Marguerite Lockwood. In truth, he'd reluctantly come to admire her over the past weeks. But she was involved with Anthony Sokorvsky, and he had more than enough grievances against Minshom to spare.

Ah, Anthony. Part of the thrill of fucking Sokorvsky was that even in extremis, he had always tried to resist Minshom, to prove that he could deny his sexual impulses even when his body said differently. And perhaps, seeing as he had obviously found sexual comfort with a woman, he had been correct to resist. He'd insisted that he had the right to choose his own sexual destiny, to walk away from Minshom, to make him a laughingstock . . .

The carriage stopped and Minshom stared coldly at Robert and Jane. Tonight would be different. He would show Jane that he really had no soul or compassion left in him. He would show everyone.

Jane licked her lips as she was ushered up the wide white steps and into the brothel. Wedged between Minshom and Robert, she could see very little except intriguing glimpses of well-polished marble and wood floors and scarlet silk wallpaper. The house and its surroundings certainly weren't quite as she had pictured them. The neighborhood looked far too upper class to contain a bawdy house.

"We'll go in to the receiving room and wait for Madame."

Minshom sounded irritated, but then he so often did when he was near her. Despite his insistence that he didn't care about her anymore, he still reacted to her presence. She'd felt him respond to her earlier, enjoyed the way his heated gaze had lingered on her exposed breasts. For one thrilling moment she'd thought he was going to grab her and take her to the ground.

Jane lowered her hood and went to warm her hands in front of the fire. Men's breeches gave her a freedom of movement she hadn't experienced before. Maybe she should take a pair home and wear them to ride astride or climb onto the roof or any of those other thousands of tedious jobs that became impossible in a skirt and petticoats.

"Good evening, Lord Minshom."

Jane turned around to find one of the most beautiful women she had ever seen coming through the doorway. The vision was blonde, petite and had a husky French accent that only added to her allure.

"Good evening, Madame Helene." Minshom bowed but didn't make an effort to kiss the goddess's hand. "I wish to bring a guest into your house this evening."

Madame inclined her head. "Which of these gentlemen is it?"

"I believe you've met Robert before." Minshom waved a casual hand in Jane's direction. "It's this one."

Madame's delicate blue gaze fastened on Jane and her eyes widened. "'This' isn't a man."

"No."

"I don't think I've ever seen you bring a woman into my establishment before, my lord." Madame paused and directed her next question at Jane. "Are you sure you want to do this?"

Minshom frowned. "Madame, that is scarcely any of your business . . ."

Jane moved in front of her husband and dropped an awkward curtsey in her breeches. "I'm sure, thank you."

An amused smile hovered on the paragon's lips. Jane realized she was being scrutinized very carefully and that close-up, Madame was not quite as young as she looked.

"Do you know Lord Minshom well?"

"Very well." Jane said. "We've been married for ten years."

"You are his wife?" Madame pressed two fingers to her mouth as if to stifle a laugh. "Forgive me; it never occurred to me that a man such as Lord Minshom would be interested in having a wife."

Jane gave her a sunny smile. "It's all right. He's not really interested in having me—that's probably why you've never heard of me before."

"I think Madame has heard enough about our private affairs, don't you, my dear?"

Jane tried to resist as Minshom took her by the shoulders and propelled her toward the door. She craned her head around to see her hostess. "Thank you, Madame. Perhaps we will become better acquainted soon."

"I certainly hope so, Lady Minshom. In fact, I look forward to it."

Minshom marched Jane up the wide staircase and then flattened her against the wall and placed his bent arm over her head caging her in.

"I told you to be quiet. Do not tell anyone else who you are. Do you understand?"

"You don't wish to acknowledge our relationship?"

"Of course I don't."

"Why not?"

He sighed. "Because you are going home and I don't need more gossip circulating about me than there already is."

"I thought you never listened to gossip." He was so close that she distinctly heard his teeth click together when he set his jaw.

"For once in your life, swear to me that you will be quiet and do as you are told. If you don't agree, I'm going to send you home right now." She opened her mouth and he placed his hand over it. "When you have seen enough to convince you to leave, ask the way down to the main hall or the kitchens and Robert will take you home. Now nod if you understand me."

Jane managed a nod and he released her. She looked up into his handsome, brutal face and fought a smile. He was trying so hard to intimidate her that he was obviously running scared. She'd known him long enough to understand that the more she tried to get close to him, the harder he pushed her away. It seemed that nothing had changed.

He held her gaze. "We will be going up to the third floor where the most extreme of the sexual activities take place."

"Can we just walk through the other levels first?"

"Jane, what did I just say to you about keeping quiet and not asking questions?"

She obediently closed her mouth and tried not to look pleading. He knew she had always been sexually curious and he was simply being his usual arrogant, overbearing self by not allowing her to look around. She waited until he stalked away from her toward the next staircase and simply took herself in the other direction into the first of the public salons. He wouldn't be happy when he realized she wasn't behind him, but at least she'd get a quick glimpse of the delights of the pleasure house before he caught up.

The salon was decorated in tones of scarlet and gold, and an opulent buffet occupied one third of the far end of the room. Large cushions piled up into one corner housed a variety of couples and groups engaged in sexual intercourse or play. Jane paused to stare at a man who was being sucked off by a naked woman while he sucked off another man.

When he winked at her she felt herself start to blush. As she progressed farther into the room, warmth continued to creep into her face and other more interesting parts of her body. She had never seen such unguarded public sensuality before; realized she was both attracted to and appalled by her instant arousal.

She almost gasped when a heavy hand descended on her shoulder and spun her around. It was Blaize, of course, his blue eyes arctic and promising retribution.

"We are going upstairs. If you don't choose to obey me, I'll pull down your pantaloons and spank you."

Jane licked her lips. "Right here in front of everyone?"

"Yes."

"I'm almost tempted to stay." She saw his eyes flicker, and the depth of his sexual awareness of her was revealed before he masked it.

"Jane . . . don't provoke me."

"Why ever not?"

"Because you don't really know what I'm like anymore, or what I'm capable of."

She held his gaze. "Then perhaps you should take me upstairs and show me."

He bowed. "Perhaps I should."

Robert sat down at the pine table in the warm welcoming kitchen of the pleasure house and sipped at the cup of mulled wine the cook had just given him. He couldn't help but wonder what his employer was up to, bringing his wife to such a scandalous place. He could only guess that Minshom was trying to frighten Jane into going back home. That would be just like him.

He took another sip of the wine, enjoyed the tartness of the apple and the warmth of cloves and cinnamon against his tongue. But her ladyship had always had a way of getting around his lordship. Robert suspected that she might enjoy the pleasure house far more than Minshom anticipated.

"Robert, is that you? I thought I saw you in the hall."

Robert got hurriedly to his feet and smoothed down his hair.

"Captain Gray, sir."

He stared into the smiling face of the very man he'd hoped to avoid. The man who haunted his dreams, whose face he imagined every time Minshom fucked him. Captain Gray was blond, his hair clubbed back in an old-fashioned queue, his skin bronzed and weather-beaten from his days at sea. He was about the same age as Minshom, but there the comparison ended.

Captain Gray gestured at the mulled wine. "Is there any more of that?"

"The wine, sir? I don't know, you'll have to ask the cook." God, he felt like such an idiot. He was probably blushing like a girl as well.

"If you don't object, perhaps I might sit with you?"

Robert shrugged and sat back down, watched as Captain Gray laughed and flirted with the elderly cook in perfect French and then brought not only a cup of wine back to the table but a whole jug full.

"I haven't seen you for quite a while, Robert."

"No, sir, you haven't."

"Have you been down in the countryside working at Minshom Abbey?"

"No, sir." Robert stared down at his cup. "I've just been busy, sir."

"You haven't been here for ages."

"As I said, I've been busy."

Captain Gray finished his wine and poured himself another cup, offered the jug to Robert.

"Is something wrong?"

"With me, sir? No."

"Then it's just that you don't want to talk to me."

For the first time, Robert lifted his gaze from the tabletop and found Captain Gray's calm blue eyes fixed on his.

"It's more the other way round, isn't it, sir? I'm not quite sure exactly why you would want to talk to me."

"Because last time we met, you told me to leave you alone and that you were quite happy with Minshom." Captain Gray smiled. "I didn't believe you then, and I don't believe it now."

"Because you can't believe I'd stop wanting you?" Robert blinked hard. Didn't Captain Gray understand that he'd done what was best for all of them?

Before he could continue, Captain Gray spoke. "I'm not that conceited, Robert. I think you wanted me to be free of Minshom, and you sacrificed what you desired for yourself to achieve that."

"You're wrong, sir. I'm perfectly happy where I am."

"Being fucked by Minshom, being at his beck and call, being *used*?"

Defiantly, Robert met Captain Gray's skeptical gaze. "Just because you decided you didn't like it anymore, doesn't mean that I had to, *sir*."

"My name is David. You've always had my permission to call me that."

"In bed, maybe, but out here in the real world? You're the son of an earl and I'm the son of a parson. You like fucking me; Minshom likes to fuck me. We'll never be equals, will we, *sir*?"

Captain Gray stood up and pushed away from the table. "Ah, yes, hide behind your class, pretend that I view you in the same light as Minshom does. You know it wasn't like that between us."

"Wasn't it, sir? Perhaps you remember it differently than I do."

"Are you suggesting that I forced myself on you?" A muscle flicked in Captain Gray's cheek and his eyes narrowed. "That is one of the most insulting things anyone has ever said to me."

Robert tried to shrug away the pain. "What would you like me to say, sir?"

"I'd like you to tell me what you really think and I'd like you to kiss me, but I doubt I'll get either of my wishes."

"I don't know, sir. If you ask Lord Minshom nicely, perhaps he'll hire me out for your use."

Captain Gray briefly closed his eyes. "Robert, I can only apologize for making such a mull of this. If you ever want to talk to me about *anything*, please come and find me. I am truly concerned about you and I want to help." He hesitated, his gaze flicked to the cook who seemed oblivious to the drama going on behind her. "I know some of the reasons why you stay with Minshom, I have some of the same memories, but I . . . God, I miss you and I'm afraid for you."

Robert returned his gaze to his cup and kept it there, his whole body shaking with the urge to get up and find comfort in Captain Gray's embrace. He heard the captain sigh and then walk away. Not chasing after him, not taking this second opportunity for freedom, was one of the hardest things Robert had ever had to do.

6

Jane's steps faltered as the doorman opened the last door at the end of the narrow dark hallway. Blaize placed his hand in the small of her back and urged her firmly over the threshold before closing the door behind him. Jane stared at the black and red painted walls, the bare birch floorboards and the racks filled with instruments for sexual pleasure, and slowly swallowed.

She'd never imagined such a place existed, but now that she was here, she could see how her husband might thrive in such threatening sensual surroundings. Even with her, his sexual tastes had run to the unusual and the extreme. And here was a place where there seemed to be no boundaries except those imposed by the men and women inhabiting the space.

It took her longer to focus on the people in the room, most of whom had stopped what they were doing to stare at her and her husband. A tall brown-haired man wearing just a long shirt came toward them and went down on his knees.

"Lord Minshom."

Jane looked back at Blaize, who barely acknowledged the

man kneeling at his feet. His gaze scoured the room as if he was looking for some particular person. Was he hoping to see the infamous Lord Anthony Sokorvsky, expecting his lover to come back to him after all? Jane prayed he hadn't. She had plans for her husband that didn't include a previous lover.

Minshom took her hand and walked her farther into the room until she faced the largest wall of implements. He selected a short whip and then turned back to the man who had remained on his knees by the door.

"Mr. Shaw. Did you miss me?"

"Yes, my lord."

Jane shivered at the silken anticipation in her husband's voice and pressed herself back against the wall. She watched as Minshom strolled across the room, the tip of the whip tapping against his thigh.

"Why did you miss me?"

"Because you give me what I need, my lord."

"And what is that, Shaw?"

"Pain, my lord."

Shaw shuddered as Minshom trailed the whip over his shoulders and down his back. Jane licked her lips and drew her arms around her waist as if to protect herself from Minshom's beguiling tone.

Minshom glanced over at his wife, smiled when he saw her attention was riveted to the scene he played out for her benefit. Well, not entirely for her benefit—he was enjoying it too, enjoying her watching him even more, if he was honest. Shaw was an easy mark, his pleasure at being thrashed a legacy of his school days that required little effort to satisfy. But Jane didn't know that. He hoped she'd only see the man cowering before him and hate him for what he was about to do.

"Place yourself on the punishment horse, Shaw."

The man got up and went across to one of the black leather contraptions in the center of the room. He laid facedown, arms on either side of the horse.

"Grasp the restraints."

Minshom came up behind Shaw and stared down at the prostrate man. He kicked Shaw's feet apart until he could stand between the man's legs and raised the whip. Shaw made no sound at first as the whip flicked over his arse and back. But Minshom knew all the signs, how he gripped the restraints, his knuckles whitening against the black leather as the whip landed on his flesh.

After another quick glance at Jane, Minshom lifted Shaw's shirt and stared down at his reddened buttocks and sweaty, quivering skin. Sexually, Shaw did nothing for him. He was far more interested in the effect his actions were having on his wife. How much would Jane be able to watch before she fled the room in horror? How far would he have to take this suddenly unappealing charade before she broke?

"Please, my lord."

Shaw's stuttered words brought Minshom's attention back to his victim.

"What do you want, Mr. Shaw?"

"More of the whip, please, my lord, more pain."

Minshom drew back his arm and landed a perfect blow on Shaw's right buttock.

"Like this, Mr. Shaw?"

"God, yes, please . . . just like that."

Minshom put a little more effort into his strokes until Shaw was writhing on the horse and moaning. Red lines marred his skin and he shoved his hips forward with every stroke. Minshom drew the tip of the whip down between Shaw's buttocks and then lower to nudge his balls.

"What else do you want, Shaw?"

"To be fucked, my lord? Please, I beg of you, fuck me."

Jane hadn't moved, her gaze was still fixed on him and Shaw. Minshom contemplated his options. If he fucked Shaw, she would probably run. Even though he was hard and ready, it wasn't because of the pathetic man in front of him. It was because Jane was watching. That gave him much more sexual satisfaction than he had anticipated; made him even more determined to finish it and get rid of her.

He took a step backward and snapped his fingers.

"Come here, Jane."

She walked slowly to his side, her expression calm, her hands clenched at her sides. Minshom ran his hands over Shaw's buttocks until he moaned.

"Do you think I should fuck him?"

"I think you should do whatever you wish."

She sounded far too composed for his liking. He pointed at a chest of drawers set against one of the walls. "Go and get me the second drawer and bring it back here."

He waited until she returned with the shallow drawer, gestured for her to place it on the floor between them.

"You see that black ebony phallus there in the center?"

"The big one?"

"Yes, pick it up and give it to me."

Jane bent to do his bidding and handed him the thick engraved phallus; her fingers trembled when they brushed his. Ah, so she wasn't as unaffected as she pretended to be.

"Now go and find me a bottle of oil—there should be some in the top drawer of that same cabinet."

She brought back the oil and held it out to him. He shook his head.

"Put some oil on your fingers and cover the tip of the phallus with it."

She moistened her lips with her tongue and failed to meet his gaze. "I'm not sure I want to do that, my lord."

"I don't believe I gave you a choice."

She looked at him then, her hazel eyes unnaturally bright in the dim lighting. "And if I don't?"

He smiled at her. "You wish to take Shaw's place?"

She swallowed convulsively and opened the bottle of oil, poured a small amount onto her fingertips. Minshom opened his hand and let the phallus lie in his palm. Felt his own cock harden as he watched her fingers work over the engraved surfaces of the ebony, turning the dull blackness to a glistening, glowing sheen.

"That's enough."

She withdrew her hand and hastily wiped it on the back of her breeches.

"Now slide the phallus into his arse."

She made no move to take the phallus from him, simply stared at him as if he had run mad.

"I . . . I can't do that."

"Why not? He wants to be fucked—you heard him beg for it."

"He wants you to fuck him, not that thing."

"He'll take whatever I give him, and in this case I'm going to fuck his mouth while you, my dear, fuck his arse." He raised his eyebrows. "You did promise to obey me this evening, didn't you? To humor my perversions so that you could see what kind of a man I've become."

"If I do this, I'll expect something in return."

"Like what?" *God, he was enjoying this far more than he should.*

"An hour of your time for an honest conversation?"

He laughed and weighed the phallus in his hand. "No."

"An evening out at a proper ball?"

He studied her carefully, admitting a reluctant admiration for her sheer persistence and courage under circumstances he had deliberately arranged to undermine her. He let the whip drop to the floor and held out his hand.

"Done. Now fuck him."

Jane put out her hand for the oiled phallus and tried not to look at the prostrate, half-naked man stretched over the leather horse. Minshom strolled to the man's head, unbuttoning his placket with his long elegant fingers. His erect cock emerged and he fondled himself for a moment, his eyes closed, a small smile on his lips.

"Slide it in, Jane."

She looked up and met his challenging stare, knew all at once that he expected her to bolt, to forfeit their arrangement to hopefully run all the way back to Minshom Abbey with her tail between her legs.

"Please, my lady."

Shaw's whispered words affected her more strongly than Minshom's gloating. He wanted this, God knew why, but he did. She wouldn't be hurting him, at least she hoped she wouldn't. With a quick prayer to the heavens, she lined up the tip of the phallus with Shaw's arse hole and gently pushed it in a half-inch.

"God . . ." Shaw's gasp was cut off as Minshom slid his cock into his mouth. To her shame, Jane couldn't help but watch his shaft disappear into Shaw's mouth, couldn't help pushing the phallus in just as deeply. As if she'd been trained, Jane matched her movement to the thrusts of Minshom's cock, kept her gaze on his swollen red flesh rather than on what she was doing.

When she risked a glance up at Minshom, he was watching her, his blue eyes half-closed and laced with lust. She couldn't look away, felt her own insides convulse and melt as they worked the man between them to a straining gasping climax. Jane slammed the phallus home one last time as Minshom came too, his gaze still fixed on her as if it were her mouth receiving his hot cum and her arse filled with the phallus.

Jane stepped back, shaking her head, and retreated to the wall as Minshom buttoned his pantaloons and Mr. Shaw gasped out his thanks to both of them. Without acknowledging the man at all, Minshom went toward the door and Jane followed. They descended the stairs in silence until they reached the main hallway.

A footman gave Jane her cloak and she covered herself as quickly as she could. A door banged to the side of the hall and Robert emerged. He looked almost as grim as Jane felt. What on earth had she done? How had she allowed herself to be drawn into one of Minshom's little sexual games?

"Are we all ready?"

Minshom put on his hat and exited through the main door, Jane and Robert following in his wake. She hoped he wouldn't try to bait her on the carriage ride home. She didn't have the strength to resist him anymore.

As soon as they entered the house, Minshom dismissed Robert for the night and opened the door into his study.

"Would you care for a nightcap, Jane?"

Torn between her desire to talk to him and her fear about what would happen next, Jane reluctantly entered the study. She paused by his desk, surprised by the amount of papers still spread out on it as he went to pour two brandies from the decanter set on his book shelves. He held one out to her and raised his own in a toast.

"Here's to an enjoyable evening."

Jane gripped her glass more tightly and wondered how much it would hurt if she threw it hard at her husband's conceited, arrogant head.

"I'm not sure if that is quite the way I saw it."

He paused, his glass halfway to his sensual mouth. "You didn't enjoy yourself?"

"You didn't want me to enjoy myself. You wanted me to run out of there screaming."

He laughed and put his glass down on the desk. "But you didn't, did you? Why is that, I wonder?"

"Because I am a fool?"

He came closer and she found herself caged against his desk. "You're no fool, Jane." He took the glass out of her unresisting fingers and placed it beside his own. "Were you too afraid of what I might do to you if you ran? Did you imagine yourself almost naked and facedown like Shaw?"

"Of course not!"

She gasped as he grabbed her arm and spun her around until her upper body and face were pinned to the desk top. He stepped closer, kicked her legs apart and leaned down to drop a kiss on the back of her neck.

"How does it feel, Jane, to be held down, to be at my mercy?"

She knew what he was trying to do. Knew he was about to hammer home the lessons she had already learned, that he was dangerous and unreliable, a player of sexual games that she could never compete with. She tried not to breathe as his still familiar scent surrounded her, brandy and cigars, the faint aroma of sex, of leather, of pure aroused man. His cock was hard again and nudged at her buttocks.

"Let me up, Blaize."

His soft chuckle stirred the hairs on the back of her neck and she shivered.

"Not yet. Did you like it when Shaw begged to be fucked?"

"No." She closed her eyes as he nipped at her ear and then licked the sting away.

"Strange, because you used to beg for me."

"I . . ." She yelped as he bit her earlobe, harder this time, leaving it throbbing in time to her raised heartbeat.

"Don't you remember? Even during that first weekend we met, you begged me to kiss you again, to touch your breasts, to suck them into my mouth."

Waves of humiliation rolled over her. Trust him to take some of her most special erotic memories and try to use them against her. She tightened her lips, refused to speak, refusing to cheapen those first overwhelming days with him.

"You begged, Jane. You begged for my fingers between your legs making you come, begged for my cock in your mouth, begged me to take your maidenhood."

She tried to buck him off, but he only settled over her more completely, his slender muscular body far stronger than hers had ever been.

"So what makes you any different from Shaw?"

Minshom shifted the arm he had around her waist upward until it grazed her breasts. Her nipples hardened in a sudden aching rush. God, not now, she couldn't give in to him now.

"Let me go, Blaize." She sounded weak and unsteady, knew he'd notice and revel in her discomfiture.

"Why, because I have disgusted you? Because after years on your own, you have forgotten how it feels to want to be fucked?" He slid his hand down between her legs and curved his fingers over her sex. "Are you dry here, like an old maid? Does the thought of sex frighten you?"

She fought him then, tried to turn her head and bite his fingers, fought even harder when he shoved his fingers inside her breeches and sank into the thick wetness of her arousal.

He went still and ripped his hand away, his breathing now as unsteady as her own.

"Damn you, Jane Minshom. Damn you to hell."

7

As Minshom recoiled, Jane slid out from under him and ran for the stairs. Her booted feet sounded loud on the marbled floor and her breathing echoed as she pounded up the stairs. She glimpsed the first landing and then gasped as Minshom tackled her from behind and brought her down onto the stairs, his arms wrapped around her bracing her fall.

The side of her face lay against cold stone yet the rest of her body was far too hot. Minshom's hand settled between her legs again.

"I should've known you wouldn't be disgusted, shouldn't I? You were always something of a sexual voyeur." The palm of his hand ground against her sex and he flexed his long fingers. "I should have tied you up beside Shaw and had you both."

Jane tried to take a breath and found it even more difficult than she had anticipated. Between Minshom's weight and her own excitement, she was barely able to function.

His other hand moved to her breasts and slid under her waistcoat, searched for her already-hard nipples and pinched hard. Mortified, Jane closed her eyes as a climax shook through her beleaguered and sensually starved body.

With a curse, Minshom rolled off her and pulled her to her feet. God, she was blushing so hard he must be able to see it even in the darkness. She waited for the tirade about how pathetic she was, how needy to come without even being penetrated. Instead, he retained her hand and marched her along the hallway, pushed her inside his bedchamber and closed the door.

She backed away from him and collided with the corner of his massive oak-framed bed, had to steady her hands on the elegant brown satin comforter. He reached her before she could get her body to obey her and turned her facedown into the side of the bed, his hands quick and rough as he stripped off her boots and breeches and flipped up the tails of her long white shirt.

"Don't worry, Jane. I'll give you want you want."

God, what did she want? Why couldn't she move? Why wasn't she screaming at him not to touch her rather than passively allowing him to fondle her buttocks to slide his fingers between them and rub against her wet, swollen, needy sex?

He reached across her to move the single candle into a better position for him to look at her and uncapped a small glass bottle with his teeth. The scent of lilacs invaded her nostrils and then she felt the coldness of an oiled fingertip inserted in her arse.

Blaize's teeth grazed her throat and she jumped, the smaller ache seemingly more invasive than his finger.

"You liked being fucked here, didn't you?" He slid another oiled finger alongside the first. "In truth, you were so eager to be fucked before our marriage that this was the only way I could appease you."

"You make me sound like a wanton."

"You were a wanton. You were begging for it."

Jane moaned as he moved his two fingers back and forth, widening her and preparing her for the far bigger penetration to come.

"You remember what to do. Relax and breathe deeply, don't fight me. Not that you ever did. You allowed me every sexual liberty I ever asked of you." He chuckled, the cynical sound so close it vibrated through her skull. "You even begged and pleaded for more."

"I wanted to please you. I was your wife."

"And you did please me." He added a third finger. "Why do you think I married you?"

Jane closed her eyes and focused on the motion of his fingers, the way he pushed her mound against the hard edge of the bed with every skilled maneuver. She knew with sudden desperate clarity that she wasn't going to stop him, was going to take what he offered her, even beg if he demanded it. She had gravely miscalculated the effect he had on her and she been denied sexual release for far too long to give up even a small dose of it now.

Minshom worked another finger in and admired the delicacy of Jane's buttocks in the candlelight; her skin was so pale he wanted to sink his teeth into it, knew she'd probably climax again if he did. He tore his hand away from her breast and brought it under her knee, bringing her right leg higher until her foot rested on the bed frame. Her cunt was exposed in all its swollen wet glory. He wanted to shove his tongue into the creamy wet heat and swirl it around until she screamed, to set his teeth on her clit and make her come a thousand times before he deigned to enter her. His cock throbbed and pushed at his breeches as he slowly unbuttoned himself.

He wasn't going to stop. Even knowing what she was and what had happened between them to bring them to this place wasn't going to stop him fucking her arse. Perhaps this was the best way to remind her of why she needed to leave. The best way to bring her to her knees.

That thought brought a graphic image of her servicing his cock, made him want to crawl onto the bed and enact it in real life. He smoothed a shaking hand over his wet shaft and eyed his embedded fingers. No, he'd take her arse, show her how he took a man, remind her and perhaps himself that she meant nothing more to him than somewhere to shove his prick.

"Are you ready, Jane? Ready to take my cock?"

She didn't reply so he slid his hand up inside her shirt, shoved under her bandaged chest and pinched her nipple between his finger and thumb. She shuddered underneath him, her back arching, her buttocks pressing against his cock.

"Tell me you don't want it, Jane, and I'll stop." He removed his fingers and inserted the first inch of his cock, felt her tighten around his crown. He wrapped her long braid around his hand until her head angled off the bed.

"I want you." She whispered, "God help me, I always have."

He stared down at the vulnerable curve of her neck. Damn her for being so soft. Didn't she know him well enough to understand that her submission only made him worse, that he gloried in mastering her? He shoved his cock deep into her arse, heard her gasp as he took her, fucked her, filled her.

He held still, his shaft fully embedded, his tight cum-filled balls pressed up against the satin of her skin. She wasn't fighting him at all. He drew back his hips and plunged into her again, gave it to her like he gave it to a man, hard, fast and selfishly. But she'd come for him, he knew that, even if he didn't touch her clit at all.

She was panting now with every hard stroke and even after all this time, he knew she was close to coming again. Damn, he was too close himself. He thrust one more time and groaned as he climaxed, his hot seed pulsing deep inside her. With a final shudder he let go and sprawled over her, let his weight push her into the softness of the bed, kept his cock still inside her.

"I know what you really want, Jane. I've known it all along, but this is all you'll ever get from me. My cock in your arse or in your mouth, never in your wet, needy little cunt. You'll never get my seed in there even if you beg on your knees. Do you understand?"

He pulled out, used the tails of her shirt to wipe himself clean and went over to open the door between their suites. He returned to the bed, picked her up and took her through to her own room. He dropped her right in the middle of the bed.

"Good night, Jane."

She lay where he had placed her and looked up at him. Her cheeks were flushed and tears glinted in her eyes. He wanted to look away from her but found he couldn't. Some part of him wanted to take her into his arms and comfort her; his baser side wanted to fuck her again. She licked her lips as if trying to speak but then rolled away from him onto her front, shutting him out, dismissing him.

He bowed even though she wasn't looking at him and headed back to his own room. In the dim light, he stripped naked and grimaced as his cock continued to throb, and grow, and want. He stroked his shaft, smelled Jane and instantly got even bigger. With a curse, he walked over to his dressing table and broke the ice on the jug of water stationed there, poured it into the matching china bowl.

He leaned over the bowl and splashed some of the freezing water onto his stomach and groin. His breath hissed out as the icy droplets settled on his skin like shards of glass. God, he wanted to go back in there and fuck her all night . . . He closed his eyes, forced himself to remember why he needed to remain in control.

Whenever he lost a fight, his father had taken him out to the stables, thrashed him again and forced him to clean himself up with one of the coarse brushes used on the horses. Minshom found himself reaching for his hairbrush, wanting to scrub at his groin until he bled, until the sense that he had somehow lost to Jane was obliterated in the rough pain he knew he deserved for treating her so badly.

But he wasn't going to do that to himself anymore. He wasn't going to let his father win. Better to call Robert and have him rather than to give into that old urge to harm himself to take the taste of defeat and shame away. With a grimace, Minshom cupped his balls and dunked them into the water as well, watched his cock shrivel and his desire fade.

It was well past time to go to bed and sleep. The morning would show him whether he had achieved his aim. Would Jane be leaving and, if not, what the devil was he going to have to do next?

Jane lay still until she heard Minshom softly close the door between their two suites. Waited a moment more until she heard the second door into his bedchamber close, and then allowed herself to cry. She'd been manipulated and outmaneuvered by a sexual expert. How could she have thought she could remain unaffected when he touched her? She'd never managed it before and apparently her body was just as overeager as her seventeen-year-old self.

She groaned and hurriedly covered her mouth, not that she thought he'd be listening; the walls were far too thick for him to hear her unless she screamed. She felt like screaming and pummeling her pillow or, preferably, his head. How quickly he'd disabused her of her notions of controlling him, of getting what she wanted without a fight.

His smell, his taste, the press of his body over hers, had all combined to render her useless, to turn her into just the sort of woman he despised. Her hand drifted between her legs, felt the wetness he'd left there and also the steady throb of unsatisfied desire. *And* he was wrong; she hadn't just come after him for his *seed*. She managed a tremulous smile. How arrogant an assumption was that? And how very like him.

There were other matters at Minshom Abbey that required his attention and he had to face them before it was too late. She bit her lip and realized he hadn't kissed or caressed her once, had denied her the intimacies of love and mutual satisfaction simply because he could.

What had happened between them changed nothing. She still had to talk to him. Relieved to have regained a modicum of her composure, Jane rolled onto her back and stared up at the canopy over her bed.

Even though part of her shuddered at the thought, she would have to try a more direct approach. Despite his apparent disinterest, she guessed Blaize wouldn't appreciate her widening her sexual experience without him. She'd liked Madame Helene. Perhaps she could persuade the good lady to help her fool Blaize. Jane stripped off the damp shirt that smelled far too potently of Blaize and threw it as far away from her as she could. And if Madame Helene couldn't help, perhaps it was time for her to renew her acquaintance with Captain David Gray.

8

"Good morning, my lord."

Minshom flicked his newspaper an inch to one side to reveal Jane dressed in her highly respectable yet dowdy blue gown, about to sit down opposite him. The white-paneled breakfast room was bright at this time in the morning. It was positioned to take advantage of the sun at the rear of the house and overlooked the small garden between the house and the mews.

"Good morning, my lady. I see you are dressed for travel. May I bid you a heartfelt good-bye?"

"Not at all, my lord. I'm going out with my friend Emily this morning to help at the charity school for orphan girls she cofounded in Blackheath."

He put his paper down. "You are staying?"

She met his gaze, her hazel eyes as clear as the morning sky, knife raised over her plate. "Yes, my lord."

"Even after what happened last night?"

She continued to butter her toast. The scraping sound set Minshom's teeth on edge. He motioned at the solitary footman to get him a fresh pot of coffee, waited until the door closed behind the man and returned to his perusal of his wife.

"Even after I fucked your arse?"

She stopped buttering the toast and neatly cut it into four triangles. "You are my husband; you were merely exercising your marital rights."

He carefully folded his newspaper and put it down on the linen cloth beside his plate. "Oh, we're back to that, are we? Your unconvincing portrayal of a martyred wife. Don't ever go on the stage, Jane, you'd be laughed off."

"I have no intentions of going on the stage, sir. I'm quite happy as I am."

"Last week you told me that you weren't happy at all. What's changed?"

She looked at him, her expression thoughtful. "Me, I think. I've realized that I've done without sex for far too long."

"*You've* realized? Don't you mean that I've showed you?"

She waved an airy hand at him. "You certainly helped, but it isn't always about you, Blaize. You also reminded me of how much I've always enjoyed sex."

"Wait a minute, are you suggesting that you haven't had sex since I left you?"

She blinked at him as if he were a half-wit. "Of course I haven't."

He sat back in his chair to study her more completely. "I don't believe you."

"Just because you are an adulterer doesn't mean that I have to be one as well."

"I still don't believe you."

"Believe what you like, but it's true." She bit into a piece of toast, chewed slowly and swallowed. "I would've thought you'd like to know that you were irreplaceable in my bed."

"That's the part I don't believe. You loved fucking, Jane, almost as much as I did. God, you were desperate for it from the day I met you."

"You make me sound like such a great marital catch." She swallowed hard and looked across at him. "I didn't feel like that about any of the other men I met. Only you."

Minshom got to his feet, aware of that sensation again, the one when he stood far too near the edge of a rapidly crumbling cliff. He picked up his newspaper and tucked it under his arm.

"Gratifying as this display of emotion is, Jane, I'm not changing my mind. You still need to go home."

"Because you don't want to bed me."

"Because you are interfering where you are not wanted. Haven't we had this discussion before?"

"But as we just discussed, you have stirred my sexual appetite."

"So?"

"So what am I to do?"

"I could tell you, Jane, but I try not to be too coarse in front of a lady, even my wife."

She raised her chin to stare at him. "You were certainly coarse last night and I didn't complain. And if you are talking about pleasuring myself, I know how to do that; how do you think I've survived the last few years?"

Minshom stared at her and deliberately licked his lips. "Perhaps you could show me one day. I'd be delighted to critique your performance." He strolled toward the door and put his hand on the ornate gold handle.

"That's hardly the point, is it?" Jane said. "If you will not oblige me, I think it's time I found myself a lover."

He let go of the doorknob and swung around, felt his temper start to rise. "You will do no such thing."

"Why not?"

"Because you are my wife."

"You are my husband and yet gossip says you have fucked almost everyone in the *ton*."

"I'm a man."

"And that makes it different?"

"Of course it does." He gave her his most patronizing smile. "You know the rules. I get your money, your body and your fidelity."

"And what do I get in return?"

"The glory of bearing my esteemed family name?" God, that was a joke; his family was almost as notorious as the disgraced murderous Ferrer's. "The joy of my occasional presence?"

"That's not enough."

He scowled at her. "I don't care. That is the way it is and that is how it will stay."

She glared right back at him, her hands clenched together on the tablecloth, her color high. "And what if I choose to disobey you?"

He took two deliberate steps back toward her until he towered over her chair, but she didn't draw back. "It's within my husbandly rights to beat some sense into you."

"You wouldn't do that, Blaize."

He raised his eyebrows at her. "You are certain of that? Didn't you see me wield that whip last night?"

"That was for a different purpose altogether."

He stared down at her and exhaled sharply. She knew him rather too well. He would never beat her in a rage, would never allow himself to lose control like his father had with him. He'd learned that there were far better ways to dominate and master people. Proving that to Jane would almost be a pleasure.

"If you are so eager to enlarge your sexual experience, I'm quite happy to keep on fucking your arse and letting you suck me off." He brushed a hand over the front of his buckskin breeches and cupped his balls. "You can start now if you like."

"But I haven't finished my breakfast yet."

"So?"

"You wouldn't want toast crumbs in your shirttails, would you?"

He had to stare up at the ceiling so that she wouldn't see the urge to smile that had almost escaped him at her prosaic reply. She was incorrigible. Sometimes he simply wanted to strangle her.

The clock on the mantelpiece chimed the quarter hour and Jane shot to her feet, almost catching him under the chin with her head.

"I have to go and get my bonnet on. Emily is calling for me in five minutes."

Minshom caught hold of her wrists and held her captive. "You are not taking a lover."

She took a long time examining his face before she sighed. "I can't promise that, Blaize, and you can hardly expect me to. You've had everything your own way for far too many years."

"How many years, Jane? Would that be the seven since I've left you, or do you consider our marriage the start of my good fortune?"

She blinked hard and then refocused on him. "There were . . . elements of our marriage that I consider very fortunate indeed."

Damn her and damn the constriction in his chest. How dare she make him remember? He tightened his grip. "There's another excellent reason why you won't ever take a lover. They'll be no cuckoos in my nest or in your womb."

"You . . . you don't ever want to have another child?"

"Of course I don't."

"Blaize . . ."

The shock in her eyes almost made him feel relieved, as if he'd finally gotten through to her, as if she finally understood that there were some mistakes he never intended to repeat. He released her wrists and stepped back. It was time to drive the knife home and make her stop. His smile was calculated to hurt.

"I thought you'd be relieved, Jane."

"Because you say you don't want another child?"

"In truth, I can almost understand why you would want another man to father your child. God knows, if I got you pregnant again I might murder this one as well."

She twisted her hands together, her face as white as his cravat. "I shouldn't have said that, I was distraught, I was hysterical, I . . ."

". . . Was right. I *was* the last person to see Nicholas alive, wasn't I? The last person to hold him and watch him die."

"Don't say it like that, don't make it sound as if you wanted him dead . . ."

Minshom bowed and turned back toward the door. He had to get away from her before he said something he might regret or gave her the opportunity to press him further. Much better to leave now, take his anger and pain with him and . . . and what? Inflict it on Robert? He strode into his study, slammed the door behind him and sat down at his desk. He stared at the stacks of correspondence, the bills, the ledgers, and saw none of it, only the small white face of his son, Nicholas, asleep but not asleep, in his arms but far, far away.

Minshom shoved his hands into his hair and focused on his breathing. Sometimes it was the small things that saved you, the small necessities of life that helped you realize you were still alive and could bear any pain inflicted on you. He'd learned that lesson young and it had always stood him in good stead.

He breathed in time to the tick of the clock until his gaze refocused and his heart stopped pounding like that of hunted prey. He'd known in the depths of his soul that this day would come, that Jane would eventually come after him and want to talk about the "tragedy." He smiled bitterly at his blotting pad. He'd thought seven years would've deadened the pain, but it hadn't.

He raised his head and took another deep breath. If he wanted to survive this, he'd have to pretend that seven years had been more than enough time to forget his son Nicholas had ever existed. If he wanted to survive Jane, *his* very existence might depend on it.

Jane stared at the door Blaize had exited through and sank back down into her chair, one hand covering her mouth. How on earth had she allowed that to happen? The conversation had veered off course with all the randomness of a ship in a storm. And what a pile of wreckage she had created.

Blaize was angry with her and she couldn't blame him. She'd only mentioned taking a lover to annoy him, not considered all the ramifications of her potential liaison. Oh God . . . She wrapped her arms around her waist and rocked slowly back and forth. He didn't want another child and it was all her fault.

"My lady? Are you all right?"

She looked up into the concerned face of one of the footmen who had returned with a fresh pot of coffee.

"I'm not feeling quite well. Would you be good enough to give Lady Millhaven my apologies when she calls and tell her I can't accompany her out today?"

"Of course, my lady." The footman hesitated by her chair. "Would you like me to fetch your maid?"

She managed to smile at him. "No, I'll be fine in a moment. I think I'll take myself upstairs to bed."

"If you're sure, my lady."

She waved him away. "Thank you, I'm sure I'll be fine."

He withdrew, leaving her to get to her feet and walk unsteadily to the door. She glanced toward the end of the long hallway to her left. Blaize's study door was shut. She looked uncertainly at the stairs. She couldn't give way to weakness and go and hide in her room now. Blaize was already angry with her. By confronting him now she couldn't make anything worse, could she?

She tiptoed down to his study and slowly opened the door and slipped inside. He sat at his desk, his profile toward her. One hand was in his black hair, the other tapped out a driving rhythm on his blotter.

"If that's you, Robert, go to hell, but fetch me a bottle of brandy first."

Jane bit her lip and walked around to where he could see her. He stopped tapping and slowly raised his head. His eyes were so cold she almost stopped breathing.

"Get out, Jane."

"I wanted to apologize to you."

He raised one disinterested eyebrow. "Apology accepted, now get out."

She took a step closer. "After Nicholas died I was hysterical with grief, willing to blame anyone, his nursemaids, you, God. Anyone for his death except myself. In my sorrow, I said things that were untrue and accused you of something unforgivable."

"I know what you did and what you said. I was there."

"But once I realized that I was Nicholas's mother, that I should've *known* . . ." She struggled to carry on in the face of such total disinterest. ". . . That I should have protected him."

"From me?"

"No!" Jane swallowed hard. "I know you loved Nicholas, Blaize. I wronged you greatly when I said that you didn't."

A muscle flicked in his cheek. "You did far more than that, my dear. You accused me of murdering him."

She held his gaze, searched for some sign of softening toward her, some sign that he understood what she was trying to say. "And that's why I'm apologizing, because I was wrong and because I have regretted those words ever since."

"So?"

"So I came to London to make amends, to assure you that I never thought you killed Nicholas." She sighed. "I should never have listened to your father's wild imaginings and turned my ridiculous suspicions toward you."

His mouth twisted at one corner. "My father could be very persuasive when he wanted to be."

She felt as if she was trying to run uphill in wet sand and tried again to reach him.

"Still, I should have ignored him. I was very young, but that doesn't excuse my lack of faith in you."

Blaize stood up and walked across to the window.

"But my father was right, wasn't he?"

"I beg your pardon?"

"I did dismiss Nicholas's nurse and insist I was left alone with him that night. And you heard the fight that morning when I swore to my father that he would never get an heir from me."

Jane's stomach did an uncomfortable flip. "What are you saying?"

He shrugged, his expression hidden in the glare from the window behind him. "I think you know."

"But I don't want to blame you anymore," she whispered. "I truly don't."

"That's very generous of you, my dear, but it doesn't really make any difference, does it?" He held her gaze. "Nicholas is dead and I'm responsible."

Jane shook her head as his figure blurred and trembled before her tear-filled eyes. "No."

"And while we're on the subject of exactly why you are here, Jane, why don't you just tell me the rest?"

"The rest of what?" she managed to whisper.

"Your plan."

"I have no plan."

He walked toward her and handed her his handkerchief. "Don't lie to me. I know the way your mind works."

She dabbed at her cheeks and tried to gather her wits. "I came to tell you I was sorry, that's all."

"And what did you expect me to do? Immediately fall at your feet, renounce my evil ways and return home with you?"

"I don't know what I expected." Not this, not him apparently accepting and embracing his guilt. She shuddered as he placed two hard fingers under her chin and brought her head up to look at him.

"And I have disappointed you again, haven't I? Isn't it time for you to go home now?"

Jane closed her eyes to avoid his mocking expression and slowly shook her head. "You're right. I didn't just come here to talk about Nicholas."

"Ah, I thought as much. Is this when you try to persuade me to have another child?" His tone grew frosty. "I believe we've already had that discussion."

She opened her eyes. "That's not what I wanted to discuss at all." His skeptical and patronizing smile gave her the impetus she needed to fight back, if only for a moment. "I wanted to talk about your father."

His smile vanished and was replaced by unreachable coldness. "My God, your curiosity and desire to pry has no boundaries, does it?"

"Blaize, there are things that need to be decided—his last wishes, his debts, his belongings . . ." God, his belongings. She thought about the diaries she'd discovered, the drawings, the hidden secrets of her husband's family that had tainted their relationships for generations.

He walked to the door and flung it open. "Good morning, Lady Minshom."

She held her ground and tried not to cower when he strode back toward her. At least reading the diaries had confirmed things about her husband's past that explained some of his behavior. She could never forget that when she dealt with him now.

He frowned down at her as if he could read her thoughts.

"What the devil is wrong with you? I am not discussing my father with you."

"But, Blaize . . ." She gasped as he picked her up and deposited her outside his door then shut it firmly in her face. She stared at the dark wood paneling, resisting an urge to pummel her fists against it and scream her frustration aloud.

She was back to wanting to scream again and she wasn't going to be allowed back into that study today. With a sigh, she picked up her skirts and headed back along the hallway and up the stairs. She had a lot to think about. Perhaps Blaize was right after all and it really was time for her to leave.

She entered her room and her steps slowed. But wasn't that exactly what he wanted? She took a deep breath, followed it with another, waited until her body stopped shaking so violently. She was no longer an innocent seventeen-year-old bride. She'd fought to become a better woman, survived the double tragedy of losing her son and her husband.

She sat down on the bed and allowed her mind to replay Blaize's answers. He'd suggested that her apologies meant nothing because he'd deliberately killed Nicholas. Instantly her mind rejected his statement. She'd seen him with Nicholas, knew that he would never harm his son, whatever he now said.

Then why say it with such conviction? Jane opened her eyes and frowned. That was the part she didn't understand. The doctor who had examined Nicholas's body had found no marks of violence on him, nothing to indicate that he had been murdered in a rage. He'd been a sickly baby, prone to catching colds and fevers that Jane had been unable to prevent. It was if he had simply given up the struggle to live.

She rose and paced the carpet, her thoughts in a whirl. Even if she couldn't understand why Blaize felt the need to blame himself, it explained why he had never returned to her. She'd imagined it was her harsh and hysterical accusations that had kept him away, but had he simply used her as an excuse when it was his own guilt that paralyzed him?

She stared unseeingly out of the window into the small garden below that led to the mews. It was true that Blaize was found alone in the nursery with Nicholas in his arms and that Nicholas was dead. Jane wrapped her arms around herself and slowly rocked back and forth. How would she have felt if their positions had been reversed? Would Blaize have instantly believed the worst of her, called her a murderer, forced her to leave? In her heart, she suspected he would have defended her against the devil himself.

Jane straightened her shoulders and raised her chin. She wasn't leaving yet. Blaize might have shaken her resolve and destroyed her attempts to sexually resist him, but she wasn't giving up on him. How could she believe that he was really at peace with her and his family when he still refused to talk about his father?

Her gaze slid to her clothes chest and the box concealed there. Unable to resist the compulsion to check that the contents hadn't been disturbed, she locked her bedroom door and retrieved the ornate red leather box. It smelled old and musty and the lid creaked when she opened it.

Despite having viewed the contents more than once, she still had to brace herself to look at them. Blaize's father, the Earl of Swansford's diary lay on the top. THE LITTLE GENTLEMAN'S CLUB was embossed in faded gold lettering on the front. She took it out and opened it at random. Each page was very similar, containing the date of the meeting, the boys involved in the fights and the name of the eventual winner.

Blaize figured on almost every page and she'd charted his horrific progress from his twelve-year-old self to eighteen when the diary abruptly stopped.

She traced his name and the list of other boys, twelve in all on this particular page, all called by their first names as if to protect the identity of their fathers, the fathers who made them fight each other until only one boy remained conscious.

Under the list of boys and the knockout schedule came a description of each fight, its duration and a list of the bets placed on each contestant. The huge sums made Jane wonder anew at the cruelty of men and their obsession with winning, even wagering on their son's lives.

In the beginning, being one of the youngest, Blaize had lost all the time. By the end of the journal he was winning consistently and beating all the older boys. Jane shuddered at the thought of just how he had achieved that supremacy. It wasn't surprising that he wanted to dominate everyone around him. He'd learned that lesson far too young and from a man who should've been protecting him.

She put the book aside and stared at the pile of documents underneath. And this wasn't the worst of it. The Little Gentleman's Club had been run by the same group of aristocratic families for at least three generations, each father putting one of his sons into the ring, each father passing on the legacy of violence.

Had Blaize been horrified at the thought of carrying on such an appalling tradition? Or could he have decided, while in a rage, that his son would never live to be forced into participating in such a horrific legacy? Jane shuddered. She would've fought him on that, fought him with every weapon at her disposal rather than let any child of hers be deliberately hurt. But she still couldn't imagine him killing his own child purely to prove a point to his father. He'd be far more likely to refuse to resurrect the club completely.

She stuffed the book back into the box and couldn't bear to look at the sadistic little pen and ink drawings showing various boys being beaten to a pulp. But who had fought for Blaize? No one. His mother either hadn't known or hadn't cared what happened to him every summer. And she'd died when he was thirteen. He'd had to fight to survive and she suspected his father hadn't made it easy for him at all.

She replaced the heavy box back at the bottom of her clothes chest and shut the lid. She was staying. Despite her doubts, she had to convince Blaize to face his past and deal with the twisted legacy his father had bestowed on him. With renewed energy, she rang the bell. Somehow she doubted Blaize intended to have dinner with her tonight. She had to be ready to go out with him whether he wanted her company or not.

9

"What exactly do you think you are doing, Jane?"

Minshom studied his wife who was dressed in her men's clothing, hair braided tightly down her back. She'd invaded his bedchamber uninvited and was now interfering with the ritual of his dressing.

"I'm coming out with you."

"You damned well are not."

He allowed Robert to help him into his dark blue coat and settle it over his shoulders. Before Robert could step back, he deliberately swung him around to face Jane and ran his fingers down the front of Robert's breeches to cup his balls. Robert's breath hissed out as he squeezed hard.

"I'm not in the mood to bear with you tonight, wife."

She swallowed, her eyes fixed on the unsubtle movements of his hand as he forced Robert's cock to swell between his fingers. After downing half a bottle of brandy to quell the maelstrom of unwanted emotions she roused in him, he still felt dangerous, needed sex, needed to dominate.

"I want to come with you."

He gave Robert's cock one last yank and released him. "So does Robert, but I'm going to deny him release all night and keep him erect like this so that everyone can see how much he wants it."

"That's cruel."

Minshom shrugged. "I know. So don't come out with me."

"But I want to."

"Because you are still feeling guilty?"

She met his gaze. "Perhaps."

He bared his teeth at her. "If you come out with me this evening, I'll take your guilt and use it against you."

She nodded as serenely as the queen. "I understand."

He smiled at her and inclined his head, sudden excitement thundering through his veins at the thought of having her, the source of all his sorrows, at his mercy again. "No, you don't, but you soon will."

He took Jane back to the pleasure house and played with Robert's cock during the short carriage journey just to annoy her. Robert's hips surged forward off the seat and Minshom immediately stopped touching him, watched as sweat broke out on his valet's forehead.

"Don't come, Robert."

"No, sir. I won't."

Jane touched Robert's arm and glared at Minshom. "You should, Robert. It can't be healthy for a man to be denied release like that."

"Are you offering to suck him off?"

Jane raised her eyebrows. "If you like."

Minshom's own cock swelled at the challenge in her voice "But then you'd both enjoy yourselves too much."

"And you prefer others to suffer."

"You know me so well, my dear."

Jane ignored him and turned back to Robert. "Please don't

make yourself ill just because of my husband's stupid obsession with being in charge."

Minshom laughed. "You think he doesn't like it? You might know me, but you don't know Robert very well at all. He's more than content to be mastered, aren't you, Robert?"

"Unfortunately, his lordship is right, my lady." Robert stared at him for a long moment. "He is my master and I'm quite content with that."

"You could learn a lot from Robert, my dear."

"In what way?"

"Complete obedience to my will, a desire to give me sexual release whenever and however I want it."

"I am being as obedient as I can, my lord." Jane answered as if the words were being forced from her lips.

He stopped smiling, "We'll see about that won't we?" Robert shifted uneasily in his seat and Minshom reached for his cock again. "Now where were we?"

"Wait here."

Robert frowned as Lord Minshom escorted his wife into one of the more intimate rooms on the third floor and shut the door in his face. What was he supposed to do? Stand here all night watching hardened sexual libertines pass on their way down to the more public salons on the lower floors?

He knocked on the door and Minshom opened it, his expression irate.

"What?"

"What do you want me to do, my lord?"

"I told you to wait."

"Do you wish me to strip for the pleasure of others or simply stand here like an invisible footman guarding the door?"

Minshom's blue eyes turned to chipped ice. "I don't like your tone, Robert. Perhaps you *should* take off your shirt and leave your breeches unbuttoned for anyone who wants to grope you."

Robert exhaled. "I didn't mean it like that, my lord. I . . ."

"Do what I said." Minshom indicated a hook high up on the wall. "And keep your hands up there."

Minshom waited as Robert stripped off his coat, waistcoat and shirt. He shivered as Minshom nonchalantly pinched his nipples. There was a coldness about his master tonight that didn't bode well for his wife and yet it excited Robert—it always had. Robert lifted his arms and grasped the lamp hook above his head. Minshom took the discarded cravat and secured Robert's wrists to the metal, then stepped back and nodded.

"Have a pleasant evening, Robert."

Robert exhaled as Minshom stepped back inside the room and shut the door. His beleaguered cock was already throbbing with the anticipation of being touched, of being handled without his consent. A deep shame burned low in his gut. He craved this and Minshom knew it, understood him better sometimes than he understood himself. He closed his eyes and settled back against the wall to wait.

Minshom circled Jane, who had remained in the middle of the room, one hand resting on the leather contraption he intended to bind her to. By the pleasure house standards, it was a small, intimate room. The narrow bed was only meant for one, the floor space dominated by the leather horse in the center and the various sexual toys hung on the darkly painted walls.

"Are you sure you want to do this, Jane?"

"Yes, my lord."

He placed his hand on her shoulder and she jumped before turning to look at him.

"Are you quite sure? Because once I tie you down, that's it; you're my plaything for as long as I want."

"I know that."

He admired her courage even if he knew it was a front. "Then as long as we understand each other . . ." He stepped back and settled himself into a chair by the small fire. "Strip."

He watched her slender pale body emerge from its male trappings until she faced him, her expression calm, her skin tinted pink like the finest Italian marble. He deliberately allowed his gaze to wander from her head to her toes, paused to study her breasts and the neat triangle of brown hair at the apex of her thighs.

"You've remained remarkably slender, Jane."

"I've been too busy managing your estate, my lord, to lounge around eating sugar plums."

He wagged a lazy index finger at her. "From now on, you'll only speak when I ask you a direct question. Do you understand?"

She nodded, her mouth set in a determined line that amused him greatly. Jane loved to talk, loved to use her quick wits to confound him. Being unable to speak would go hard on her. But he wasn't in the mood to be pleasant and accommodating tonight. She'd raised the dual specters of his past and now his body seethed with the memories, with the regrets, with the anger. He yearned to lash out, to share his pain, his anguish . . . Yet hadn't Jane suffered alongside him? Hadn't they ploughed parallel lines of despair?

Minshom shook off the memories and pointed at the leather horse. "Lie facedown on it." He waited until Jane did what he had asked and then strolled over to her. It took him but a moment to readjust her position, to place her chin on the very edge of the leather and to spread her legs so that the curve of her sex was visible from behind. Her arms hung down on either side of the central section.

"Cross you arms as if over your breasts."

She complied, her palms flattened on the side of the cylindrical shape and her fingers almost touching her shoulders.

"Hold still."

He took several long leather ties and bound her torso and crossed arms to the leather, kept her immobilized from neck to hip. He walked around to where she could see him and took off his coat and waistcoat. Her hazel eyes looked wide and vulnerable as she watched him.

"Did I tell you that this room is open to the public?" She blinked at him but didn't speak. "Yes, anyone who wants can come in here and watch us, touch you, even fuck you if I permit it."

"You would let another man do that to me?"

"I told you not to question me." She sounded breathless. He liked that slight hint of vulnerability far more than he should have, wanted more, wanted it all. "It depends on how you perform, my dear. How good you are at taking what I give you without complaining."

He trailed his fingers over her hair and down her spine, enjoyed the way her skin rippled and responded to his touch, the slight arch of her hips, and the catch in her breath. He let his hand rest on her buttock and squeezed hard.

"I believe I owe you a spanking. So let's start there, shall we?"

Jane tried not to react as Blaize's hand connected with her left buttock and then returned to strike her again. The regularity and accuracy of his strokes had her biting her lip and tensing her muscles against the next blow. He stopped and spread his fingers out over her heated flesh.

"Stop fighting it, Jane. Take the punishment, accept it, embrace it. Didn't you want that, didn't you want to show me how sorry you are?"

She wanted to scream at him, to ask him what the hell he was talking about, but she'd promised not to question him hadn't she? She moaned as he started on her right buttock and then alternated between the two. His voice floated over her, so calm, so persuasive, so incredibly inviting.

"Breathe through it. Stop resisting and you'll enjoy it."

She closed her eyes tight and let her body sink down onto the leather, wondering if it would help absorb the sting of the slaps. His rhythm didn't falter and soon it became a white and red haze of motion behind her eyes, inside her skin.

"That's right, Jane. Take it."

Strange how she couldn't feel each individual slap now, only the tempo of the whole, the way her mound rubbed against the leather with each forward motion, the way her breathing had slowed until she felt almost detached, as if she were floating in the red molten heat.

She gasped when she felt his fingers flick over her clit and circle her opening.

"You're wet for me now."

The satisfaction in his voice should've annoyed her, but she could do nothing to stop him touching her, nothing to stop the need and the wetness flowing from her over-sensitized body. It had always been like this. Since the first day she met him she'd wanted him, opened her legs and her heart to him without a second thought.

She opened her eyes as he appeared in front of her, her gaze on level with his pantaloons, the bulge of his cock all too evident in the close-fitting garment. He moved closer until the satin brushed her lips.

"Lick it. Take me into your mouth."

She licked at the satin, tasted his arousal seeping through the tightly stretched fabric and tried to suck him into her mouth. She felt a tug on her braid as he wrapped it around his fist, bringing her head slightly farther back. She moaned as he loosened the ties and used his other hand to play with her breasts, to pinch and fondle until she could no longer tell if it was pleasurable anymore, just endure the waves of sensation.

He released her braid and moved away to the far side of the small room and opened a drawer, selected several items and returned to her. He crouched down so that she could see his face and held up the ornaments in his hand.

"These are for your nipples. They re-create the sensation of a man's teeth pulling on you."

He pinched her right nipple between his finger and thumb and slid the metal clamp on. Jane's breath hissed out as the teeth sank into her aching distended flesh. She tried to jerk backward. Blaize cupped her skull, brought her face back to his.

"Breathe through the pain. I'm going to do the second one now."

"No."

"Don't argue with me, Jane."

She gasped as he ignored her and fixed the second clamp. She focused, instead, on mastering the sharp burning ache. Eventually, she stopped shuddering and Blaize slid a finger under her chin.

"Don't fight me anymore, or I will let them touch you."

Frantically, Jane tried to look to the side. Were there other people in the room? She'd totally forgotten about that possibility during her struggle to deal with Blaize's sexual games. He stood and walked away from her and she almost panicked. Was he leaving her?

"I will not . . . fight you." she whispered.

"Good. Now I'm going to put a clamp on your clit."

He came up behind her, his hand firm on her reddened buttock. His fingers plucked at her clit and added the clamp and she climaxed. She felt him slide something inside her pussy while she was still pulsing and writhing. God, she couldn't even ask him what he'd done, what he'd penetrated her with. She knew only that it wouldn't be his cock.

She moaned as he fingered her arse and oiled her before pushing something cold and big inside her again. Her lower body throbbed with the double sensation of fullness, with the pinch of the clamps and the still stinging heat from her buttocks. She felt exposed, as if all her sensuality had been brought to the surface, the tip of her clit, her nipples, her . . . God, her sex, all open, raw, greedy and available to Blaize.

He appeared before her again, a long thin whip in one hand as he slowly unbuttoned his pantaloons with the other. She swallowed hard as she glimpsed the rounded metal head of the piercing underneath the foreskin of Blaize's cock. How would that feel in her mouth, would it choke her?

She had no time to think as he cupped her jaw and rubbed the wet purple crown of his cock against her lips until they were wet with pre-cum.

"Open your mouth, Jane."

Helplessly, she did as he asked and he leaned into her, fed his thick length into her mouth and headed for the back of her throat. She could feel the hardness of the metal stud against her tongue, but it wasn't unpleasant. As she started to suck, she wondered when he had decided to pierce his cock, wondered if she'd ever get the opportunity to ask him.

Her thoughts were abruptly directed back to the present when the whip glided over her buttocks, reigniting the earlier heat and energy. She sucked harder as her whole body started to throb. She wanted to scream but couldn't make a sound around the thick cock filling her mouth.

Was this truly what she wanted? Was this really about showing Blaize she was sorry or was she simply satisfying her own peculiar sexual desires? She couldn't remember anymore, didn't care anymore as he came into her mouth and she climaxed so violently her whole body convulsed as if she were being invaded by demons.

Minshom looked down at his wife as she writhed and twisted against her bonds. He wanted her again. Wanted to take her until she begged him to stop, until she begged him to never stop. He dropped the whip and eased his still half-erect cock from between her lips. His anger had dissipated, blown away in the salacious delights of arousing his wife, of taking her beyond her sexual limits and making her climax for him alone.

Disturbed by the direction of his thoughts and Jane's obvious enjoyment of her captivity, he pushed his hair back from his face. Jane would be leaving him soon. His current fascination with her was just that, an interlude, a passing fancy, an urge that sexual familiarity would soon destroy.

He stuffed his cock back into his pantaloons and stalked toward the door. Jane wasn't going anywhere, and he desperately needed to get away from her.

Robert sighed as he strained to hear Lord Minshom's quiet voice through the door. Lady Minshom had stopped speaking a while ago, either gagged or otherwise occupied. Robert frowned down at his half-erect cock. Was he jealous of Lady Minshom? Did he truly wish to be in her place when his master was in this kind of temper?

Robert raised his shoulders to ease the ache in his back. In truth, he'd never seen Lord Minshom in this kind of a mood over a woman.

"Robert."

He looked up into the familiar face of Captain David Gray and tried to smile.

"Sir."

"Are you waiting for someone?"

"Yes, sir. I'm waiting for Lord Minshom."

"Like this?" Captain Gray frowned. "Where is he?"

Robert jerked his head to one side to indicate the door. "In there, sir."

"With a new man? He left you out here while he dallies with another man?"

"No, sir, he's with a woman."

Captain Gray's expression was almost comical. "A woman?"

"Yes, sir."

A group of rowdy drunkards came down the narrow passageway and shoved Captain Gray to one side. Robert groaned as the Captain's thigh connected with his exposed cock.

"God, I'm sorry, Robert." He groaned again as the Captain's fingers closed around his already-throbbing shaft. "Did I hurt you?"

"No, sir, God . . ."

David's fingers stilled as his thumb brushed the wetness oozing from Robert's slit. He brushed at it again, swirled the tip of his finger into the mess. He sucked his fingers into his mouth and stared at Robert.

"I want my mouth on you, Robert."

"I have to stay here, sir. I can't . . ."

"That's not a problem." David slid down to his knees, hardly an effort when his knees were already shaking. "I'll manage."

He closed his eyes and used his tongue and fingers to locate Robert's cock, shoved aside his half-open breeches and licked him from tip to balls. Robert's answering groan emboldened him and he sucked each tight ball into his mouth, drew on them, until Robert's hips surged forward. He returned to lick Robert's cock, took him deep into his mouth with one swift hungry swallow.

God, he felt good. David curved one arm around Robert's hips to keep him close, not that the man was trying to escape him—far from it. But he'd missed Robert's unique taste, the thickness of his shaft, the way he thrust himself so deeply and urgently into David's willing mouth as if desperate not to miss a moment of his attentions.

"God."

Robert's cock bucked against the roof of David's mouth and he started to come, his shaft pumping hard, his hot seed pouring down David's throat. David felt an answering kick in his own cock but kept his focus on Robert, denying himself satisfaction for his lover.

He gave Robert's shaft one last lascivious lick and got up, found Robert staring at him, his brown eyes still hazy with lust. David leaned in and kissed his mouth. "Thank you."

Robert sighed. "Sir . . ."

"My name is David." He glanced at the still-closed door beside them. "And it's all right. Minshom didn't see anything so you don't have to worry." He turned to leave and felt sick to his stomach when he realized he had achieved nothing except to make himself horny and angry all over again.

"I'm not worried about myself," Robert muttered. "I'm worried about what he'll do if he finds you here."

"What else could Minshom do to me? I've already given him everything he demanded, endured everything he ever threw at me."

"But I don't want you to have to deal with that again."

"Because I escaped?" David grimaced. "And what if I realized that I'd lost more than I'd gained?"

Robert's gaze flicked away from him. "Don't say that."

"But it's true. I lost you."

"You never had me. I was always Minshom's creature, you know that."

"Because he saved you or because he damned you for all eternity?"

"He saved me, sir. He stood up to his father and saved my life, took a beating for me that would've finished me off."

"I know. I was there. I was part of that horror too." David rubbed his hand over his mouth to erase the taste of those memories, tasted Robert instead. "But it doesn't mean he still owns you."

Robert's face lost all expression. "I promised never to leave him."

"And he's abused that promise on numerous occasions, why can't you see that?"

David struggled to mask his frustration and to present the calm face he showed to the rest of the world. But there was something about Robert that had always exposed him for what he was, a man who was hopelessly in love with a man completely committed to someone else. Someone who didn't even deserve such loyalty and love.

"Good evening, Captain Gray."

David swung around to find Minshom at the door, his expression frosty. God, how much had the man heard and what did he intend to do to Robert?

"Good evening, Lord Minshom. I was just annoying your servant." He nodded brusquely at Robert. "He had the good sense to ignore me."

"Was that before or after you had sex?" Minshom leaned forward and licked David's lips. "I can taste Robert's cum."

David tried to hide his instant physical reaction to Minshom's touch and raised an eyebrow. "If you leave him alone in a hallway, with his breeches open and his chest exposed, what do you expect?"

Minshom stared at him for a long moment and then nodded. "Would you like Robert to suck you off?"

"I beg your pardon?"

Minshom glanced at his valet. "Robert needs to learn some self-restraint and he's always had a soft spot for you. I was in need of a diversion. Come inside and Robert will oblige you."

David knew he should walk away, but the thought of Robert touching him, combined with his curiosity as to what on earth Minshom was doing with a woman, proved too strong for him to resist. He nodded his agreement and stepped into the small black-walled room.

10

Jane heard the door slam behind Minshom and struggled to turn her head. Had he left her? Had he really had the nerve to walk out and leave her tied up and alone in the pleasure house? She tried to breathe away the panic but couldn't, tried to fight the leather straps but remained captive.

She'd done what he wanted, she hadn't argued with him after he'd warned her, so where had he gone? She licked her lips. Was he intending to leave her to the mercy of the other guests, to let them fondle and fuck her at will? Part of her trembled at the thought, the other more basic parts of her stirred with anticipation. She sighed, the sound loud in the small room. Blaize knew her too well, played her with a sexual expertise that exposed her willingness to submit, her eagerness to be dominated . . . her inability to say no to him.

Voices sounded outside the room and the door opened. Instinctively, Jane shut her eyes until she realized she recognized at least two of them, and vaguely a third. She jumped as someone slapped her buttock, knew it was Blaize when he chuckled at her reaction. He came to stand in front of her.

"Did you think I'd left you for good?"

She didn't speak, but she knew he'd like her to challenge him by the gleam in his eyes.

"Were you becoming aroused at the thought of other guests coming in here and touching you?" He smiled. "In extremis, you often confessed to a desire to be fucked by more than one man. Whether to make me punish you or because you really craved it, I don't know. And, quite frankly, it doesn't matter."

He turned to the chest of drawers on the wall and retrieved a silk scarf. "I'm going to gag you now so that no one is tempted to fuck your pretty little mouth."

He tied the silk in a tight knot at the back of her head and then untied her braid, allowing her hair to slither and slide down to her hips.

"Come here, Robert." He clicked his fingers and Robert appeared in Jane's sight. "Now strip."

Jane watched in reluctant fascination as Robert took off his clothes to reveal his strong narrow frame and already-erect cock. Blaize was taking things out of the drawers again, his back to Jane as he talked.

"Robert needs to learn to keep his cock and his hands to himself." He beckoned to Robert. "Put this on your cock and balls, make sure it is tight."

"Yes, my lord."

Jane watched as Robert tried to stuff his erect cock and balls through the metal rings and spirals Minshom handed him. He grunted as he tried to shove the largest of the rings down to the root of his shaft to join the two smaller rings already encompassing his balls.

"It hurts less when you aren't constantly hard, Robert. Perhaps you should bear that in mind."

"Yes, my lord."

In the flickering candlelight, wetness gleamed on the tip of Robert's straining cock, emphasized the tightness of the rings constricting his blood flow and keeping his balls tight and high against his body.

Blaize walked over to examine Robert's cock, pushed the rings lower and closer together until Robert groaned.

"Please, my lord."

"Please what? You know the rules, Robert. I'm the only man who is allowed to make you come. You disobeyed me and now you must suffer the consequences."

The other man cleared his throat. "He didn't disobey you. He was tied to the wall. I took advantage of him."

Jane frowned as the lower half of another man came into view to stand between Robert and Blaize. He sounded familiar as well. Had she met him before? Would he recognize her tied facedown and naked?

"It seems you have a champion, Robert, but then David was always very fond of you, wasn't he?"

"Sir . . ." Robert sounded agitated.

"Don't interrupt me. Get down on your knees, put your hands behind your back and use your mouth for something useful." Blaize bowed to the man he'd called David. "If you want him to suck your cock, I suggest you unbutton your breeches."

There was a long silence broken by David's soft curse and the sound of him undoing his placket.

Blaize stepped out of her way and she was treated to the sight of Robert on his knees in front of a tall blond man dressed in naval uniform.

"Are you enjoying this, Jane? You always liked to watch Robert suck me off; perhaps this will be even more arousing for you."

For a moment, Jane was glad she had been gagged as she couldn't think of a thing to say. David cradled Robert's head in one hand and guided his motions, his gentleness in stark contrast to the more domineering way Blaize insisted he was serviced. His cock was big too, stretching Robert's lips as he sucked and pulled on it.

She jumped when Minshom's hands closed on her hips and his satin pantaloons brushed the insides of her spread thighs.

"Keep watching Jane."

She shivered as he removed the thick dildo from her arse and drove his cock inside her instead. The heat and motion of his throbbing shaft felt so different from the cold stone. He began to thrust and each movement sent a jolt through the dildo in her pussy and the clamp on her clit. He reached around her hips, his hard body almost flat on top of hers and plucked at her nipples. She climaxed instantly and kept climaxing as he continued to pound into her.

"You like it, don't you, Jane? You like the thought that they can see you being fucked, even as you enjoy watching them."

She couldn't deny it, even as pleasure flooded through her and then rebuilt, forced her to a higher plane of awareness where pain and pleasure bonded into a white-hot wire of ecstasy. She whimpered as she watched David's hand tighten in Robert's thick red hair, saw his hips start to lose their smooth rhythm and just slam into Robert's mouth.

"Come in his mouth, David, do it right now," Blaize commanded.

David groaned and thrust one last time; Robert's throat worked convulsively as he swallowed the other man's cum. Behind her Blaize stopped moving and held himself deep and still inside her.

"Get up, Robert."

Robert rose, his hands clasped behind his back, his trussed-up cock dripping with pre-cum and straining against his bonds.

"Do you want to come?"

"Yes, sir."

"But you won't until I tell you to, will you?"

"No, sir."

Blaize laughed. "You see how obedient he can be, David?"

"I'd be happy to make him come again."

"But that wouldn't be the point would it? Robert has to remember who his master is."

"He is a free man, not a slave."

"What did he say when you told him that?"

"That he was bound to you. That you were his master."

"And yet you still pine for him after all these years?"

"Yes."

How could David say that out loud? Why didn't he sound weak when he said it? Minshom shifted slightly to remind Jane that he still hadn't come, to demonstrate his superior control, to impress upon her that all the power was in his hands. He'd originally considered letting one of the other men have her as well but realized he had no intention of sharing her at all. A surprising discovery that he refused to examine too closely, let alone impart to Robert and David.

"Perhaps you need to understand that Robert will do anything I tell him to. Come and stand by Jane's head, Robert."

Jane's view of David was blocked by Robert's naked stomach and groin.

"What do you want me to do, sir?"

"Take your cock and place the head against the silk scarf covering her mouth. When you are ready, take your hands away and brace them on the side of the leather horse."

"This is hardly necessary," David said abruptly.

"Ah, but it is. Jane needs to accept my orders as well. Both of them have shown far too much of an independent streak recently."

A muscle flicked in David's cheek. "And what am I supposed to do while you 'punish' them?"

"Your cock is already erect again, so either fuck Robert or manage for yourself."

"I don't get to fuck you?"

"You'll never get to fuck me again."

"Again? You remember that, do you?"

David's blue eyes met his and Minshom refused to look away, refused to acknowledge his slip about the past and their shared pain.

He rocked his hips. Both Jane and Robert moaned as Robert's cock brushed the already sodden silk scarf across Jane's mouth.

David took a step back. "I'm not going to fuck him, Minshom."

"Why not? Are you afraid he still prefers me?"

"No. I'm not going to fuck another man without his consent and I swore long ago never to take orders from you again."

Minshom raised his eyebrows. "But you came here at my bidding and you let Robert suck your cock. Why stop now?"

"Because I've realized I am a fool." David sighed. "I should've learned to keep away from you by now."

Blaize held his gaze and started to slam his shaft into Jane, pushing her inexorably against Robert's trapped cock. Robert started to groan and bowed his head, his shoulders shaking with the effort to restrain his desire to come.

David didn't move but seemed unable to tear his eyes away from the scene. Minshom felt his cum gather at the root of his shaft and pumped harder, kept his eyes open as he climaxed in thick pulsing waves deep inside Jane's arse. Robert groaned and fell to his knees, almost banging his head against Jane's as he collapsed to the floor.

Before Minshom could recover and order him to stand up, David knelt beside Robert and pushed him onto his back, used his hands and then his mouth to rid Robert of the cock rings. Minshom smiled as Robert appeared to struggle against the other man and then realized his servant was simply trying to reposition himself so that both men could take each other's cocks in their mouths.

Blaize slowly pulled out of Jane and studied the two men. Why hadn't he realized that David was completely obsessed with Robert? It explained why he had put up with Minshom for so long when it had been obvious that his tastes ran in different directions. Part of him wanted to join in, take charge, fuck them both until they screamed. Jane would probably enjoy that and it certainly might make her run for home.

He tucked his cock back into his pantaloons and turned to untie Jane and remove the dildo and gag. The two men were oblivious at the moment, too engrossed in bringing each other to a climax, with expressing lust long withheld.

Jane collapsed back against him and he wrapped his arms around her nakedness and drew her close, her buttocks nestled against his groin. She turned her head to whisper in his ear.

"Aren't you going to stop them?"

"How do you suggest I do that? Throw a bucket of water over them?"

"But . . ."

"I'd rather join in. Would you like to see that, Jane? Three men fucking each other while you watched and pleasured yourself?"

He allowed his fingers to drift down over her slightly rounded stomach, felt her tremble and then her sharp intake of breath when he removed the clamp from her clit and then the ones on her nipples.

"You liked the pain of these, didn't you?"

She turned her head away, her long hair covering her face, her answer almost indistinct. "Yes."

"I liked watching you squirm and pant and come for me." He glared at the men on the floor but felt curiously unmoved. "I think we should leave them here, to wallow in their sordid passion, don't you?" He hoisted her higher in his arms, stepped over Robert's outstretched leg and headed for the door.

"But I'm naked."

"And I'm not stopping to find your clothes." He liked the thought of her sitting in his lap on the way home, her long hair sliding through his fingers, her body open and available to him and only to him. He gathered her closer and went down the first flight of stairs.

How strange that the thought of a naked Jane was far more exciting than the men fucking on the floor behind him. He paused on the landing and stared down the next flight of dimly lit backstairs. What the hell was wrong with him?

Robert shoved at David's breeches, pulled them as far down as he could to feel the other man's taut buttocks under his hands. His cock was on fire, the need to fuck and be fucked unavoidable.

"Please, Robert," David groaned around his cock.

He sucked harder, drew David's shaft as far down his throat as he could manage, wanted to give him so much pleasure he'd scream. Too late to stop now, too late to worry if Minshom was going to punish him. This gloriously forbidden and long-dreamed-of liaison would have to end tonight, but by God, he was going to enjoy it for as long as Minshom let him.

David bucked his hips and slid his fingers between his cock and Robert's teeth to release himself. He rolled onto his stomach. The invitation to have him was too much for Robert to resist. Turning, he used the thick pre-cum from the tip of his own cock to edge his way inside David, deeper and deeper with each urgent push of his hips until he was gasping with the closeness and tightness, his balls pressed tight against David's.

"God, I've wanted this." He thrust harder, determined to give David everything so that he'd never forget the moment, would have his own memories to carry him through his dark days with Minshom. "God, I've wanted to fuck you like this so much."

"Don't stop then, don't ever stop." David sounded as desperate as Robert felt. "Touch my cock, make me come for you."

Robert slid his hand around to grasp David's thick wet shaft and pumped him in time to his own movements, gripped his cock as tightly as David's arse was gripping his.

He came hard, roared as his cum spilled deep inside David, felt David's climax spurt between his fingers. He bit David's shoulder as he shuddered and shook and finally collapsed over David's back. He tried to get his breath, half waiting for the sting of a whip on his back or the thud of Minshom's boot in his side, but nothing happened. He rolled off David and dared to look up.

There was no sign of Lord Minshom or his wife.

"Where did Minshom go?" David asked, his expression puzzled.

"I don't know. He must have left while we were . . ." Robert sat up and groped for his clothes, dread coalescing in his gut. "I have to go after him, I have to explain."

"Explain what? That you wanted to fuck me?"

Robert went still and reluctantly faced David. "This doesn't change anything, sir. You know that."

"Why the devil not?" David stared at him and then did up his breeches, tucked his shirt in and stood up. "Wasn't I good enough for you?"

Robert grabbed David's hand. "Please don't do this. I fucked you only because Lord Minshom didn't stop me."

"Ah, I see, it's all about Minshom, is it, and nothing to do with how you feel about me."

Robert stood up, his clothes clasped to his chest, his voice sounded as raw as he felt. "I *can't* feel anything for you. I belong to Minshom, don't you understand?"

David shrugged. "I understand that you are afraid and I know how that feels, but I don't understand why you can't walk away from him."

"Perhaps I'm more loyal than you are."

David's expression darkened and he shoved Robert up against the wall. "Don't you dare talk about loyalty to me. I've been waiting for you for years!"

Abruptly he let go of Robert and stepped back, rubbed his hands on his breeches. "Why are you the only man in the world who still makes me angry? I've tried so hard to bury that part of myself, to accept who and what I am and live with it. But you, you make me want to rage, to strip you naked and chain you to my bed and fuck you and fuck you until you can't see or hear anyone but me, crave only me and despair when I'm not inside you."

David drew a deep shuddering breath. "But you don't care about that, do you? You want the familiar, the safe, the known and I can't give you that. Only Minshom can."

Robert wet his lips tried to speak. "You're right, I am a coward. I don't deserve your loyalty."

"Do you think I don't know that?" David touched his cheek. "And yet here I am, still hoping, still loving you."

David's smile made Robert's chest ache and his throat close up. Robert looked at the door. "I have to go. I have to find him, explain . . ."

David bowed and put on his coat. "Good night, Robert. I'll try not to bother you again." He walked out and shut the door very gently behind him.

Robert slid down the wall to the floor and covered his eyes with his hands. He had to get dressed and find Lord Minshom, but how could he when his master would sense the sexual satisfaction he had achieved? What the hell would he do then? Would Minshom finally push him too far or push him away? Robert started to shake as he forced his feet into his stockings and breeches.

Jane tried to move away as Blaize dropped her on the seat of the carriage, then squeaked as he pulled her back onto his knee and held her close to his body. He'd used his cloak to cover her nakedness against the chill of the night air, but she was still shivering, her body reacting to the sexual excesses he had put her through, sensations she would never forget, that she would now crave.

"Stop wiggling, Jane, or I'm going to spank you again."

Blaize's soft words made her go still and allowed him to gather her closer, one hand anchored around her waist, the other on her thigh. His thumb rose to caress the underside of her breast and she shuddered. He knew what he was doing, was a master at stoking sexual fires and then dousing them.

She endured his deliberate touching without speaking even as her sex throbbed and wanted. She'd revealed far too much about her sexual needs for one night; he didn't need to know how much she craved him again. His fingers brushed against her clit, and then again, until she wanted to grab his hand and rub herself shamelessly against his palm until he pushed his fingers inside her and made her come.

She closed her eyes against her rising need. Had she really thought of this as a night of punishment to show Blaize how sorry she was or had she wanted something else? A way to indulge in her most forbidden fantasies with the only man who would ever sexually understand her? She should be ashamed of herself, but she wasn't. Had she become greedy and willing to grab anything he offered her? Did she somehow believe that gaining his sexual interest would persuade him to take her back?

The carriage stopped and he picked her up again, ignored the startled greeting from his butler and carried her straight up the stairs to her room. The ease with which he carried her made her feel weak and very feminine, made her want to cling to him like a limpet, which would never do.

When he bent over to place her on her bed, she didn't let go and he had no choice but to follow her down, her arms around his neck, her legs wrapped around his hips.

"Jane . . ."

She kissed him hard until he kissed her back, his tongue drilling into her mouth, as hot and demanding as her own. She arched her back until her sex rode his erect cock, until her wetness soaked his already-damp pantaloons and she could feel the heat and strength of his pulsing shaft. He groaned into her mouth and she nipped his lip, gloried in her moment of power of being in control of his hard, sinful body.

He wrenched his mouth away from hers and levered himself up on his hands and away from her.

"Stop it, Jane."

She stared at him, her eyes wide, her breathing uneven. "Stop what?"

His lower body was still chained to hers, his cock so close to penetrating her that she wanted to scream at him to do it.

"Trying to get my cock inside you."

"Why would I do that?"

"Because you want me."

She stared into his eyes, suddenly outraged by his smug confidence, his arrogance, and his assumption that she needed him, even if he was right. She reached between them and grabbed for his cock, rubbed him so hard he started to come in thick jerking pulses against her hand. She kept her fingers there and enjoyed every erotic moment of his loss of control.

When he'd finished, she let go of him and looked back up at

his face. "Oh dear, perhaps I was a little too enthusiastic. Now you're the one who is covered in cum."

"And you're not." He climbed carefully off the bed and this time she didn't try to stop him. "And you won't be coming at my hand again tonight." He bowed. "Good night, Jane, and sweet dreams."

She allowed her hand to drift down between her legs and cover her mound, saw his eyes narrow as she plucked at her clit.

"Good night, Blaize. I'm sure my dreams will be sweet—I'll make sure of it."

He turned away from her and muttered something under his breath as he slowly walked toward the door. She could only imagine how uncomfortable he must be feeling and she was so glad. He might win the war but she'd certainly won the last battle. She resumed her stroking of her sex and climaxed quite quickly, smiled and went to sleep.

11

Jane picked up the skirts of the dreary bottle green gown she'd chosen to wear specifically to annoy Blaize, and entered Emily's carriage.

"Jane, dear, whatever are you wearing?"

She smiled at Emily's horrified expression and settled herself on the seat. "Good morning, Emily. This is the dress I usually wear to feed the chickens at Minshom Abbey Farm."

"It certainly smells like it." Emily held her lace handkerchief to her nose. "You are going to change, aren't you?"

"If you have something else for me to wear?"

Emily gestured at the bundle by her side. "Of course I do. Can you change in the carriage?"

"If you help me." Jane wiggled out of the bodice of the green dress. "It was worth resurrecting this gown. You should've seen Minshom's face when I appeared at the breakfast table and announced that I was going visiting with you in it." She laughed. "He almost forbade me to go. I could see the words trembling on his lips before he stalked out. I do so enjoy teasing him."

She thought about the night before, the sheer sexual intensity of Blaize's expression when she'd made him come in his pantaloons. That was another kind of teasing altogether and far more dangerous.

"You should be careful, Jane. Minshom has never struck me as a man who likes to be trifled with."

Jane dropped the green dress on the seat beside her and reached for the brown patterned Indian muslin Emily had chosen for her at Madame Wallace's.

"You were the one who encouraged me to defy him, so why this sudden change of heart?"

Emily frowned at her. "Because I don't want you to get hurt again and disappear."

Jane reached out to clasp Emily's gloved hands. "You won't lose me. I'm a much stronger person than I was then. I'll never lose faith in myself like that again."

Emily's smile returned. "You'd better not, or I won't come after you this time." She sighed. "All right, I probably will, but you'd have to beg awfully hard to make me forgive you this time."

"And I would beg, Emily, never doubt it. I don't want to lose you either." Jane knelt on the carriage floor and turned her back so that Emily could tie her laces and the three buttons at the top of the bodice. She flinched when Emily touched her throat.

"What have we here? A love bite? Have you and Minshom actually been . . . ?"

"Been what?" Jane struggled to her feet and sat down opposite Emily again. "Biting each other?"

"Are you actually blushing, Jane?" Emily gave her a sly wink. "Perhaps I was wrong in my assumptions. Obviously you are more than capable of bringing Minshom to heel without any assistance from me."

"I wish it were that simple." Jane sighed. "So far all he's proved to me is that I am still a fool where he is concerned. He just has to look at me and I'm contemplating climbing into bed with him and doing anything he wants."

"But that's good, isn't it? Isn't that what you want?"

"Not on his terms, Emily. I'd be selling myself to him for nothing." After last night's adventure, Jane realized the truth of that anew. What on earth was she going to do to stop herself craving him?

She smiled at Emily, determined to forget her irritating husband and enjoy her outing. "Where exactly are we going today?"

"To visit my orphans school and then have lunch together?"

"That sounds delightful." Jane smoothed the fine fabric of her new gown and pulled a face. "Perhaps I should've kept my old gown on after all."

"It's all right, Jane. You don't actually have to do anything except look gracious and smile."

Jane shot her friend a mischievous look. "And when have I ever managed to do that? You know I'll want to play with them." She took another glance at her discarded dress. "I think you'd better help me change back after all."

"Good morning, my lord."

Minshom raised his head and stared steadily at his valet. He'd got up and dressed unaided, had breakfast and started work, all without Robert's assistance. In truth, he'd instructed Broadman not to let Robert into his study until he was summoned. Robert had obviously made an effort to look his sartorial best this morning. His cravat was ironed, his auburn hair tamed and he wore his favorite brown coat. If it hadn't been for the telltale rash from another man's stubble on his face, he might almost have looked respectable.

"Good morning, Robert. Did you have a good night?"

Robert sighed. "You know I got back here just after you did. You simply locked me out of your rooms."

"Did I? Maybe I assumed you'd be too busy expressing undying love to the extremely dull Captain Gray to come home."

"I wouldn't do that, sir."

"Why not? The man is obviously infatuated with you."

Robert met his gaze, his brown eyes steady. "You know why, sir."

"Because of me?"

"Yes, sir. I was worried about you."

A spark of anger ignited low in Minshom's gut. "Did you think I'd use my wife as a substitute for you?"

Robert briefly closed his eyes. "Please tell me you didn't, sir?"

Minshom smiled at the anxiety in his voice. "She certainly made me come in a rather painful manner, if that is what you mean, but she didn't provide *quite* what I needed."

"Perhaps that is for the best, my lord. Perhaps with her ladyship here you no longer need me to . . ."

"Fight with?" Minshom paused. "Lady Minshom isn't staying, Robert."

"But if she did, sir?"

Minshom hated the gleam of hope in Robert's brown eyes and moved to crush it. "You are tired of catering to my needs, then? You no longer wish to give me sexual satisfaction?"

"My lord, this isn't fair. I never said that, I just hoped you had found someone else who loves you enough to help you . . ." Robert trailed off.

"To help me." Minshom echoed, his gaze on his lover's flushed face. "I know you hate 'helping me,' Robert. Why do you still do it?"

"Because I love you, sir?"

"And if I told you I didn't care, that your 'love' means nothing to me?"

Robert half-smiled. "I wouldn't believe you."

Minshom glanced down at his hands, which were folded tightly together on his desk. He was becoming tired of Jane and Robert assuming that somehow they meant something to him. He didn't need anybody, didn't deserve anybody's loyalty and certainly had nothing to give back except pain.

After his dealings with Jane, he'd needed Robert last night, but even though he'd just had to unlock the door and Robert would come, he hadn't done it. Sometimes his own desires disgusted him. He slowly raised his head.

"Robert, did it ever occur to you that the debt you think you owe me is false?"

"You saved my life. If you hadn't intervened, your father would've beaten me to death."

"I doubt it."

"I don't. I wasn't a true member of The Little Gentleman's Club; I was just some lower class thing for you all to practice on. I was expendable. No one would've asked any awkward questions if I'd disappeared."

"Perhaps I didn't save you for the reasons you believe."

Robert frowned. "I don't understand, sir."

"Perhaps I saved you because I wanted that beating, wanted to show my father that I was tougher than you were, that I could take anything he or the other boys could hand out to me."

"I'm not sure that makes the outcome any different, does it?" Robert shrugged. "You still saved my life."

Minshom stared at him. "I didn't care whether you lived or died. All I cared about was myself. That's all I've ever cared about."

A flush mounted on Robert's pale skin. "You think I don't know that, sir? I've never had any illusions about who and what you are."

"And yet you still profess your love for me." Minshom managed a derisive laugh. "How pathetic is that?"

"As pathetic as Captain Gray loving me probably." Robert shrugged. "But that's how it is, and that is how it will remain."

"Unless I dismiss you."

Robert stilled, all the color draining from his face. "Sir?"

Minshom sat back and stretched. "I'll think about it and let you know after I've dealt with my wife."

Robert swallowed hard. "If you wish me to leave, I'll go."

"Really? Has the estimable Captain Gray offered you a refuge?" He paused. "Of course he has. He is a far more honorable man than I'll ever be."

Minshom tried to imagine his life without Robert and found it surprisingly difficult. Then he remembered Captain's Gray's face as Robert had sucked his cock. The man had looked as if he was in ecstasy. How could he deny another man that? Because he had been denied, because he'd never been allowed to choose what he wanted, apart from his decision to marry Jane. Damnation, why did everything come back to her? She'd even started affecting his relationship with Robert!

He shrugged and picked up his pen. "It's up to you, Robert. Stay or go; I care not."

Robert simply turned and walked out, leaving Minshom alone. He contemplated the carefully closed door. What would Robert do? And why the devil should he care? He tried to return his attention to his work, realized his ears were straining to hear any sound of Robert returning, or worse, leaving for good.

A knock at the door interrupted his thoughts and he sat up straight. "Come in."

Broadman, his butler, appeared, his round face anxious.

"I'm sorry to disturb you, my lord, but there is a gentleman who would like to see you."

Minshom held out his hand. "Did he give you his card?"

"Indeed he did, sir." Broadman deposited it in his palm and quickly backed away.

Minshom read the engraved black writing and almost stopped breathing. It seemed that all his demons were coming back to torment him this year. He let the card slide through his fingers onto his desk.

"Tell Major Lord Thomas Wesley that I am not at home."

"But you are, sir."

"Tell him I am not and if he calls again, keep telling him, do you understand?"

"Yes, sir. But if I might say, sir, he seems like a very nice gentleman. He's just returned from India."

Minshom fixed Broadman with a quelling stare. "I don't care what he's like. I don't want to see him. Is that clear?"

"Yes, sir, very clear." Broadman backed out of the room, his face troubled. "I'm not the best liar, sir, but I'll tell him you're not home."

Minshom hid his face in his hand and groaned. Sometimes he wondered why he put up with Broadman and his chatty nature. Despite his years of service, he seemed more at home acting like a meddling nurse than a snobbish London butler. Perhaps it was time to pension him off along with Robert and start anew.

His gaze fell on the card again and he couldn't repress a shiver. Thomas was a distant cousin of his whose titled father had died the previous year. Thomas had obviously decided to make the long journey from India to settle his father's affairs. But why the hell did he want to see Minshom? True, they'd once been good friends despite their two-year age gap, but the yearly summer fighting tournaments had put paid to that, made them the deadliest of enemies, each one vying for superiority.

Minshom sighed. He couldn't face another potential battle of wills today. Robert had sucked out his energy and Jane continued to defy him without seeming to do anything at all. The dress she'd worn down for breakfast that morning had been fit for only a pigsty. It had taken all his hard-won restraint to allow her to leave the house in such a garment. And she'd known it, had smiled triumphantly at him as she left.

Too restless to settle to his work, he rose from his desk and went to the window. His life seemed to be dissolving around him. Jane had done this to him once before when he'd first met her and wanted her and married her. Perhaps it wasn't surprising that now she was here again he was floundering. And then there was Sokorvsky, Robert and his new visitor, Thomas Wesley . . .

Damnation, he was going to take a long ride in the park and forget the lot of them. Surely after some physical exercise his beleaguered brain would start working and he'd come up with some new strategies to beat them all. Because his father was right: winning was everything. He'd stake his life and soul on that. He smiled savagely at his faint reflection. In truth, he already had.

"It's all right, Emily. I'll go and change."

Jane picked up the skirts of her old green dress and laughed out loud. After her highly successful morning at the foundling's school, she was covered in glue, feathers and other unmentionable messes she didn't want to identify. After all the incessant tugging from the younger children, her hair had come unpinned and streamed down her back.

"Yes, go up immediately, Jane, you look like a ragamuffin!" Emily tried to shoo Jane up the stairs whilst simultaneously sneezing into her handkerchief.

"Good afternoon, Emily. What on earth is going on? Have you started keeping chickens in the house?"

Jane froze, her bottom foot on the stairs, and turned slowly around. A tall blond-haired man in naval uniform stood laughing in the hallway batting at the feathers swirling in the draughts.

Oh God, would Captain Gray recognize her from the night

before? She met his sea blue gaze, watched his eyes widen and a faint color appear on his cheeks. Oh dear. It appeared that he did. She smiled brightly and sketched a curtsey.

"Captain Gray. How delightful to see you again."

Emily nodded at her brother-in-law. "You remember Lady Minshom, don't you, David? She was at my wedding."

He bowed, hat in hand. "Of course I do, Emily. It's a pleasure to see you again, my lady."

Emily gestured to Jane to keep moving. "Go and get changed and meet us in the small dining room. David will be joining us for lunch so you can enjoy a quiet chat."

"I'll be as quick as I can, Emily." Jane trudged up the stairs behind the maid Emily had asked to help her and was ushered into one of the spare bedrooms. Now what was she going to do? Pretend that she knew nothing about David and his complicated love life, or admit it all?

As the maid helped her out of the old gown and started to brush the feathers from her hair, Jane stared at her stricken face in the mirror. The situation was already difficult and involving Emily would only make it worse. She would have to take care to ask enough questions to satisfy her friend without betraying the rest.

With a sigh, Jane allowed the maid to lace her into the new dress and pin up her hair. It was time to face Captain Gray, whether she wanted to or not.

David rose as Lady Minshom entered the sunny dining room and took the seat opposite his. She looked completely different now, her brown hair tamed, braided and pinned tightly to her head, her dress immaculate. He wondered if he would have even recognized her if he hadn't seen her laughing in the hallway with her distinctive long hair swirling around her hips.

And how the hell had she ended up at Madame Helene's with her estranged husband? David wasn't normally a man who enjoyed gossip, but even he was intrigued by this aberration in Minshom's behavior. He'd never seen Minshom with a woman in a sexual situation before. Did the man after all have a streak of morality, that he wouldn't fuck a woman when he had a wife?

David realized he was still standing behind his chair and quickly sat down. Emily raised her eyebrows at him. She wasn't stupid—he would have to be careful about how he dealt with the fascinating Lady Minshom in front of her. Absentmindedly, he served both ladies some wine and helped pass the dishes abound the table, lapsed into social small talk as if he hadn't just experienced the most shattering night of his life.

Emily sat back when the last of the servants withdrew and smiled at Lady Minshom.

"Jane, I'm sure that David would be happy to talk to you about anything you wish, wouldn't you David?"

For a fleeting second, David met Lady Minshom's hazel eyes and tried not to look as panicked as he felt. Had she just winked at him? Surely not. He took a deep breath, remembered he'd been in worse situations than this before, far worse, and inclined his head.

"I'd be delighted to help Lady Minshom in any way I can, Emily."

"Good, because, if you'll excuse me for speaking so frankly, we, I mean *she*, wants to know all there is about the relationship between Lord Anthony Sokorvsky and Minshom."

"About Sokorvsky?" God, was he actually stuttering? "I thought..." Never mind what he'd thought, he needed to adapt to this sudden change of tack.

"It seems that my husband took it very badly when Lord Anthony left him."

Lady Minshom's quiet voice steadied David, allowed him a few moments to marshal his thoughts. "He did. I think Anthony was the first man who had ever left him for a woman."

"But not the first man to ever leave him."

David nodded. "I left him, but that was to preserve my sanity. He was like an addiction for me, an addiction I needed to rid myself of."

"And you succeeded."

"I'm not sure if I did." David sighed. "Your husband is a very difficult man to forget."

"I know."

Her smile flashed out, surprising him with its warmth and beauty. Why on earth had Minshom married this woman? She seemed far too nice and normal, but then she had been at Madame's last night . . .

"He left me seven years ago and here I am, still trying to understand him and get him back."

David put his wineglass down on the crisp white tablecloth. "In truth, it was about seven years ago when he started to change, to become more cynical, more inclined to dominate everyone around him." He shrugged. "Although he had those tendencies when we were boys together."

"You've known him that long?"

David blinked at the intensity of her question. What else might he betray? What else didn't she know about her husband? "Yes, we were at school together and our fathers . . . our fathers were friends." *God damn them both to hell.*

She sat back, her expression distant as if trying to recall something important. "Of course, I should've known that. But Minshom wasn't at school with Lord Anthony, was he?"

"No, Anthony is much younger than us, about six and twenty I believe."

"Really? I'd pictured him as older. He isn't far off our age. Emily, do you know him?"

"I've met him a couple of times." Emily looked thoughtful. "He is a very handsome man and from an excellent if slightly eccentric family."

"What did Minshom see in him to make him want him and then resent losing him so badly?"

David sighed. "Because originally Anthony seemed to crave what Minshom likes to give—pain. But as Anthony matured, he realized that Minshom's way wasn't the only way to gain sexual pleasure, and that he had to choose his own path."

"And he found it with a woman?"

David smiled. "That is certainly part of the equation, though I'm not sure if it is the whole of it."

"And this woman doesn't object to that?"

"Obviously, I can't speak for her, but I do know that she loves Anthony and is willing to allow him to explore more unconventional avenues for sexual gratification than may perhaps be the norm."

"As long as they don't include my husband."

He looked at her and she smiled again. "Exactly."

Emily cleared her throat. "Do you know if they fought? Minshom and Sokorvsky?"

David grinned at his sister-in-law, who was never averse to a bit of gossip. "I'm not sure. Sokorvsky mentioned that he'd punched Minshom in the face and inadvertently knocked him down a flight of stairs, but apart from that . . ."

Emily looked triumphant. "That must've been when Minshom hurt his ribs, Jane! And that's why he didn't say anything to anyone—how embarrassing to have to admit to that."

"Did you help Anthony escape my husband?"

David's gaze was drawn back to Lady Minshom. "The initial decision was his, my lady, but I must admit that I did offer him the benefit of my advice and my experience when he needed it."

"Your sexual experience?"

"All my experience," David said firmly.

"Do you think Lord Anthony will ever go back to my husband?"

"No, I don't, and I'm not sure that Minshom would want him anymore anyway."

"Because he humiliated him?"

"Yes and because I believe that somewhere, deep inside him, Minshom respects Sokorvsky for standing up to him."

Lady Minshom nodded as if he made perfect sense. "It's always better to stand up to Blaize."

Emily giggled. "Lord Minshom's first name is Blaize? How unusual."

David held Lady Minshom's gaze even as he answered Emily. "Saint Blaize is the patron of wool makers, didn't you know that? A very important saint to the farmers in Cheshire, where the Minshom family comes from. I believe Saint Blaize allowed himself to be torn to death rather than renounce his faith."

Emily sniffed. "I can't see the current bearer of that name behaving in quite such a self-sacrificing manner."

David kept staring at Lady Minshom. "I don't know about that. He can surprise you."

"Well, if you don't think Minshom will ever get Sokorvsky back, then Jane has nothing to worry about." Emily declared as she dabbed her mouth with her napkin. "I told you David was the right person to ask, didn't I?"

"You did, Emily, and Captain Gray has been most helpful."

David smiled at his sister-in-law. She expected her life to be a certain way and so it was. No doubts for her about her position in society, her husband's fidelity or the love she had for her children. She had no concept of the far murkier world he and Minshom inhabited, although he guessed Lady Minshom did.

As if she'd read his mind she smiled at him. "Captain Gray, are you free to walk me home after lunch?"

12

Jane glanced up at her silent companion as he ushered her through the doorway of Emily's townhouse and down into the busy square below. If Anthony Sokorvsky was not a threat, would David still be prepared to help her or would his obvious dislike of Blaize and his entanglement with Robert make him unwilling to be involved?

She crossed the deserted road into the park at the center of the square and allowed David to open the high spiked wrought iron gate for her. A couple of children played catch on the still-shaded frozen grass, their nurse watching from a nearby bench. Jane strolled farther into the garden until she reached a patch of rippled sunlight and a rustic stone seat.

She used her gloved hand to clean off a scattering of faded leaves, sat down and beckoned David to join her. She'd changed back into her disreputable green dress and was quite happy to let the skirts trail in the mud and the dew. She gave David an encouraging smile.

"Just in case you were wondering, it was me you saw in the **pleasure house** last night with Minshom."

"Ah." His answering smile was guarded.

"Aren't you going to ask me what I was doing there?"

He shrugged. "That would be incredibly hypocritical of me, wouldn't it? I don't believe in judging anyone else's sexual choices."

"Except perhaps Robert's."

His blue gaze hardened. "I'm not prepared to discuss Robert with you."

Jane sighed. "I didn't mean to pry. Although, to be fair, I believe Minshom does care for Robert in his own particular way."

"I know."

"Love is so unfair sometimes, isn't it?"

"Indeed it is."

Jane smiled. "You are a man of few words, Captain Gray, or is it simply that you don't wish to talk to me?"

He studied her for a long moment. "It isn't easy for me to share confidences with the woman who is married to my worst enemy."

Jane nodded. "It isn't easy for me being married to him sometimes either, but I persevere."

"I can imagine." His blue eyes searched her face. "But you care about him, don't you, or else you wouldn't have been there last night."

Jane realized that if she wanted to get anything out of this complex man she would have to take him into her confidence and reveal more about her complicated relationship with Minshom than she had anticipated. She took a deep breath.

"I am trying to persuade my husband to come back to me."

"Why on earth would you want to do that?"

"Because seven years ago I wronged him, and I believe that how he is now is partly my fault."

"With all due respect, I can't imagine you having the power to affect him so deeply." Captain Gray grimaced. "He has always been like this."

"I told him to leave me and never return. I accused him of unforgivable crimes against his own family." Jane swallowed hard. "I drove him away."

Captain Gray's expression softened. "And yet you came after him."

"I had to. I can't bear to see him ruin his life like this, as if he is incapable of feeling and incapable of loving when I know that isn't the truth."

"You love him, don't you?"

"Yes."

"Then I almost feel as sorry for you as I do for myself." Captain Gray hesitated. "But I don't believe you should blame yourself entirely. Your husband was . . . already damaged long before he married you."

Jane took a deep breath. "That is the other thing I wanted to talk to you about. Do you know anything about The Little Gentleman's Club?"

Captain Gray went still. "What do you know about that abomination?"

"I was tidying up some of the old accounts in Minshom's father's study and I found a whole box of diaries and pictures and . . . trophies and . . . I made the mistake of looking at them. I recognized Blaize's name—it is quite distinctive." She fought the tide of sickness back down her throat. "There was also a David . . ."

"And you thought it might be me."

His flat statement alarmed her more than any anger he might have shown. Impulsively she placed her hand on his sleeve. "I'm sorry if I have offended you."

His large callused fingers closed over hers, patted them and then withdrew. "You haven't offended me at all, but there are some things a man might choose to forget happened to him even though they still haunt his nightmares." His smile was tight. "Did you know that Robert was involved as well, and that's why he won't ever leave Minshom?"

"Robert?" Jane frowned. "Are you sure? I don't remember seeing a Robert on the lists."

"That's right, I'd forgotten. Robert wasn't considered a true member of the club because of his class. They didn't use any of our full names though, did they? Only our Christian names. It was supposed to protect our fathers' identities, although we all knew exactly who we were." His mouth twisted. "We all went to school together, for God's sake, except Robert."

"Then how did Robert become involved?" Jane had to ask the question although she suspected she wouldn't like the answer.

"He worked on the estate. Minshom's father took a fancy to him and made him fight as well." A muscle flicked in Captain Gray's cheek. "Although more as a punching bag than as a true opponent. It's hard to fight back when you're naked and blindfolded."

"And yet Robert became devoted to Blaize, the son of the man who forced him into such a dangerous situation."

"Robert's devotion stems from an appalling incident when Minshom saved his life. Or Robert thought he did. I've long wondered at your husband's reasons for his supposedly heroic act."

"You really don't like him at all, do you, Captain Gray?"

"Call me David, my lady, and I wish it were that simple. I don't like Minshom, but I understand him, and that makes me both a threat and a weakness in his eyes. He kept me in thrall for years, pushed me into performing sexual acts I hated simply to win his praise, to have his mouth over mine, his cock . . ." David straightened abruptly. "I apologize. I'm sure you don't want to hear about my personal life."

"I suspect you stayed for Robert's sake as well, didn't you?"

He sighed. "And much good that did. Robert refused to listen to me and refused to leave. Eventually I had to break away from them both before I destroyed myself."

Jane contemplated him in silence until he returned his gaze to her face. "If I can free Robert for you, I will."

"But you shouldn't have to do that." His smile was bitter. "Robert must make that decision for himself or he isn't worth having." He took a deep breath. "I realized that last night after we'd made love and he still had to rush back to Minshom."

Jane frowned. "I wonder why? He must've known Minshom was with me."

"That's one of the things I've never been able to understand either. Gratitude has its place, but why does Robert stay with a man who treats him so abominably? It's not as though Robert is the kind of man who craves pain."

Jane raised her head. "Perhaps their relationship has sides to it that we don't know about."

Captain Gray laughed. "Here I am insisting I'll not talk about Robert and then spilling my guts to you about everything." His expression sobered. "If I can help you with Minshom I will, but remember, my interests are not going to run completely parallel with yours. You might want Minshom back, I simply want to end his domination over me and other people that I love."

Jane stood up and held out her hand. "I understand that and I'd be glad of your help."

He bowed and shook her hand. "I was the David in the papers you found. I'm the fourth son in my family. For some reason, my father wasn't particularly fond of me. He enjoyed seeing me beaten to a pulp and always bet against me, always hated it when I won."

He placed her hand on his sleeve and walked slowly across to the other exit from the park that would lead them onto the street containing Minshom House. The streets were quiet and only the rumble of the occasional carriage or delivery cart marred their journey.

"I'm sorry, David."

"For what? None of this is exactly your fault, is it?"

"I know that, but it still seems wrong that you have suffered and that no one acknowledges it." She frowned into the sun. "If I had a pistol, I'd find each one of those fathers and shoot them myself."

"Ah, but as I'm sure you noticed from the contents of the box, Minshom and I weren't the first generation of 'little gentleman'—we were the third. Our fathers had survived and their fathers before them."

"But that doesn't make it right, does it?"

"No, it doesn't." David sighed. "Do you want me to escort you right to the door or leave you discreetly at the next corner?"

"Are you afraid Minshom might see you?"

He smiled. "No, I'm afraid of what he might do to you if he sees you consorting with a ramshackle fellow like me."

Jane stopped walking and stared up at her companion, her brain racing along with her heart. "He wouldn't like it, would he?"

David's smile widened. "He's never been particularly good at sharing."

"Are you brave enough to face his wrath?"

"If you are."

She smiled back at him in perfect accord. "Then let's go and wish him a very good afternoon."

Minshom checked the clock in his office again. It was past three o'clock and neither Robert nor Jane had yet returned to the house. In truth, neither of them had told him exactly what they were doing or pledged to return at a certain time, but he was still on edge. He pictured Jane in her awful green dress drawing the whispers and attention of the *ton* in some fashionable park or gallery. She wouldn't care if his reputation suffered as a result of her martyrdom; in truth, she'd be delighted.

He frowned into the silence. Yet when had he ever cared about his reputation? Was it possible that he was worrying about hers?

He put down his pen when he heard the sound of the front door being opened and rose to his feet as Jane's laughter rang out. Another voice laughed alongside hers and it definitely wasn't Emily's.

Minshom shoved his chair back and strode toward the door. In the center of the hall, Jane stood talking to an all-too-familiar figure. Minshom slowed down and stopped.

"Good afternoon, Captain Gray."

"Good afternoon, my lord. I'm just returning Lady Minshom safely home."

"So I see."

Gray had the audacity to smile at him and bow. Minshom strolled farther into the hall until he was next to Jane and glared down at her. Her dress looked even worse than he remembered it, the skirts streaked with mud and covered with feathers. Her hair was falling down as well, long tendrils escaping her bonnet.

Minshom raised his quizzing glass. "Are you sure this is my wife? It looks rather like a street urchin."

"Don't be silly, my lord. Of course it is me." Jane smiled at him and took off her bonnet. Her hair cascaded over her shoulders, sending pins everywhere. "Oh lord, I knew that would happen."

"Then one might wonder why you took the damned thing off. You are embarrassing Captain Gray."

Jane had the temerity to laugh up at him. "I suspect he doesn't embarrass easily, my lord. Shall I ask him?"

Minshom shot her a quelling look. "No. Now perhaps you

might go upstairs and make yourself respectable again while I bid good-bye to Captain Gray in your stead."

"But I was going to ask him to dinner."

Captain Gray cleared his throat. "As I've already mentioned, my lady, I do have a previous engagement."

"Oh, no matter, then. You must come another night." Jane started for the stairs and then twirled around. "Perhaps we could have supper together before you take me to the theater on Friday?"

Captain Gray bowed as if unaware of Minshom's frosty gaze on his face. "What an excellent idea. I'll send you a note when I have everything arranged."

While they blithely smiled at each other, Minshom held his tongue as unaccustomed emotions shook him. Jane was his wife. How dare she arrange to go out with another man while he was standing in the hall right beside her?

"Good *day*, Captain Gray."

His voice came out more harshly than he had anticipated and Jane stared at him.

"Are you all right, my lord?"

He ignored her and turned to Gray, who at least had the brains to start for the door. Minshom waited until it was shut behind him and then grabbed Jane's wrist.

"Come with me." She pulled away from him but he didn't relax his grip.

"I thought you told me to get changed."

"I've changed my mind." He nodded at Broadman. "Call me a hackney cab at once."

"What are you doing?"

He enjoyed the tremor in her voice, the fact that for once she was the one off balance and not him. "I'm taking you out."

"Why?"

He stepped outside, bringing her with him and manhandled her into the cab, giving the driver his direction while Jane was still trying to remonstrate with him. He sat opposite her in the cramped dirty space, one hand clamped around her knee to stop her escape.

"Are you going to throw me in the Thames?"

He smiled at her. "No, although that would certainly take care of that appalling dress once and for all."

"And possibly me." She hunched a shoulder at him. "I'm not a very good swimmer."

"Ah, well, sometimes one has to suffer to be fashionable."

She glared at him, her tangled hair around her shoulders, her cheeks flushed. "Then where are we going?"

"Patience, my dear, has never been your strong suit."

"Or yours, my lord."

"We'll have to see about that, won't we?" He tossed her a handful of the pins his butler had returned to him from the hall floor. "Perhaps you'd like to pin up your hair?" He settled back into his seat. Oh, he liked her like this, with her feathers ruffled, enjoyed being in control even if it was fleeting. The carriage stopped and he opened the door. "Here we are."

He tossed some coins to the driver, then hauled Jane out of the carriage and into the shop and rang the bell. A young girl appeared, gaped at them and ran straight back out again. Minshom sighed as the pitch of excited female voices behind the pink curtain started rising.

"What are we doing here, my lord?" Jane said.

"What I want."

"You wanted to bring me to a dress shop? I thought I was an extravagant minx who was trying to ruin you."

"You are."

A disturbance occurred at the rear of the shop and a thin older woman with a face like curdled milk came toward them.

"Lord and Lady Minshom?"

Minshom nodded his head at her. "Indeed. I assume you are

Madame Wallace. I know my wife is hard to recognize dressed in this abomination. She needs a new gown for tonight."

Madame's expression tightened. "And you expect me to produce one from thin air? I am a genius, sir, not a magician."

"And I am a busy man who is willing to pay whatever it takes to get her something decent to wear." He gestured at Jane's green dress. "Look at her."

Madame shuddered and then stared at him hard and he held her gaze.

"I do have something for Lady Minshom that is almost finished. I was intending to send it to Lady Millhaven early next week. Perhaps that will suffice."

"But . . ." Jane started to say something and then stopped when Minshom squeezed her arm and talked over her.

"I'm sure it will be delightful." He drew Jane closer and frog-marched her across the floor. "Come along, wife, let's not waste any more of Madame's valuable time than we have to."

Jane found herself in the largest of the fitting rooms with Minshom lounging on the chaise, his critical eyes on her as Madame helped her out of the green dress.

"You will burn that, Madame, won't you?"

"Of course, my lord."

"But I like it." Jane protested as the offending garment was whisked over her head and taken away by one of the hovering girls. "It has stood me in good stead for years."

Madame patted her arm. "I'm glad to see that you are wearing the new corset and petticoats I made for you. At least we have something to work with."

Without thinking, Jane's gaze collided with Blaize's and she watched his eyes narrow. Perhaps he wouldn't pay attention to Madame at all and miss her pointed remarks. And perhaps a cow might jump over the moon. Madame left the room and Jane braced herself for her husband's next question.

He rose from his seat and walked a slow circle around her and paused right behind her, his breath warm on her neck. She shivered as his finger traced the lace edging her corset.

"I'd already paid for my undergarments before you ordered me to stop buying anything else."

His derisive chuckle made her want to step away from him and slap at the hand that played with the laces of her corset. "Did you think that making a quick confession would absolve you of plotting and planning with your friend, Emily, behind my back?"

"I haven't been plotting or planning anything." She gasped as his teeth settled over the bruise he'd made on her throat and he bit down hard. God, she shouldn't be aroused by such a deliberately possessive gesture, but she was.

"I don't believe you. And by the way, Captain Gray only fucks men. He's hardly a suitable paramour for you and I'd never believe he was having you."

"I know what he is and what he likes. Am I not allowed to have friends?"

"Not without my permission." He licked the bruise his teeth had made, probing the slight indentations with the tip of his tongue.

"That is hardly fair."

"Marriage isn't fair. You know that."

"I thought you would approve of Captain Gray. He knows all your secrets and now some of mine."

"That you like to be fucked in public?" She shuddered and he slid his arm low around her hips bringing her body into close contact with his. "That you like to be spanked?"

"Yes."

He spread his fingers wide over her hip bone. "And what if I don't want anyone else to know what my wife does or doesn't like?"

"Surely it's too late for that? David knows and you said that anyone could walk in on us at the pleasure house."

The door behind them opened and Minshom stepped back and resumed his seat, leaving Jane feeling suddenly cold. Madame and one of the girls appeared carrying a pale blue gown over her arm.

"Here we are, Lady Minshom. It is almost complete, so you may try it on and then I'll set one of my girls to finish it for tonight."

"Thank you, Madame." Jane managed a smile although it was hard with Blaize sitting there, judging her, assessing her. She closed her eyes as the dress was slipped over her head with a slick whisper of silk.

"I still need to sew the hem and the bodice seams and then it will be perfect."

Jane opened her eyes and stared at her reflection in the mirror. She looked most unlike herself, almost dainty and elegant.

"It is beautiful, Madame." She cleared her throat. "I haven't owned such a lovely garment for years."

Madame spoke through a mouthful of pins as she continued to mold the dress more tightly to Jane's figure. "It is true, I am a very talented woman and you are lucky to have acquired my services."

Blaize moved restlessly on the couch and she caught his eye in the mirror. "Do you like it, my lord?"

"It is very nice, although I'd appreciate a lower décolletage."

Madame tuned to look at him and Jane wanted to laugh. "Lady Minshom isn't your mistress, sir, she is your wife."

"A fact that I am well aware of, Madame, never doubt it." He got to his feet and consulted his watch. "If you could have the finished garment at my house by nine this evening I would be most grateful."

Madame nodded and began to ease Jane out of the altered gown. "Nine it is, sir."

"Thank you, Madame." Jane smiled and tried to make up for her husband's lack of warmth, realized she'd been doing that ever since she married him.

Madame didn't bother to curtsey, just marched out of the room, her head held high as if neither of the Minshoms mattered to her. And perhaps they didn't. As a businesswoman, she must have learned to deal with the most unpleasant of customers over the years and at least Minshom paid his bills on time.

In the sudden silence, Jane looked around for her dress and then remembered it had been disposed of. She folded her arms across her chest.

"Now that you have deprived me of one of my favorite dresses, what am I supposed to wear on the way home?"

Blaize looked down at her as if surprised she was still there. "You have nothing to wear?"

"Only your cloak." She gasped as he whipped that out of her reach. "Blaize . . ."

"I'm going to my club for an hour or so. I'll meet you at home for dinner at eight and then we'll go out."

Jane frowned. "Is *that* what the dress is for?"

"Of course, why else would I bother to clothe you decently if I wasn't going to be seen with you?"

"But where are we going?"

"To a ball—you did say that you wanted to be seen in society, didn't you?" He tied the strings of his cloak securely around his neck and put his hat back on.

Jane took a step toward him and touched his sleeve. "Why this sudden change of heart?"

His smile wasn't reassuring as he firmly removed her hand from his coat sleeve. "That is none of your business, is it? Just be ready to leave when I tell you to."

"I'm not sure I like this, Blaize. I don't trust you when you are being conciliatory."

"You shouldn't ever trust me." He stared at her, his expression hard. "I will certainly let you down." His half-smile was bleak. "You of all people should know that." He tipped his hat to her and turned for the door. "Good afternoon, Jane."

For a startled moment, before her senses returned in a furious rush, she just stood there like a fool and watched him leave. Then she opened the door and ran after him.

"I have no clothes. How am I supposed to get home?"

He paused at the main entrance to the shop and swept her a beautiful bow. "I have no idea, my lady. Perhaps Madame Wallace can find you another dress to wear? I'm sure she has something in your size, seeing as she is obviously still making your clothes for you."

Goodness gracious, so he had noticed Madame's little revelation about Emily. "Perhaps I'll walk home in my corset and petticoats."

"I wouldn't recommend it. It's just about to rain."

"I've never minded a spot of rain." She held his gaze and hoped he could see the fury emanating from hers. "I live in the countryside."

He bowed again. "Then good luck. I'll see you at dinner, if you don't drown in a pothole." He closed the door behind him with a definite snap and disappeared into the street. Jane took a deep breath, suddenly aware of the interested eyes on her and dove back into the fitting room. She sat there for a few minutes until she was sure she was in control of her temper and then went to find Madame Wallace. She was in the main work room surrounded by bolts of fabric, trimmings of every description and a hoard of chattering young girls.

"Madame, would it be possible for you to lend me one of the uniforms your employees wear?"

Madame looked up from the blue silk dress she was still pinning into place and frowned at Jane. "Why on earth would you want to do that?"

"To make a point to my husband who is behaving insufferably."

"Ah, he is the reason why all your bills are going through Lady Millhaven's account, then?"

"He is, and now he has left me here with nothing to wear home."

Madame's lips twitched as if she was fighting a smile. Jane tried to look stern. "I'd bring it back, of course."

"I'm sure you will, otherwise I'll put it on your bill."

Jane looked hopeful as Madame continued to study her. Then she sighed. "Oh, all right then." She clapped her hands and the workroom went silent. "Marie-Claude, go and find your spare uniform and help Lady Minshom into it. Daisy, go and call her ladyship a hackney cab."

Jane curtsied low and smiled at Madame Wallace. "Thank you."

Madame snorted and rolled out a bolt of orange-flowered muslin on one of the big cutting tables. "Your husband strikes me as a man who needs to be put in his place."

"That's right, Madame, he does." Jane retreated to the door when she saw Marie-Claude reappear and beckon to her. "I look forward to seeing you again and thank you for all my dresses."

"Good-bye, Lady Minshom."

Realizing she had been dismissed, Jane allowed herself to be laced and buttoned into the clean pink-striped gown, declined the apron and headed for the door. She was looking forward to sitting down to eat her dinner with Blaize immensely.

13

"You look like a servant."

Jane stopped sipping her soup and smiled agreeably at Minshom.

"I know."

He drank the rest of his wine and refilled his own glass before the footman stationed behind him could do it for him. "Why is that?"

"Because you left me at the modiste's with nothing to wear?"

In truth, she looked remarkably charming in the simple striped muslin, far too young to be a wife of ten years and a mother. Minshom quashed that thought before he started to soften toward her. His father always said that women were sent by the devil to tempt men into evil, and sometimes when faced with Jane at her most Machiavellian, he almost agreed with him.

"Why didn't you pick something more appropriate to your station?"

Jane opened her eyes wide at him. "Oh my goodness, you

sound almost as prim as my grandfather. What would've been the fun in choosing something you approved of, when this gown was offered to me instead?"

"I doubt it was offered to you. You probably had to beg and wheedle it out of that old harridan."

"Madame Wallace is a saint."

He regarded her silently for a long moment before motioning to the footman positioned around the room to leave.

"You delight in disobeying me, don't you?" He hoped she could hear the snap in his words, the warning of worse to come.

"I don't quite see it like that, my lord."

"Of course you don't, but you are my wife and you owe me your obedience in all matters, is that not so?"

"If you say so, you must be right."

He put down his glass and leaned toward her. "You pretend to agree with me and yet do exactly what you want regardless."

Her smile disappeared. "What else am I to do when you give me no choice by behaving so appallingly?"

"My behavior has nothing to do with you. Yours, however, reflects on me and I don't wish my wife to become the laughingstock of the *ton*."

"Why, because you prefer to occupy that position yourself?"

His hand shot out and he grabbed her wrist, bore it down to the table, felt the delicate bones flex and yield beneath his hard fingers. "You will go upstairs and change into the dress I have provided for you. You will not substitute another gown, leave your slippers or your petticoats off *and* you will dress your hair in an appropriate manner. Do you understand me?"

She looked down at her wrist. "I understand you very well. You don't have to maul me."

He lifted her hand to his mouth and kissed her palm. "You like it when I touch you."

"Not like this."

He bit down on the fleshy mound beneath her thumb and felt her quiver. "Liar. You loved being held down, being tied up, being fucked . . ." He released her and sat back, aware of the blood surging through his cock and the lavender scent of her skin now clinging to his lips. "Go and get ready. I'll meet you in the drawing room in an hour."

"And if I choose not to accompany you and plead a headache?"

He held her gaze. "I'll come and find you, and by God, I'll dress you myself."

Jane rose to her feet, her cheeks as pink as her dress. "I don't appreciate being manipulated, Blaize."

"Neither do I, and since you've done nothing but manipulate me since you arrived, perhaps it's time to turn the tables."

She stormed out of the room, head held high and her back as straight as the queen's. Minshom let her go and lit a cigar, settled down to a glass of brandy and his solitude. Whether she intended it or not, Jane certainly kept him amused. Sometimes her ingenuity in getting around him made him furious, and other times it made him want to laugh. The laughter was dangerous; he couldn't afford to fall under her spell again and give her what she truly wanted, another child.

His faint smile died and he took more brandy. A tap on the door made him glance up. Robert appeared with a fresh bottle of brandy, which he set on the sideboard. Then he bowed and retreated for the door.

"Where are you off to, Robert?"

"Back to the kitchen, my lord, to eat my dinner."

"I thought you'd left to set up house with Captain Gray."

Robert stared at some distant point over Minshom's shoulder and refused to meet his gaze. "No, my lord."

"Then where have you been all day?"

"It was my afternoon off."

"But you chose to return."

"Yes, sir, I told you I would."

"Captain Gray didn't want you after all, then?"

Robert swallowed hard, "I didn't go to him, sir."

"Then where did you go?"

Robert finally looked at him. "I believe that is my business, sir, not yours."

Minshom stared at him for a long moment, aware of a sense of relief, of finally being able to breathe again. It was the same feeling he'd had when Jane arrived unharmed and full of plans at the dining table. Was he stupid enough to care about them after all? Were all the lessons his father had taught him worth nothing?

"I want you to accompany me tonight."

"If you wish, sir." Robert bowed. "Is Lady Minshom coming too?"

"I believe that's my business, not yours." Minshom deliberately parroted Robert's words back at him. "After you've helped me dress, get yourself ready and meet me by the carriage."

"Yes, sir."

Minshom got to his feet, wondering if Jane was actually getting dressed or had already escaped from her bedroom window simply to annoy him. "Go and check that Lady Minshom is in her rooms before you come to me."

"Yes, sir."

Robert went out and closed the door behind him. Minshom hated it when Robert retreated into his servile mode. He took another slug of his brandy and finished smoking his cigar. Keeping them both waiting was important, keeping them off guard essential if he wanted to remain in control. And he would need all his control this evening as he guided his wife through the intricacies of a *ton* ball.

* * *

"Am I late?" Jane smiled graciously at her husband as she descended into the hall.

"No. Open your cloak."

It seemed Blaize had forgotten how to be charming again, at least to her. Jane spread the folds of her black velvet cloak wide. "I'm wearing the right dress and I even found a pair of slippers to match. Will I do?"

Blaize studied her from head to toe. "I suppose so."

Jane sighed. "High praise indeed when I went to so much trouble to look nice for you."

"You didn't do it for me. You did it because you are an incredibly curious little cat who couldn't resist the lure of an evening out with me."

"I do believe you are right. How perceptive you can be when you want to."

He placed her hand on his sleeve and led her toward the open door. "Are you suggesting I lack perception in other areas of my life?"

She gave him her most dazzling smile. "Yes, would you like me to list them?"

"I'm well aware of my faults, Jane." He helped her up the steps into the carriage and climbed in after her. Just before he shut the door she saw Robert appear.

"Don't you want to let Robert in?"

"No, he can travel outside. If he wants to act like a downtrodden servant then he can ride like one."

Jane arranged her skirts carefully on the seat around her. Despite Blaize's highhanded orders, she was enjoying wearing the beautiful dress and the prospect of an evening out. From the barbed comments he was now throwing out, she sensed she was starting to get under his skin. It was a dangerous occupation, but she had to risk it, had to make him see that she wasn't going to give up until he really talked to her.

Despite his reputation, he wasn't known for losing his temper; he prided himself too much on being in control. Jane frowned as she tried to remember if she'd ever seen him in a true rage and couldn't.

"Aren't you going to ask me where we are going?"

"No, because you'll only tell me it's none of my business. I'm happy just to wait and see."

His faint smile didn't quite reach his pale blue eyes although he sat at his ease, long muscled legs encased in tight black satin knee breeches and white stockings and buckled shoes, his coat a dark blue and his waistcoat dove gray.

"You look very fine this evening, my lord. Are we perhaps going to court?"

"Not quite."

Jane sighed. "You really should work on improving your conversation. You have become almost as silent as Robert."

"Robert should be silent. He is a servant."

"He is far more than that."

Blaize raised his eyebrows. "Because I allow him to service my sexual needs? I hardly think so."

Jane refused to look away. "He is also your friend. Captain Gray told me that you saved Robert's life. Is it true?"

A muscle twitched in Blaize's cheek and he went still, one hand braced against the toll of the carriage. "When did you have the opportunity to converse so intimately with Captain Gray? I thought he just escorted you along the street."

Jane shrugged. "He did escort me home, but I actually had lunch with him at Emily's. He *is* her brother-in-law."

Blaize's smile was dismissive. "Why on earth would Captain Gray mention Robert?"

"We were discussing Robert's devotion to you. I suspect he was trying to explain the unexplainable."

Blaize sat back but he was no longer at ease. "And exactly what did he say I'd done?"

"He wasn't very specific." Jane pretended to look interested, knew he would be suspicious if she was too agreeable or pretended to be surprised. "Why, is there something he didn't tell me?"

"Not at all. It was all rather boring, really, a bit of boy's high spirits that got out of hand."

"And you saved Robert's life."

"Robert has always seen it like that. Personally I think he exaggerated the incident, I have no idea why."

"But it explains why Robert is so attached to you when you treat him so abysmally."

Blaize shrugged. "Has Robert been complaining to you? He is a servant; his feelings are of no concern of mine."

"Robert hasn't complained. It just seems strange that he hasn't gone and worked for Captain Gray, when they seem so well suited to each other."

"You mean that drivel that they are 'in love.'"

Jane regarded him steadily. "Yes. Why do you say that with such contempt? Do you not believe two men can love each other?"

"The Bible would say not. And I don't believe in love. It is a foolish waste of a man's time and energy."

"You have never loved anyone, then?" The carriage started to slow and Blaize turned to put on his hat before looking back to her.

"Fishing for compliments, Jane? That's not like you."

His eyes were as hard as glass, the cynicism in his gaze hard to take. Heat rose in Jane's chest until it consumed her, blossomed on her cheeks.

"I know you don't love me, but what about Nicholas? You loved him, I'd stake my soul on it."

"Then you'd be in hell now, right along with me, wouldn't you?"

Before the footman could oblige, Blaize shoved the door of

the carriage open and jumped out. When he turned to help Jane down the steps, all signs of emotion had been bleached from his face. She hesitated before setting her fingers on his arm and bent forward to whisper.

"I'm sorry, Blaize, that was cruel of me."

His reply was as quiet as hers. "No, it was the truth. I kill the things I 'love,' Jane, don't ever forget it."

She struggled to stop her voice from trembling. "Then perhaps I should be grateful that you don't love me. Is that what you are saying?"

He inclined his head and guided them both forward toward a set of white stone steps leading up to a well-lit doorway. Jane forced herself to move forward even as she knew he would never reply to her. His silence was far more eloquent than any words, and it hurt more than she could've imagined. But she hadn't come back to him expecting to be loved, had she?

She took a deep steadying breath as they merged into the crush of guests flooding into the grand mansion. A maid took her cloak and offered to show her to the lady's retiring room. Jane declined. She was far more interested in seeing why Blaize had brought her to this particular ball at this particular house.

He reclaimed her gloved hand and led her up the wide staircase and to the left where the house's ballroom obviously had its own wing. Even in her distress, she couldn't help but notice the attention they were receiving, the buzz of excited conversation that increased as Blaize headed for the receiving line. Was it simply because he had brought her out in society for the first time or was there more to it?

"Good evening, Lord Minshom, what a . . . nice surprise to see you here."

"Good evening, ma'am." Blaize bowed. "May I present my wife, Lady Minshom?" His smile was beguiling. "My dear, may I introduce you to the Marchioness of Stratham?"

Jane curtsied low and held out her hand to the pleasant-faced, dark-haired marchioness whose gaze flicked worriedly between her and Blaize as if she feared she was being made fun of. Jane smiled. "It is a pleasure to meet you, my lady."

"And I you, Lady Minshom. In truth, I didn't recall that Lord Minshom was married."

"It's not widely known, my lady. I choose to live in the countryside. I find it better for my health."

The marchioness managed to smile. "Well, it is a pleasure to meet you, my dear, and I hope you enjoy your evening."

"Are both your sons here tonight, my lady?" Minshom asked. Lady Stratham visibly started.

"I'm not sure, Lord Minshom."

"Don't worry, I'm sure I'll find them."

They passed on, met the marquis who scowled at Minshom down his long nose but managed to be polite to Jane, and kept going. While they waited for the line to proceed, Jane tapped Minshom's arm with her fan.

"Do you know their sons? Is that what the ball is for?"

"I believe the ball is for the coming out of their youngest daughter, Lady Mary, but yes, I do know their sons."

"And they do not like the relationship."

"No one likes me being friends with their sons." His smile was almost feral. "I can't imagine why."

Jane curtsied and smiled at Lady Mary, a dark-haired girl dressed in the palest of pink gowns with a strong look of her mother. She found herself with no one else to greet at the end of the line, Blaize at her elbow.

"I don't see her brothers."

He shrugged. "We arrived quite late. They have probably been told to mingle with the guests until the dancing begins."

Jane stopped walking. "You don't expect me to dance, do you?"

"Why not?"

"Because I haven't danced in public for years!"

Blaize raised his eyebrows at the shrillness of her tone. "Then perhaps it is time you relearned."

As if on cue to torment her, the orchestra stuck up a resounding opening chord and the marquess and his daughter and the marchioness and a younger man stepped out onto the polished wood floor. Jane glanced at Blaize who had stiffened, his attention now firmly focused on the smiling couples in front of him.

The music started and he relaxed and turned back to her, his expression so amiable it instantly made her wary. After a short while, other couples joined the Stratham family, and Blaize swept her the perfect bow.

"Would you like to dance, my lady?"

"No." She scowled at him for added emphasis, but he, of course, ignored her, grabbed her hand and led her onto the now-crowded floor.

"You know this one; it's an old country dance. We even danced it together once before."

He was right; her feet instantly remembered the steps. "You remember that?"

The dance took her away from him, provided her with another partner whom she performed the same set of steps with. She watched as Blaize did the same and was drawn farther away from her with every beat of the music. He danced with a natural grace; he always had when he bothered to try. She had to stop watching him and concentrate on her steps.

Eventually they were reunited and his hand clasped hers again. She realized she was enjoying herself now, was even glad that for just a few moments she could pretend that she had a satisfying life, a husband who wanted to dance with her, a future to compensate for the awfulness of the past.

All too soon the music stopped, leaving her a little breathless. Blaize bowed again and placed her hand on his arm. She noticed how quickly people got out of his way, the lack of welcome in the glances directed at them both and wondered anew why he had chosen to attend this event.

"Lady Minshom?"

Jane looked up to see Captain Gray approaching, a smile on his face. "Good evening, Captain."

"I did not expect to see you here, sir." Captain Gray nodded at Blaize, his smile disappearing.

"Why? A man has a perfect right to escort his wife to a ball."

"I'm just surprised you chose this particular one."

"A debutante's ball?" Minshom patted Jane's fingers. "My wife never had a London Season. I thought she might enjoy seeing what she missed."

"How kind of you," Jane murmured. "And how very like you."

Captain Gray frowned. "Are you sure you wish your wife to witness anything that might happen?"

"My wife is no sheltered little bird. She knows me very well, Gray. I don't understand what any of this has to do with you."

"Because I have an acquaintance with you both?" Captain Gray answered. "Because I would hate Lady Mary's debut ball to be marred by the kind of ugliness I know you can create."

Blaize's eyes narrowed. "May I suggest you keep your nose out of my business, Gray? I'm perfectly capable of behaving like a gentleman when I choose to."

Jane looked to her left where a gap had opened up in the crowd and saw a tall dark-haired man striding toward them. His eyes were blue and his mouth was set in a grim line, belying the pleasant angles of his face. When he reached them he bowed.

"Lord Minshom."

Blaize inclined his head an inch. "Lord Anthony Sokorvsky. Aren't you pleased to see I'm alive? You could've killed me the last time we met."

Anthony Sokorvsky shrugged. "If I had, I'm sure I would've heard about it before now. And, by God, you deserved it."

"And you'd do it again if I let you."

"Exactly. Now what do you want?"

Blaize opened his eyes wide. "To enjoy the ball, of course. To show all the doubters and gossips that I'm not afraid to breach the very stronghold of the Stratham family to prove that I'm not weeping over you."

Jane tensed as the two men continued to stare at each other, felt the fine tension quivering through Blaize's whole frame. To her surprise, Anthony Sokorvsky smiled.

"Then you have proved your point, haven't you?"

"Indeed."

"And now you can leave."

Blaize laughed softly. "Are you afraid you'll change your mind if I stay?"

"No, I'm as done with you as you are with me." Anthony's contemptuous glance passed over Jane. "It seems as if we have both moved on, although I must say, I didn't expect you to take up with a woman."

Blaize's expression turned deadly and beside him Jane tensed. "This isn't just any woman; this is my wife."

Anthony's smile wasn't pleasant. "You got married to prove a point?"

Captain Gray cleared his throat. "Sokorvsky . . ."

Jane stepped forward and placed her hand on Blaize's arm. "In truth, we were married a long time ago. Ten years to be exact." She lifted her chin and gave Anthony her most open and engaging smile.

He sighed. "I apologize, ma'am. I let my unruly tongue run away from me." He bowed stiffly to Blaize. "And I apologize to you too, sir."

"Don't bother," Blaize said. "Is Lady Justin Lockwood here with you tonight?"

Anthony straightened and looked over his shoulder. "Yes, she is here—why?"

"You haven't persuaded her to marry you yet, then?"

"That is none of your business."

Blaize laughed. "Then I assume the answer is no. Not that I find that surprising."

"I'm not going to discuss Lady Justin with you, Minshom, so don't try to rile me."

"As if I would." Blaize nodded and squeezed Jane's fingers. "Shall we go and get some refreshments? I understand there is a most superior buffet set out in the supper room."

With expert ease, he drew her away from Anthony Sokorvsky and past the crowd of gawkers into the next room.

"You don't need to defend me, Jane."

His arctic tone made her glance up at him. "Why not? You are my husband."

"And I'm quite capable of defending myself."

"You weren't the person being insulted."

"Yes, I was. This wasn't about you at all and you know it."

Jane looked away from him and focused on the line of people moving along the sumptuously laden tables. The smell of the salmon and the rich cream desserts made her feel slightly nauseated. "It's never about me, is it?" She realized she was somewhere between bursting into tears and slapping his face. "I thought you brought me here to enjoy myself, not settle old scores."

He placed his hand in the small of her back, forcing her to keep moving. "Then you were mistaken. I never do anything I don't want to, Jane."

"And you don't wish to be pleasant to me, do you?"

His smile was almost sympathetic, but she could see the anger and frustration in his gaze. She knew him well enough to tell that his meeting with Anthony Sokorvsky had shaken him far more than he would ever admit.

He sighed. "We've had this conversation a thousand times. I want you to go home. Why would I go out of my way to make your stay here pleasant?"

"Because you promised to attend some normal social functions with me if I participated in your sexual games."

He brushed one gloved finger over her lips. "Ssh, do you want everyone to know our secrets? And by God, you enjoyed every minute of our outing. You begged, don't you remember?"

"That is hardly the point, is it?" She smiled at him, showing her teeth. "You haven't fulfilled your part of the bargain."

His eyebrows rose as he handed her a glass of white wine. "You're here, aren't you?"

She met his gaze. "I refuse to be used as a kicking bag simply because you can't have Anthony Sokorvsky."

"I don't want him."

"It didn't seem that way to me." Jane thrust the glass back into his unresisting hand and curtsied. "I'm going to the ladies retiring room and after that I'm going home. I'm sure you'll find someone else to oblige you with a fight, but it won't be me."

She walked away from him, struggling to keep the calm smile on her lips, aware of everyone still staring and whispering. She was a fool for hoping, for wanting, for *needing* Blaize to change.

"Lady Minshom?"

She looked up, aware of a large male body blocking her retreat. It was Anthony Sokorvsky, his expression concerned. "Are you all right, my lady?"

"I'm fine, my lord. I'm just tired and ready to go home."

Anthony sighed. "I'm sorry. It was appalling of me to put you in the crossfire like that. There is something about your husband that brings out the worst in me."

She couldn't look up at him, replied instead to his chest. "It's all right, truly. I know how he is."

"And yet I have upset you and spoiled your evening." He took her arm and walked along with her, nodding at his acquaintances, doing more to restore her reputation in one second than Blaize would ever do or ever care enough about the opinions of others to try. They reached the entrance to the ballroom and Jane withdrew her hand. Despite his kindness, she couldn't let Anthony Sokorvsky know how she really felt. She curtsied low and even managed to smile at him.

"You haven't ruined my evening. I enjoyed it immensely. Please give your sister my good wishes for a successful Season. Good night, my lord."

He stared at her for a long moment and then smiled. "I can see why Lord Minshom married you. You are tremendously brave."

"Not really, but thank you for the compliment."

He bowed low. "The pleasure was all mine. Now, before I return to the ballroom, can I arrange for your carriage to be brought round?"

"It isn't necessary, sir. My servant is down in the hall. I'm sure he can take care of it for me."

He nodded. "Then good night, Lady Minshom. I'm glad I met you. I'm beginning to think that with a champion like you there might be some glimmer of hope for your husband after all."

Robert lounged in the cavernous hallway, his back against a black-and-white marble pillar, his gaze fixed on a hideous portrait of an old lady with fifteen pug dogs surrounding her. He hadn't settled on fifteen yet. Every time he examined the picture he spotted another of the little buggers lurking in the drapery.

Minshom's dismissal hadn't bothered him, although the ride to the mansion clinging to the outside of the ponderous coach had proved somewhat cold. In truth, he wasn't sure how he felt about his master at the moment, was even relieved not to have to face him. And Minshom knew him far too well for such unruly thoughts to be hidden and would only exploit them, drive him into a corner, reduce him to begging again.

Robert sighed. Why couldn't he just leave? Hadn't he paid his dues fifty times over?

"Does anyone know a Captain David Gray?" The footman's voice shattered Robert's musing. "There is an urgent message for him."

Robert put up his hand. "I know him."

The footman looked relieved. "Can you take this note to him immediately? I'd prefer not to have to announce this to everyone."

Robert took the note and headed up the wide staircase, ignoring the occasional look of surprise or deliberate sneers at his somber attire from the invited guests. He had to help didn't he? He couldn't pretend he didn't know Captain Gray when there was obviously an emergency.

He spotted the captain almost as soon as he entered the ballroom and hastened to his side.

"Captain Gray."

His lover—his ex-lover—turned around slowly as if bracing himself against the sound of Robert's voice.

"Yes?" For the first time, there was no hint of warmth in David's face, no indication that they were anything more than master and servant. Robert concealed his immediate pang of hurt. He'd told David to leave him alone, had begged him to, in fact, so why should he hate it?

Robert bowed. "I apologize for interrupting, Captain, but I was asked to deliver an urgent message to you." He handed over the sealed note and stepped back.

"Thank you." There was no inflection in David's voice as he turned back into the circle of his acquaintances, leaving Robert standing alone. God, it stung to have to walk away, to not have the privilege of asking what was wrong, of offering his help.

Robert made his way back down the stairs and took up his previous position by the marble pillar. At least Lord Minshom hadn't seen his humiliation—that was one thing to be grateful for. He glanced up at the entrance to the ballroom and saw Captain Gray descending the stairs with great speed. He couldn't help stepping into the light and into his path.

"Are you all right, Captain?"

David looked at him and swallowed hard. "Apparently my father has suffered another stroke. I've been ordered to attend his bedside. He is not expected to live."

Robert touched his arm. "I'm sorry. Can I do anything to help?"

Briefly, David's hand sought his and squeezed hard. "No, I thank you. Just pray for him."

"I will do that, sir." Robert hesitated. "Are you sure you do not need me to accompany you? You seem a little shaken."

"Thank you for the offer, but I'm fine." David's smile was fleeting but meant the world to Robert. "Good night."

Robert watched him leave and fiercely contemplated his choices. If he'd been brave enough, he would have the right to comfort Captain Gray, to hold him in his arms and tell him that everything was in God's hands. But he didn't have that right, did he? He'd squandered it with his obsession with Minshom.

God, he wanted to follow David more than he wanted to breathe. He took a step toward the door and then another.

"Robert?"

He made the mistake of looking back, saw Lady Minshom coming down the stairs and reluctantly faced her.

"My lady?"

She swallowed hard. "I want to go home. Can you take me?"

What on earth had happened to shake her considerable composure? He should've known there would be trouble when he'd realized exactly whose ball Minshom had decided to attend. He bowed.

"Of course, my lady. Just let me fetch your cloak."

Minshom strolled down the staircase and spied his wife and Robert in the doorway. Jane looked surprisingly well in the blue dress, not a diamond of the first water, but certainly elegant. But marrying her had never been about her beauty, had it? He'd simply fallen in love the moment he saw her.

He pushed his way through the crowds. Just as Robert was shutting the carriage door Minshom yanked on the handle and let himself in, smiling at their startled expressions.

"Good evening, my dears. I decided to join you after all."

For some reason, after his confrontation with Sokorvsky and Jane's exit, the ball had lost his interest. His fingers flexed as he settled into the seat next to Robert and eyed his wife. She was pretending he wasn't there, which was most unlike her. Normally she met every one of his barbs head-on and repaid them in her own unique manner.

He studied her averted profile. Had he really ruined her evening? He supposed he had. The strangest thing was that she hadn't expected him to, had imagined they could spend a conventional evening in each other's company like a normal husband and wife.

He transferred his gaze to Robert who looked equally displeased to see him. He'd wanted them both to stop worrying about him and yet he had never liked being ignored.

Anger threaded through him. Sokorvsky had made him look like a fool hiding behind his wife, his wife who had defended him without being asked. Sokorvsky would think him weak. God, he felt weak, beleaguered by the dual demons of lust and guilt his wife managed to drag from him without even trying. His father's derisive laughter echoed in his head, made him close his eyes to escape the shame.

Mercifully the carriage stopped and Robert hopped out to open the door for his betters. Jane descended, her head held high, smiled a thank you and a good night to Robert and stalked into the house. Minshom stepped down and caught Robert's shoulder as he shut the carriage door.

"Meet me in the cellar."

"My lord . . . I don't . . ."

Minshom grabbed the front of Robert's coat and snarled, "Just do it."

For the first time ever, Robert shoved him away. "All right."

By the time Robert joined him in the half-empty wine cellar, Minshom had already stripped off his coat, cravat, waistcoat and shirt. Robert set the small lantern down on the floor, causing their shadows to loom and tremble like giants on the damp brick walls.

Minshom didn't bother to wait for Robert to strip down; he just lunged at him and shoved him against the wall.

"Fight me."

"I don't want to."

"A moment ago you seemed quite keen on the idea. What changed your mind?"

"Because this is ridiculous; it changes nothing and only re-opens old wounds and hurts."

Minshom closed his fingers around Robert's throat. "And if that is what I want? Don't you want to remember how it feels to lose so that you'll never want to be in that place again?"

"My lord . . ."

Minshom backed off and fisted his hands at his sides.

"Fight me, you bastard. Fight me, because without me in your life, you could go and suck David Gray's cock all day long."

Robert sighed. "Don't do this."

"Do what? Remind you of what you have lost? How it feels to have the lover you want moving inside you, pleasuring your cock, moaning into your mouth, instead of having to deal with me?"

"Stop it, Minshom. Just shut the hell up."

Minshom opened his eyes wide. "You know how to stop me. There is only one way or I'll keep talking, keep reminding you of what you've given up."

"Fuck you." Robert held his gaze and stepped away from the wall, fists raised. Minshom closed his eyes as the first punch landed on the side of his head, almost knocking him over. He kept his hands by his sides as Robert hit him again and again until he could no longer stand and could taste his own blood in his mouth. He fell to his knees and Robert came down with him. Pain exploded in his chest as he took another punch.

"Are we done now?" Robert sounded curiously emotional, his voice thick and hoarse. "Can I leave?"

Minshom managed to open one eye. "You are the winner. You know what comes next."

Robert used Minshom's shoulder to stagger to his feet. "No."

"You don't want your prize?"

"God damn you, no! This is wrong, this is . . . unhealthy."

"You don't want to fuck me?" Minshom rolled onto his back and cupped his cock, squeezed hard enough to hurt, to torment, to punish, and felt his body's automatic response.

Robert braced one arm against the wall. "No. I . . . can't do this anymore. I can't hurt you. I'm sorry." He turned and walked out, slamming the old wooden door behind him.

Minshom stayed where he was and stared up at the ceiling.

He felt none of his usual exhilaration after the fight, none of the intense need to be sexually dominated either. What the hell was wrong with him? He winced as his tongue swept over his bloodied lower lip.

All he could think about was going upstairs, finding his way to Jane's bedroom and fucking her just as he was—bowed, bloody and bruised. Would she welcome him between her thighs, hold him close and offer him another way to forget the past? He'd married her with that hope, had foolishly believed she would help him conquer his demons, only to have their son die in his arms . . .

So he'd turned back to his other forbidden pleasures, used them to replace her because men didn't have children, men weren't soft. Men couldn't break your heart when they cried as if they would never stop over the death of a child.

Minshom rolled onto his stomach and groaned. He had to get himself up the stairs and into bed before anyone noticed his absence. He had to stop thinking such soft, foolish thoughts and remember where they had led him—to lying in a cellar begging his servant to fight him and fuck him.

God damn it. He grabbed hold of one of the shelves and hauled himself to his feet. If he kept in close contact with the wall, he was sure he could make it up the stairs. He got as far as the door and opened it. Robert stood in the shadows outside leaning against the wall. Silently he offered Minshom his shoulder to lean on. Without another word, Minshom placed his trembling fingers on Robert's arm and allowed him to lead him to bed.

14

Minshom breakfasted early to avoid Jane and any potential questions about the stiffness of his movements and the bruises on his face. It was a relatively fine day so he decided to ride to visit his bankers rather than go in his carriage. The horse ride would either loosen his tight muscles or make them worse, and he could always claim that his horse had butted him. He didn't really care which excuse he used, just that he would have one if anyone asked.

He sipped his coffee. Not that anyone apart from Jane would dare to ask him how he did. He wasn't the sort of man who inspired intimacy in others or invited personal questions.

After finishing his breakfast, he stepped out into the bright sunshine and adjusted the angle of his hat. He heard the faint jingle of his horse's bit and the clatter of horseshoes on the cobbled pathway as his horse was brought up from the mews at the back of the house.

"Lord Minshom."

"Yes?"

He shaded his eyes from the glare and turned to the other

direction, tried to keep his expression blank as he focused on yet another unwelcome visitor.

"I'm not sure if you'll recognize me, but I'm Major Lord Thomas Wesley."

"I remember you."

Unwillingly Minshom studied the bronzed features of his old childhood friend. Wesley wore his army uniform and his face was lined by the harsher climes of India. His brown eyes remained as direct as ever and were fixed on Minshom.

"You remember me but you'd prefer not to."

"I'd say that was fair."

Major Wesley half-smiled. "I can understand that; we hardly parted as friends, did we? But I would appreciate the opportunity to speak with you."

"And if I don't wish to do that?"

"I can't force you to talk to me." Major Wesley hesitated. "But I would hope you could find it in your heart to forgive me."

"Forgive you for what?"

"You know what. But it is scarcely a conversation I wish to have in front of your groom."

Minshom looked over his shoulder, saw his horse and one of his stable hands already waiting patiently. "If I agree to meet you at Madame Helene's House of Pleasure this afternoon at four, will you agree that this will be our only meeting and not bother me again?" Minshom handed Wesley a discreet white card that contained Madame's address.

"If that is what you wish." Major Wesley shrugged. "Although I expect to be returning to India within a month, so you don't have to worry about me hanging around."

"I'm not worried."

Major Wesley smiled right into Minshom's eyes. "Of course you aren't. What do you have to fear from me?" He gestured at the houses. "This is an excellent area for a home. I must mention it to an army acquaintance of mine who is looking to rent somewhere this summer for his family."

"Indeed."

"You chose not to live in Swansford House then?"

Minshom had no intention of pursuing any topic of conversation that related in any way to his father. The thought of living amongst his parents' possessions made him shudder. "It is rented out. Good morning, Major Wesley."

"Good morning. I'll see you at four."

Minshom nodded and turned to mount his horse, aware of his visitor still watching him as he gathered the reins in his gloved hands. He kicked the horse with unnecessary force, which made his groom suck in his breath disapprovingly, and headed off toward the nearest exit from the square.

What the hell did Wesley mean about forgiving him? Surely it should be the other way round, as Minshom had ended up the victor? The whole idea of discussing their shared past made Minshom nauseated. Men didn't need to do that—they weren't like women. But he knew that Wesley would not let the matter go until it had been settled to his satisfaction. He had always been a stickler for the truth, and unlike most of Minshom's contemporaries, more than willing to apologize for his faults. And really, what was there to worry about? Only a weak man was afraid of the past.

Minshom slowed his pace as he approached the main thoroughfare and squeezed his horse past a cart carrying vegetables for the insatiable city market. But he *was* weak, his father had always said so, and he *was* afraid to discuss the past. So how was he going to survive the meeting? Challenge Wesley to a duel and shut him up that way?

Minshom shook his head and guided his horse to the side of the street where his bank was. He was overreacting; this was all Jane's fault. She'd made him start to doubt himself again. He could easily see off Wesley. He'd done it before and he'd do it again. He dismounted and headed into the bank, glad for once that the legal complexities of running his father's estates were immense and required his full attention. He had no time to worry about his forthcoming meeting now.

Jane ate her toast and slit the seal of the note Emily had sent her. There was no sign of Blaize, but from the state of the crumpled newspaper by his chair, he'd obviously eaten and left. She wasn't surprised. He knew he'd ruined her evening and was probably expecting her to rally her forces and confront him over the coffee pots.

"Oh my goodness, poor Emily and George." Jane finished reading the note and waved to the lone footman stationed by the door to come closer. "Will you go and see if Mr. Brown is available and ask him to come and speak to me?"

"Yes, my lady."

While she waited, Jane finished her toast and drank her coffee. She assumed Robert hadn't gone out with Blaize; he'd seemed out of charity with his master as well last night.

"Good morning, Lady Minshom."

Jane's smile dimmed as she looked up at Robert, who looked rather pale, as if he hadn't slept well.

"Are you all right?"

"Yes, my lady."

Jane waited to see if he would elaborate and then rose to her feet. "I had a note from Lady Millhaven about her father-in-law's death. She has asked me to go and sit with her for a while. As Lord Minshom has gone out, are you free to accompany me?"

"The Earl of Millhaven died?"

"Yes, of a stroke, I understand. The whole family was able to be with him when he passed away."

"I knew the earl was sick, my lady." Robert shifted his feet. "I was commandeered to deliver a message to Captain Gray last night at the ball."

"Oh, of course, he's David's father too." Jane sighed. "How sad for them all."

"Indeed, my lady. Now let me go and call the carriage and get my hat."

Jane went to put on her bonnet and cloak. Emily would be a countess now, her husband George the new earl. How would that feel? The sadness of death combined with the excitement of finally becoming the head of his family. She wondered how Blaize would react in similar circumstances. Would he be delighted or devastated?

"Good morning, Emily. I'm so sorry."

Robert watched as Lady Minshom drew the new countess into her arms and hugged her tight. Lady Millhaven looked haggard, her eyes red from weeping, her face lined.

"Thank you for coming, Jane. I appreciate it. Thank you for bringing her, Mr. Brown."

Robert bowed to them both. "I'll wait for you in the kitchen, if that is all right, my lady?"

He turned and walked slowly down the stairs until he reached the basement where the kitchen was situated. The greasy smell of lamb cooking assailed his nostrils and he swallowed hard. The butler was seated at the table drinking a mug of coffee, his spectacles perched on the end of his nose as he read the morning paper.

"Good morning again, Mr. Brown, and what can I do for you?"

"Her ladyship asked me to wait down here until Lady Minshom is ready to leave. I hope I won't be in the way."

"Not at all, Mr. Brown, take a seat and share some of this excellent coffee."

"Thanks, Mr. Austen, I will. I'm not sure how long Lady Minshom will be."

"Well, with all due respect, the ladies do like to talk, don't they, and on this sad day probably more than ever."

Robert sat down and accepted the mug of coffee and sweet-smelling bread roll the smiling cook placed in front of him. "So all the family was there last night when he died?"

"Well, all except Mr. Edward Gray—he's still in France dealing with that holy mess Napoleon created. But the others were all here."

"Captain Gray got here in time then?"

"He did, why do you ask?"

Robert shrugged. "I was at a ball last night, and as I know him by sight, I was asked to pass on a message to him to come home."

"He was here. In fact, he's still here. I persuaded him to go to bed rather than trying to return to his lodgings when he was obviously so upset." Mr. Austen lowered his voice. "Not that I ever thought he was particularly fond of his father, if you know what I mean. It was quite a surprise to see him so moved."

"They weren't close?"

"Not that I noticed. They barely acknowledged each other. The captain only came to the house to see his brother and his nieces and nephews."

"Ah." Robert focused on drinking his coffee and chewing through his buttered roll. Perhaps David had merely been experiencing relief. Any father who willingly involved his child in a no-holds-barred fighting contest every summer couldn't expect to be loved or mourned.

A bell rang on the crowded board above the door and the butler frowned. "That's Mr. David now, and where are James and John? Out delivering notes about the earl's demise, that's where." He sighed and put down the newspaper. "I suppose I'd better go and see what he wants."

"I'll go, if you like, Mr. Austen." Robert got to his feet and tried to look nonchalant. "I've got nothing else to do and you are needed to answer the front door."

"Are you sure, Mr. Brown? It seems a trifle rude to ask for your help, but it would be a kindness if you could aid me just this once."

"As I said, I might as well make myself useful. Which room is he in?"

After listening to the butler's directions, Robert set off for the second floor, his heart beating a little faster, his breathing uneven. He knocked on the door and obeyed the quiet command to enter.

Captain Gray sat by the window in his shirtsleeves, his back to the door, his head in his hands.

"Get me another bottle of brandy."

For a moment Robert just stood there and blinked. It was almost as if he had blundered into the wrong bedroom and was back at Lord Minshom's.

"Sir?"

Captain Gray slowly looked up. "What the devil are you doing here?"

"I'm just helping out, sir. The staff is very busy due to the earl's death."

"So?"

"I came with Lady Minshom and offered to answer your summons while the other footmen were engaged."

Captain Gray stared at him. His blond hair hung over his face in disarray and his clothes were crumpled. His sea blue eyes held a depth of anguish Robert had never seen before.

"Are you all right, David?" The name slipped out impulsively. "Can I at least get you some clean clothes and order you a bath?"

"I asked for brandy."

Robert took a step closer. "It isn't like you to drink at this time in the morning, sir. Are you sure you wouldn't prefer a nice cup of tea?"

"Damn the tea and damn you."

Robert spread his hands wide. "Damn me all you like, but at least accept my condolences for your loss."

David got unsteadily to his feet. "Your condolences? You think I cared about that bastard? The man who let me be beaten and fucked while he laughed with his cronies and bet against me?"

Robert met David's gaze and refused to look away. He deserved the other man's anger. He'd refused him so much; the least he could do was stand firm and allow his lover to berate him. "Yes, sir, my condolences, but they are for you, not for your father." He bowed. "I'm obviously the last person you want to see at this moment. I'll send one of the footmen up to attend to your needs as soon as he returns."

"Don't go."

Robert didn't exactly turn back, but he didn't move forward either. "What do you want, sir?"

"I want . . ." David shook his head.

Robert stared at David. "What?"

"I want you, but I can't have you, can I, because you love that bastard Minshom."

"That's not fair, sir. It's not just Lord Minshom; it's a whole lot of other things: your class, your aristocratic family, your profession."

David started to laugh.

Robert's hands curled into fists. "You think this is amusing, sir? You think it's easy for me to stand here and remind you of all the reasons why you shouldn't love me when inside I want to damn them all to hell and just be with you?"

David stopped laughing and turned away. "I'm sorry, Robert, I'm laughing at myself. You see, I found out last night why my father hated me so much. I'm not his son after all; I'm the product of an affair my mother had with a stable boy, so I'm not quite so far above you after all, am I?"

Robert simply stared at David, his mind in chaos. What the hell was going on? A knock at the door returned him to his senses. An out-of-breath footman dressed in the Millhaven livery bowed at them both.

"Good morning, Captain Gray, I'm sorry I'm late. I've come to relieve Mr. Brown. Can I get you some breakfast and order your bath?"

Robert took the coward's way out and left as quickly as he could. He was in no shape to deal with David's dramatic confession yet, because if it were true, and David was indeed a low-born bastard, Robert would no longer have any excuses left, no reason to protect his lover and no reason to stay with Minshom—apart from the fact that he loved them both. And where the hell did that leave him?

Minshom smiled as he entered the largest of the public salons at Madame Helene's. During the day there were far fewer clients enjoying the lush, ornate surroundings and sexual opportunities contained within Madame's wondrous house, but there was still enough going on to make a spinster have apoplexy. Major Wesley sat close to the door, a glass of red wine clutched in his hand, his gaze riveted on a man and a woman who were making love on the couch right next to him.

"Are you enjoying yourself, Major?"

Major Wesley jumped so hard that wine splashed from his glass onto the arm of the chair. His smile however was unabashed. "I must say, things have changed quite a lot since I lived in England."

"For the better or for the worse?"

"Do you think me a prude, Minshom? I've lived in India for ten years, a country that doesn't have quite the same inhibitions about sex. Not a lot shocks me anymore."

Minshom sighed. "How disappointing."

"Were you hoping I'd be too terrified to stay and meet with you?"

"Perhaps."

Major Wesley got to his feet. "That is remarkably honest of you."

"I know, I can't think what has come over me." Minshom gestured at the door. "I suspect you would like to speak to me somewhere more private. Shall we go upstairs?"

He led the way up the stairs and into one of the bed chambers and bent to light the fire that was already laid out in the grate. Major Wesley settled into one of the wing chairs beside the fire and Minshom took the other one.

"So what can I do for you, Major?"

"I hardly know where to start." Major Wesley sighed and rested his clasped hands on his knees. "I've imagined having this conversation with you so many times and yet I'm still sure that I'll get it wrong."

"Perhaps the best way is to just start talking. You've always been good at that."

"I have, haven't I?" Major Wesley smiled. "My father often said I could charm the birds from the trees, usually before he beat me for some misdemeanor, of course." He shifted slightly in his seat. "He died last year, did you know?"

"I heard of it. I wondered if you would come back."

"I haven't been in England for ten years and that was quite deliberate." Major Wesley's slight smile disappeared. "I couldn't bear to look at him."

"I know the feeling all too well."

"Of course you do. I believe we all felt betrayed by our fathers, didn't we?"

Minshom shrugged and waited for Wesley to continue, his senses alert, his suspicions aroused. The other man drew in a deep breath and slowly let it out.

"And I betrayed you as well, didn't I?"

"I don't know what you mean."

"I suspect that means you prefer not to think about it."

"About what?"

"That first summer when you were inducted into The Little Gentleman's Club. I was the first boy to beat you in a fight. The first one to fuck you."

Despite the thousand warning bells sounding in his head, Minshom kept his expression neutral and his posture relaxed. "So?"

Wesley held his gaze. "We were friends and yet I still did that to you. I didn't have the guts to stand up and refuse."

"None of us refused. Our fathers made sure of that." Minshom licked his lips, tasted his youthful terror, his blood, his total capitulation and humiliation.

"You refused longer than most. In truth, I admired you for it."

"I was a fool."

"No, I was. I destroyed our friendship."

Minshom forced himself to smile. "And is that why you wished to meet with me, to rehash our past?"

"As I said, I wanted to apologize."

"For something that meant so little?" Minshom laughed, although even to his ears he sounded strained. "I got my own back. By the fourth summer I could beat you all."

"I know."

"Why do you say that as if you feel sorry for me?"

"Because I set you on that path. I betrayed your trust and you retaliated by forcing yourself to become something you hated."

"A winner? I think you are mistaken." Minshom got up and walked across the room until he reached the well-draped window. He pretended to adjust the curtains to let in some light. "I enjoyed beating you. I especially enjoyed fucking you as well."

"I don't believe you."

"Believe what you like. If you came here feeling guilty for destroying my life, then you have nothing to worry about."

"But I did destroy it. If I hadn't . . ."

Minshom cut him off. "You weren't the first man to rape me, Wesley. My father decided that, as I objected so strenuously to being enrolled in his own personal fight school, I should understand what I was up against."

"God . . . Blaize."

Minshom turned sharply around and saw the horror in Wesley's gaze. "Don't look at me like that. In truth, I was glad that my father prepared me for the worst. Having a full-grown man fuck you is far worse than any boy."

"I'm sure it is." Wesley looked shaken. "But I still want to apologize to you. My conscience has never been easy where you are concerned."

"What do you want me to do? Forgive you, even though I have explained that I scarcely hold you accountable for the man I have become?"

"Your forgiveness would be a start." Wesley looked even more uncomfortable. "I'd also like to make amends in a more basic way."

"What exactly do you have in mind?" It took all Minshom's courage to walk back to the fire and sit down again as if nothing was wrong.

"One of the reasons I remained in India, despite my parent's pleading to sell my commission and return, is because I've realized I am not the sort of man who should marry."

Minshom raised an eyebrow. "What sort of man are you then?"

"The sort of man who prefers other men."

"Ah."

"And I would like to make love to you."

"To me?" Minshom smiled. "I don't 'make love' to men. I fuck them. They don't fuck me."

"I can understand that. But perhaps if you let me . . ."

"You think you could perform some sort of magical cure? Make me welcome another man into my body?" Minshom realized he was shaking and wondered if the other man could tell. "Make me beg for it?" He flinched as Wesley reached across and patted his knee. "Don't touch me."

"I'm sorry." Distress filled the other man's voice. "God, I'm so sorry."

Minshom managed to get to his feet. "There is nothing to be sorry about. It was a pleasure to see you again and I wish you every success in your life. Good afternoon."

He managed to make it through the door into the hall and ran for the servants' stairs. Safely behind the thick door he slowed to a walk, stopped and stared at the naked brick wall in front of him.

It hurt to breathe, hurt to think. Why the hell had he agreed to such a stupid meeting? It only raked up the past, and what was the good of that? He was who he was. He didn't blame anyone. He raised his fist and smashed it into the unforgiving brick until his knuckles bled.

Major Lord Thomas Wesley could go to the devil.

15

"Good morning, my lord."

Minshom didn't bother to answer as Jane slid into the seat opposite him and served herself some coffee.

"I said, good morning. Are you feeling quite well?"

He scowled at her over the rim of his raised cup. "I'm fine, thank you."

"You don't look it. You look like you've been out all night and have forgotten to change." She reached across the table and tried to take his hand. "And what did you do to your knuckles?"

"What business is it of yours?" Christ, this was all he needed, yet another person questioning him, expecting things of him, caring about him. "Can't you just hold your tongue for once, woman?"

"There's no need to be boorish."

"Yes, there is—if it will make you stop chattering."

Jane held his gaze, her hazel eyes full of concern. "Blaize, are you quite sure you are all right?"

"You're not my mother, Jane, now leave me alone."

"I am, however, your wife."

"A wife I don't want and don't need." Damn her, what did he have to say to make her stop? "I'm tired because I spent the night fighting and fucking other women. Is that what you wanted to know? Does that make things clear enough for you?"

She bit her lip and color flooded her cheeks, but her gaze didn't falter. "I wondered if you wanted to accompany me to the Earl of Millhaven's memorial service."

"Why would I want to do that?"

"Because he was a friend of your father's?"

Why did everything come back to his father? Why couldn't the bastard just leave him alone? Minshom gripped his cup so hard that he thought it might crack into a thousand shards.

"In truth, I'm glad when any crony of my father's dies. I hope he rots in hell."

Jane nodded and wiped her mouth with her napkin. "Then I'll go by myself."

Minshom regarded her for a long tense moment. "Why won't you fight with me today, Jane?"

She sighed. "Because I know you'd like me to and I'm not stupid enough to give you what you want."

"You usually do. You usually beg for it."

"And today I'm not going to." She stood up. "Have a good day, my lord."

He waited until she left the table and frowned into the silence. The scent of lavender and buttered toast lingered. He would've enjoyed a quarrel with Jane this morning, would've found a way to bring her to her knees and preferably his cock into her mouth. Sex with Jane always made him forget his problems and he certainly felt beleaguered at the moment.

He studied the bruised and bloodied knuckles of his right hand, remembered Robert's closed expression when he'd helped him clean off the blood last night. Suddenly there were no certainties in his life, only a reemergence of a past he had striven hard to suffocate.

Ruthlessly Minshom shoved all his turmoil aside. He had another appointment with his solicitor in less than an hour and he desperately needed to bathe and change. Where the hell was Robert?

Half an hour later, assisted by a tight-lipped Robert, Minshom was dressed and presentable. He ran lightly down the stairs and through the already-open front door to where his carriage stood waiting. His butler followed him out breathing heavily.

"My lord? Lady Minshom asked if you might take her as far as Lady Millhaven's house. She will be down in a moment."

Minshom sighed. "All right, I'll wait, but she had better be quick about it."

He strolled to the front of the carriage to inspect his horses, a new team he'd recently purchased from Tattersalls. At his nod, his coachman got down and engaged him in conversation about the prowess of the matching chestnut horses. A woman laughed to his left and he looked up expecting Jane, but it wasn't her.

Minshom couldn't help himself. He walked toward the two women and bowed. The older of the two smiled and held out her hand.

"Lord Minshom, what a surprise! I came to view a vacant property on the other side of the square with my friend, Mrs. Larksham. Her husband is thinking of resettling here after he retires from the army."

"Mrs. Larksham. A pleasure." How ironic if it was Thomas Wesley who had inadvertently sent the Larkshams here. Minshom then bowed to the smaller lady. "Lady Ellis." He kissed her gloved hand. That was all he could manage to get out. She looked as beautiful and serene as ever, and definitely more at ease than he was.

She lightly touched the dark head of the boy standing slightly behind her. "Michael, make your bow to Lord Minshom. Michael is home early from school after contracting the measles."

Minshom swallowed hard as the boy straightened and indifferent pale blue eyes met his. God, it was hard to look away. He dragged his attention back to Lady Ellis. "He is a fine-looking boy."

She met his gaze without faltering. "Yes, he is, isn't he? We are all very proud of him."

"My lord? Did I keep you waiting? I'm sorry, but I couldn't find the veil for my bonnet."

Jane's voice behind him. *God, no, not now, not like this.* He instinctively turned to face her, tried to shield her from the sight of the woman and child behind him. She stopped walking, her eyes fixed on the boy and then she brought her hand to her mouth and retreated back toward the house.

Minshom spared only a second to apologize to the trio and then sprinted after his wife. She wasn't in the hallway or in his study. He ran her to ground in her bedchamber and stood against the door fighting to catch his breath while she ripped off her bonnet and gloves. She kept her back turned to him even though she must have known he was there.

"He's your son, isn't he?"

"Yes."

"He has your eyes."

"Yes."

She turned to face him, hands clenched at her sides. "How old is he?"

"I believe he is almost twelve. He was conceived well before our marriage."

She advanced toward him, her face as pale and fragile as the simple lace trimming on her black dress. Jane in a rage was a riveting sight. He'd known she was capable of deep passion but not such scalding wrath. "And you think that makes it all right? You think that makes it better?"

"No."

Pain resonated in her fine eyes as she came even closer. "Did you ask her to come here?"

"Of course not."

She slapped his face and he accepted the blow, did nothing to stop her or hide from the sting of her words.

"She just happened to turn up?"

"Yes."

She tried to slap him again but this time he caught her wrist and held it tight. "Stop it."

"It's not surprising that you didn't care about Nicholas. You always had this in reserve, didn't you?" Jane whispered. "Another son, another child to love."

"No."

Tears slid from the corners of her eyes but she seemed unaware of them. He'd only seen her break down completely once before and had run from her to stop himself from ever having to witness such devastation again. She wrenched her hand free from his grasp and thumped both of her fists into his chest. Eventually he managed to grab hold of her wrists again.

"Stop it. This won't help."

She glared at him through her tears, her whole body shaking, her nails digging into his flesh as she fought to get free again. "You wanted me to fight you this morning, Blaize. Why aren't you fighting back?"

"I don't want to."

"Because you can't, because you know you are a lying, cheating bastard."

He tried to contain her struggles without hurting her, used the lessons he had learned as a youth to stand passively beneath her barrage of blows. He hoped in his soul that she would soon wear herself out and give in to the tears that were already threatening to disarm her.

"Jane . . ."

Her nails scraped his cheek and he recoiled, his head hitting the door panel. He moved away from the door, swung her around with him into the center of the room. Her hand closed around his cock and balls and squeezed hard.

"Is this what she did, Blaize? Did she have to hurt you to get a rise out of you, to get you to fuck her?"

"*Stop it.*" He tried to wrench her hand away but she gripped him even tighter and he felt himself respond to her violence, to her need to hurt him, to the familiar cycle of abuse. "God . . . stop."

"Is this what it takes to get you to fuck me too, Blaize? Pain? Because, by God, I'll hurt you, I swear I will."

She walked backward until she came up against the side of the bed, her fingers tangled in the waistband of his breeches, ripping and tearing at the buttons, exciting him even further. He stifled a groan as her questing fingers met his hardening cock.

"Jane . . . don't make me do this, don't . . ." His words dried in his throat as she toppled backward onto the bed, bringing him down over her, his cock nestled between the vee of her thighs. She tangled her other hand in his hair, twisting it painfully as her teeth bit down hard on his lower lip.

Despite himself, his hand dragged up her skirts to expose her sex and he didn't stop her positioning his cock at the entrance to her slick channel. He had but a second to stare down at her, to resist the temptation, to be the better man, but he couldn't do it, couldn't resist driving his cock home and hearing her scream his name into his mouth.

And then there was nothing except the tight clasp of her flesh around his, the urge to possess, to subdue, to own, to fill her with his seed. He drove into her like a man possessed, enjoyed the way her feet curled up over his buttocks and kept him deep, the heels of her boots marking the tempo of his thrusts as surely as the urgent thump of his heart. He kept his mouth over hers and plundered it as he fucked her cunt, even as she fought and bit to get closer. He caught every cry and moan as she climaxed around him and followed her, pumping deep inside her, each hot spurt feeling as if it were wrenched from his soul.

Silence, apart from his harsh breathing and the unsteady thump of his heart. His head rested on the bed next to hers, his cock was still inside her. He managed to raise himself up onto one elbow and looked down at her. She met his gaze, her eyes wide, and her trembling mouth swollen with his kisses. He wanted those lips around his cock.

He slid an arm underneath her torso and unbuttoned her dress and then unlaced her corset. She didn't resist him as he pulled everything over her head and threw it to the floor. He took his time taking the pins out of her hair and settling it around her on the bed. His cock was hard again and eager so he slid back into her now-wet cunt and fucked her again. She didn't stop him, her body as languid and liquid as any well-satisfied woman.

He closed his eyes as he pumped into her, so amazed to be inside a woman again, so different from a man. And yet why was he surprised? God had fashioned woman from Adam's rib. She was made from him and for him.

Jane awoke from her half-sleep to find Blaize fucking her again, his arms wrapped around her, her left foot balanced on his now-naked hip bone as he slid into her from behind. His endless lovemaking had blended into a series of connections she couldn't separate. Every time she woke, he was either inside her or about to be inside her or climaxing, his cum filling her until she was overflowing with his seed.

She couldn't stop him, couldn't seem to find any words other than to beg him to make her come or to move faster or harder. And she was too exhausted to fight him, too grateful to be in his arms and forget what she'd seen in the blur of his passion, to drown her pain in his lust.

A clock chimed somewhere in the house. Was it three in the afternoon or the morning? Where had the rest of the day gone? Blaize's fingers skimmed over her clit and she forgot about the time as she came for him again, felt him come alongside her.

She turned restlessly in his arms to face him, put her hand up to his face and felt the burr of his stubble. "Blaize?"

"Ssh . . ." He kissed her forehead. "Don't think, go to sleep."

Obediently she closed her eyes as he gathered her closer in his arms. His scent surrounded her and she cried silently against his chest, cried for her lost son, for the shock of finding herself face-to-face with her husband's image, an image she had no part in creating.

"Don't cry." Blaize whispered as he pushed her onto her back and spread her thighs wide. "Don't think." He slowly entered her, his hands under her buttocks holding her tightly into his languorous thrusts. She put her hands on his shoulders and held on, desperate to feel his flesh, something whole in the turmoil of her mind.

She must've slept again, as he no longer lay on top of her. She turned onto her side and searched for his warm muscular body with her outstretched fingers, felt nothing but damp sheets and his elusive scent. She opened her eyes and knew he had gone. More tears filled her eyes as she curled herself up into a tight ball. Would she ever stop crying?

She had to be strong. She had to get out of bed and face her husband. In her anger, she'd used every weapon she possessed to get him to fuck her. And that was just what he'd done. There had been no words of love spoken and no tender phrases, just base, lust-ridden demands. Jane rolled over onto her back and stared at the pastoral scene on the ceiling. Blaize called her manipulative and perhaps he was right. Hadn't she gotten what she wanted despite him? Did he imagine she was laughing at him now?

With sudden resolve, Jane thrust back the covers and swung her legs over the edge of the bed. When she set her feet on the floor, her thigh muscles trembled and quaked and she almost fell. She had to get up. She had to get to Blaize before he made up his mind to send her away.

Minshom sat in his study and contemplated the view outside his window. He'd bathed and changed, ignored Robert's concerned questions, eaten a late lunch and retired to his study to work. And yet he had done nothing except stare at the scurrying clouds and tried to re-create the image of Michael Ellis's face.

There was a knock at his door and Jane entered. She looked as worn out as he felt—hardly surprising after their night of lovemaking. Part of him was shocked she had decided to face him. The other part of him, the coward within his own heart, respected her courage more than he could ever admit.

He inclined his head a bare inch. "What can I do for you, my lady?"

She bit her already swollen lower lip and he was instantly hard.

"I wanted to apologize to you."

"Why? You got what you wanted from me, didn't you?"

"But I didn't want it like that."

"Like what?"

She sighed and sat down. "In anger, in revenge for something that happened a long time ago."

He met her gaze, keeping his expression blank. "As to that. In my early twenties I had a brief affair with Lady Ellis. I knew she was married with three children and I also knew she had no intention of leaving her husband. I believe she chose to bed me in a fit of pique because Lord Ellis had recently set up a permanent mistress."

"You don't have to tell me this, I . . ."

"Whatever her intentions, they had the desired effect. Lord Ellis became jealous and gave up his mistress and took his wife back. When Lady Ellis wrote to me to tell me she was breeding, she told me that her husband was perfectly willing to bring the child up as his own and that I was not required to play any further part in either her or the baby's life."

He swallowed hard and looked down at his desk, rearranged his pens into a straight line. "At the time I was deeply relieved and quite selfishly pleased about that. I have only seen the boy twice, both times at a distance. Yesterday was the first time I actually met him."

Jane sat down, her eyes fixed on his face. "He looks just like you."

"So it seems."

"It must have been a shock for you too."

It was hard to meet her gaze. "Yes." He busied himself rearranging his pens again before he was able to look up again. "I believe we need to renegotiate the terms of our bargain."

"I beg your pardon?"

"I fucked you."

"I know." Color flooded her cheeks. "I forced you, so surely it doesn't count?"

He raised his eyebrows. "I'm no delicate flower, Jane. I could've walked away from you at any point and I chose not to." In truth, that was a lie, but he couldn't tell her that her anger had held him as captive and submissive as a newborn lamb. "So I have decided to change the rules. You may stay here until I've fucked you enough to get you pregnant."

"What?"

"You heard me, Jane." He forced himself to continue. "We'll share a bed until you are with child again."

"And then what?"

"And then you will leave London and not come back."

"But what about the baby?"

He shrugged. "The child will be your responsibility. You will inform me when it is born and then I wish to hear nothing more from either of you."

She rose unsteadily to her feet. "That makes no sense. Why would you create a child and then send us both away?"

He glared at her, still too shaken to hide his true feelings. "Because I'll be damned if you get to have everything your own way, Jane."

"So I have to choose between you and the child?"

"Yes."

"A child that you might already have given me last night?"

"That is why I decided to change the rules." Unwillingly, his gaze fell to her belly and he wondered if she was right, if one night could make a child. Damnation, of course it could. A one-second fuck could make a child. He smiled at her bemused expression. It was almost worth all his personal anguish just to see Jane at a loss.

He walked around the desk and stood right in front of her, heard her breath catch, saw the quick rise and fall of her breasts, the breasts he'd endlessly suckled and nibbled and fondled just a few short hours before.

"Do you accept the new agreement, Jane? As soon as you are breeding, you tell me and I arrange for your immediate transportation back to Minshom Abbey."

"And until then?"

He placed a finger under her chin and raised her head until she had to look at him. "I get to fuck you as much as I like, whenever I like and wherever I like."

"You do realize it might take years for me to become pregnant?"

"I'm prepared to take the risk, and to be honest, the amount of time I intend to devote to filling you with my cum, you'll be breeding within a month."

"How nicely put."

He bent his head, licked a path along the line of her lips, and touched the tip of her tongue with his own. "You like my cum, you like being fucked. Why deny yourself the pleasure?"

She frowned at him. "Because it is wrong, because . . ."

He kissed her hard, kept kissing her until her hand buried in his hair and held him close. When he lifted his head, she was panting. "Is this how it always has to be with you, Jane? I have to fill you with my tongue, my fingers or my cock to keep you quiet?"

"You are impossible!"

He kissed her again, spread his hand wide over her buttocks and pressed her against his loins. "How about we seal our new bargain right here and now?"

She stared up at him, her eyes already clouded with desire, her intelligence for once defeated by his sheer closeness. "I don't like this, Blaize."

"Yes, you do." He maneuvered her back against the desk, picked her up and sat her on the edge, took his time opening the placket of his breeches, gave her plenty of opportunity to escape. She didn't move, her troubled gaze fixed on his working fingers and then on the swollen glory of his wet and wanting cock.

He pushed her knees wide and gathered up the soft muslin of her skirts and petticoats to expose her sex. His cock was at the perfect level to slide into her. He took her ankles and placed her slippered feet flat on the surface of the desk, held her still as the crown of his cock nudged against the entrance of her cunt.

"Are you sore?"

"Yes."

"Because of me?"

"Of course." She gasped as he pressed farther forward and pushed through the swollen folds of her flesh.

"Did you bathe?"

"Yes."

"But you're still full of my cum, aren't you?"

Her fingers dug into his shoulders. "*Yes.*"

He thrust home and held still; let her adjust to his size and thick throbbing presence. "You'll be even more full of me soon." He rocked his hips gently until she moaned his name. "So full that my cum will be dripping out of you."

She sighed and he held her tighter as he slowly entered and retreated, watched his cock work her, disappear inside her and then almost reemerge, just the tip of him in contact with her dragging wet flesh. "So you agree to our new bargain then?"

"I'm not sure."

Her breathing now was frantic, her words fragmented as he fucked her. "You agree, wife. Look down at my cock filling you and tell me you don't want it." He slid his hand into her hair and pushed her head down, let her watch the slow glide and retreat of his glistening shaft.

"I can't."

"Can't agree?"

"No, I can't stop wanting this."

A heavy surge of triumph shook through him and he grabbed her wrist. "Good, so come for me." He placed her fingers over her clit and pressed his hand on top until she began to scream into his mouth and writhe, until her inner muscles gripped his cock so hard he had to come.

When he withdrew he stared at the thick evidence of his seed that clung to her skin, to her thighs, to their entwined fingers. Strange that such an insignificant mess could produce the miracle of a child. He liked her wet like this far more than he had anticipated. Enjoyed the thought of her always being wet.

He took his handkerchief from his coat pocket and pressed it between her legs. "Don't bathe. I like the thought of you covered in my cum."

"You would." Jane slid off the desk, her color high and her expression unreadable. "I have to go and see Emily and explain my absence yesterday."

He caught her arm, both to steady her and to get her attention. "You will not tell her that we spent the day in bed?"

"Of course not and I won't mention the other matter either. Have some faith in me."

He shrugged. "You're not stupid, Jane, I'll give you that."

She sighed. "I am stupid, Blaize, because I've allowed you to get your own way again."

"I thought you were the one who had achieved her aim, not me." He tucked his cock back into his breeches and buttoned them up.

Her smile was bittersweet. "But I'm not proud of myself for what I did. You are letting me *think* I've won when in truth, you still achieve your goals. I will no longer be with you and you've created yet another cast iron reason not to come home."

"I don't need to come 'home'; my home is here."

Jane headed toward the door. "You know what I mean, Blaize. You have to come back at some point."

He turned his back on her and stalked over to the window. She sighed again and left, the door clicking shut behind her. Minshom frowned at his faint reflection in the glass. She'd regained not only her wits, but her sharp tongue far too quickly for his liking. She reminded him of a hunting dog on the scent of a fox.

Would she ever give up her campaign to make him come back to Minshom Abbey? He could only hope that the prospect of carrying a new child would take care of that, although sometimes, he doubted it. It was difficult enough to deal with her in London, let alone amongst the dark memories and still-present horrors of his family's country seat.

He moved abruptly to the door. The new bargain had been made and he had to live with the consequences. His mouth twisted in disgust. What kind of a man had he become? He was terrified of Jane conceiving another child, but even that paled in consideration to his fear of dealing with his father's affairs at Minshom Abbey. He was a coward indeed.

With a curse he flung open the door and headed up the stairs. A morning spent at Jackson's boxing salon might improve his temper. His cock twitched as he contemplated the evenings and days ahead with Jane at his beck and call. He realized, with a shock, that he was looking forward to those hours even more than he had looked forward to fucking Sokorvsky.

What the devil had Jane done to him? He slammed his bedroom door shut and glowered at Robert, who was rearranging his shirts in the drawer of the tallboy.

"I'm going out."

Robert bowed low. "Yes, sir. I'll fetch your hat."

Minshom tapped his booted foot as Robert took his time brushing the high-crowned black hat and flicking imaginary lint off Minshom's dark blue coat.

"I'm tired of your sulking, Robert."

"Really, sir." Robert handed him his hat and stepped back.

"And I'm tired of your insolence."

"Then why don't you dismiss me, my lord?"

"Because that is exactly what you want." Minshom studied his valet's obstinate face. "You'd just run straight to Captain Gray."

"No, sir, I wouldn't. He doesn't consider himself good enough for me."

Minshom put on his hat and then paused. "I beg your pardon? Surely it is the other way round?"

"I agree with you, sir, but Captain Gray doesn't want me."

Minshom frowned. Robert sounded desolate; as if his lover had been buried in the ground rather than apparently being off his head. "Are you sure about this?"

Robert shrugged. "He was drunk the last time I saw him, but very clear."

"Perhaps you should check and see if Lady Minshom has already left."

"Why would I want to do that, sir?"

Minshom pulled on his gloves and picked up his walking stick. "Because she is going to see Lady Millhaven and I insist that you accompany her." He nodded cordially at Robert and walked toward the door. "Get along with you, man."

"Why would you let me do that?" Robert said slowly.

"Because I'm tired of looking at your miserable face?"

"Sometimes, I don't understand you at all, my lord," Robert muttered as he joined Minshom in the hallway. "I doubt Captain Gray will still be at the Millhavens' anyway."

Minshom turned to face Robert. "If he isn't, you will go and find him and settle this once and for all."

"You are encouraging me to see your rival? Are you quite well, sir?"

"Obviously not." He met Robert's gaze. "And he's scarcely my rival. I just want you to . . ." He hesitated and then froze when Robert smiled. "I don't see what is so amusing."

Robert nodded. "I'm sure that you don't, sir, and God forbid that I should have to explain it to you."

Before Minshom could retaliate, Robert retreated down the hallway and knocked loudly on Jane's door. Minshom stared after him, hoped Robert could see his ferocious expression, and then departed himself, for once bereft of speech.

16

Jane stared out of the carriage window as the rain continued to fall, obscuring the sun and lowering the clouds until it felt as if the carriage were blundering through them. She contemplated her upcoming evening with Blaize. He'd left her a note telling her to be ready to leave at seven and that she should wear the new gown he would leave on her bed. Other than that, she had no idea what awaited her—apart from another night of sex.

She groaned at the thrill of anticipation that went through her body. She was a fool for him. After two weeks of constant sex, he had to only look at her and she was salivating like a bitch in heat. All her carefully laid plans, all her resolve to make him come back to Minshom Abbey with her, ruined because of her inconvenient lust for his body.

Part of her knew she should be celebrating his return to her bed, but in truth, she was ashamed of herself. She'd used her knowledge of the pain inflicted on him as a youth to goad him into action, into fucking her when he didn't really want to. Was there anything more humiliating for a woman to realize than that?

The carriage drew to a halt outside the house and Jane stepped down, nodded to the footman and ran into the hall shielded by the umbrella he carried. She didn't bother to seek Blaize out, just carried on upstairs to her bedchamber where her maid awaited her.

"Good evening, my lady."

"Good evening, Lizzie. I am dreadfully late. Can you order me something to eat while I bathe? I can have it up here on a tray before I dress."

"Of course, my lady." Lizzie nodded at the dressing room adjoining the bedroom. "Your bath is ready. I'll just add a little more hot water from the bucket warming by the fire."

Jane shivered as Lizzie unlaced and unbuttoned her before she stepped out of her damp clothes. She'd gone to visit Emily's orphans today, in Emily's stead, her friend being much involved with family matters. She'd stayed far longer than she had intended. She kept her hair pinned in place, regretted that she wouldn't have time to wash and dry it before she had to leave.

"Thank you, Lizzie." Jane stepped into the bath and sighed with relief. She would have to be quick, but she was grateful for the warmth of the water easing her tired muscles, washing away the last of Blaize's scent . . .

She opened her eyes as Lizzie reappeared at the doorway with a large towel and beckoned her to stand up. The tantalizing smell of leek soup and apple tart enticed her out of the bath as her stomach grumbled.

It took but a moment for her to devour the soup and tart while Lizzie redid her hair and efficiently laced her into a new pale green satin dress embellished with cream lace. Jane frowned at her elegant reflection in the mirror as Lizzie added two peacock feathers to her hair.

"Where did this gown come from?"

"I believe it came from Madame Wallace's shop, my lady." Lizzie waited, her expression confused. "Don't you remember ordering it?"

"I didn't order this one. I suspect my husband must have done so."

Lizzie stood on tiptoe to pin the feathers more securely in Jane's hair. "What a nice thought, my lady. Not like his lordship at all."

"Not at all." Jane laughed as Lizzie blushed. "It's all right, Lizzie, you don't have to apologize. I'm as surprised as you are." She smoothed down her skirt and held out her hand for her fan and shawl. "I'd better be off or his lordship won't be buying me any more dresses, will he?"

"No, my lady, I mean . . ." Lizzie curtsied and escaped, leaving the door wide open for Jane to follow her out. Jane had to smile. On her arrival, Lizzie had been hastily promoted to lady's maid from the kitchens and sometimes it still showed.

The clock in the hall struck seven as she reached the landing and she looked down over the banisters to see Blaize already waiting for her, dressed in the palest gray coat with a blue waistcoat beneath. She paused to look at him, aware of the coldness of his features, his contained energy as he paced the floor, the strength concealed beneath the elegance of his clothing.

Could she capture him again? Could she manage to keep him and his child? A foolish sense of hope stirred in her and refused to die. Despite what he said, he had loved her once. Perhaps he was wrong and she truly could have it all . . .

He looked up and caught her staring at him, but he didn't smile. He simply held out his hand and she obediently came down the stairs.

"You're late."

"A lady's prerogative, I believe."

He muttered something and led her toward the door and the

waiting carriage, handed her in and sat opposite her, his gaze on her gown. Jane patted the lace on her bodice. "Did you choose this dress?"

He raised his eyebrows. "Of course."

"And bullied Madame Wallace into making it for me as well?"

"Naturally."

"It probably cost you twice as much as it would've done if you'd just let me order the gowns in the usual way."

"Jane."

"Yes, my lord?"

"Are you going to argue with me all evening?"

"Surely that depends on how provoking you are?"

His lips twitched but he didn't quite smile. "I was right about keeping you quiet, wasn't I?"

"I don't remember, sir." She pretended ignorance, even as her body quickened and her breathing shortened.

He leaned forward and hooked an arm around her waist, pulled her onto his lap. "I'm sure you do." He stared at her mouth. "But what shall I fill you with? My fingers, my tongue or my cock?" His lips descended over hers and he kissed her hard until she was kissing him back. She didn't protest as he dumped her back into her seat, simply stared at him as she struggled to breathe normally.

His smile was infinitely superior and completely infuriating. "Ah, we have arrived. Perhaps you should pick up your shawl."

She bent to retrieve her paisley shawl and straightened to find him waiting outside the carriage, his expression again cold and detached. Had he always been like that? Careful to guard his face, to prevent his father from seeing him react to anything? Suddenly Jane hated that mask and hated his father all over again.

She got out of the carriage and found herself outside yet another London mansion glowing with lights. This one was distinctly smaller though, and the people going into it far fewer. Uncertainly, she looked at Blaize.

"This isn't Lord Anthony Sokorvsky's house, is it?"

"No." He kept moving up the stairs and bowed slightly to the other guests, ignoring their surprised looks. They proceeded along a dark oak-paneled hallway to the rear of the house, where the space suddenly opened up into another black-and-white tiled lobby. Beyond were double doors into a much larger set of rooms.

Jane pinched Blaize's arm. "Are you sure?"

"The house belongs to a gentleman named Lord William Feltsham. I went to school with him."

"And why are we here? Are you expecting to meet Sokorvsky?"

He looked down at her. "When you get that bit between your teeth, you are difficult to stop aren't you, Jane? I'm not here for Sokorvsky. I'm here to listen to the great Angelica Catalani sing."

Jane stopped walking and stared at Blaize, her hands clasped to her chest. "Are you serious?"

"I'm rarely anything but."

"I've *always* wanted to hear her sing."

"Indeed." He bowed slightly, reclaimed her hand and tucked it into the crook of his arm. "I had no idea." He squeezed her fingers. "And here is our host, Lord William Feltsham. Thank you for inviting us at such short notice, sir."

"A pleasure to oblige you, Minshom, Lady Minshom."

Lord William blushed and bowed so low his forehead almost bumped into Jane's bosom. He was a nondescript man dressed in a conservative manner more suited to a clerk, his hair sparse on his head and his mouth concealed by a luxurious mustache. Jane couldn't imagine how he and Blaize had ever become acquainted at school.

Jane curtsied and held out her hand. "Thank you for inviting us, sir. It has long been my ambition to hear Madame Catalani sing."

"A music lover like your husband, eh?" After a nervous glance at Minshom, Lord William kissed her gloved hand and smiled, his expression far more relaxed. "If you like, I'll introduce you to Madame Catalani afterward." He coughed and lowered his voice. "If she is in the right mood, of course—these Italians can be a little temperamental."

"That would be delightful, sir." Jane smiled. "But please don't put yourself out."

With another anxious glance at Minshom, Lord William let go of her hand and moved to greet the new arrivals who crowded the door behind them. Jane continued into the music room and sat down in the gilt chair her husband pulled out for her.

"Feltsham got rid of the mews house and converted it into this." Blaize gestured at the gilded organ with its elaborate pipes situated by the far wall. "I believe he used the Prince Regent's dragon-infested music room at the Pavilion as his guide." His mouth quirked up at the corner. "Perhaps not quite so successfully."

Jane ignored his attempt to divert her and gave him a blissful smile.

"Thank you. I think this is the nicest thing you have ever done for me."

"*For you?*" He shrugged. "I did it for myself."

Jane opened her fan with a flick of her wrist. "Why do you find it so hard to accept a compliment?"

"I am a selfish man; I please myself. Why should I accept your thanks when I do not deserve them?"

Jane continued to fan herself, for once at a loss for words. What to say to a man who denied all her attempts to reach him? Was he so unused to someone actually thanking him? Perhaps he was. She sighed and returned her attention to the elegant proportions of the room. It seemed the audience would be relatively small, far less than a hundred people.

She shivered as she glanced up at the high white and gold painted ceiling and covered her shoulders with her shawl. The acoustics in the room were well suited to music of all kinds and particularly to vocal music.

Blaize touched her hand. "I'll fetch you a glass of ratafia."

"But I don't like ratafia . . ."

He ignored her. "I'll be back in a moment."

She watched him move through the small crowd with the stealth of a big cat and with a similar effect on the people around him. He wasn't liked, his presence at such an event obviously as unusual and unwelcome as the wild animal he reminded her of. When he disappeared from view into the next room, she turned her attention to the piano where a man began to play scales to warm up.

A footman dimmed some of the lights. An air of anticipation filled the small space as the audience began to find their seats. Jane looked around for Blaize but couldn't see him. She kept the chair to her left on the end of the row free for his return.

Lord William Feltsham stepped in front of the seats, his round face beaming and his hands clasped in front of him.

"Ladies and gentlemen, thank you for coming to my musical evening and gracing me with your presence. We will begin with the Bonini string quartet, and after a short interval conclude with the great Catalani. I hope you all enjoy yourselves immensely."

A gentle ripple of applause had him bowing and resuming his seat in the front row. The string quartet took their places on the slightly raised dais and proceeded to tune their instruments. Jane looked around for Blaize, but there was still no sign of him. Had he brought her to the concert insisting it was for his own benefit and then decided not to share it with her in any way? She gripped her fan so hard she thought she might break the delicate ivory sticks.

She raised her head and stared at the musicians. Damn him. He *had* known she had always wanted to hear Catalani—she'd told him years ago. She was going to listen to a world-famous soprano sing and she was not going to let her husband ruin it for her. She fixed a smile on her face, took a deep breath and prepared to enjoy herself.

Minshom stood in the shadows of the refreshment room sipping his brandy as the rest of the guests filed into their seats, leaving him alone. Through the connecting doorway he could see Jane looking for him, but he made no attempt to attract her attention. Her willingness to believe that he would put himself out for her still startled him, her ability to smile and thank him, even more so.

He finished his brandy as the string quartet started to play and poured himself another. Jane had stopped looking for him now, her attention fixed on the stage, her face in profile. He considered her through narrowed eyes. The dress suited her, made her skin gleam like the finest porcelain. He'd told Madame Wallace it would.

Of course he'd known she wanted to hear Catalani sing, it was one of the first things she had ever told him, her eyes bright, her enthusiasm undimmed by the shadows he would stifle her with during their marriage. Then why deny it? He shrugged, even though no one was looking at him. Being thanked was not something he was comfortable with, and re-calling happier days was as pleasant as roasting in hell.

The quartet finished the short Haydn piece with a rousing chord and the audience clapped. Minshom didn't bother to ap-plaud, his attention all on Jane, who seemed to have forgotten he existed.

"Are you enjoying yourself, my lord?"

He glanced up and found Thomas Wesley at his elbow, resplendent in full dress uniform. Minshom raised an eyebrow at such magnificence.

"Dressed like that, shouldn't you be at court or guarding something?"

"I'm due to be presented to the prince in an hour or so, but I wanted to hear Catalani sing first." He grimaced. "I doubt I'll get another chance before I return to India."

"Or ever again if you wait another ten years before you return. She'll probably be far past her prime."

Thomas chuckled quietly. "Or that. Why are you standing over here? You always loved music."

Minshom gestured at the glass of ratafia he'd poured and left on the sideboard. "I came to get some refreshment for my wife."

"Ah, and you didn't wish to interrupt the musicians by returning. How very thoughtful of you."

Minshom couldn't help but smile back at Thomas Wesley. "Not quite. You give me too much credit. But then you always did, didn't you?"

"Perhaps." Thomas shifted closer and the warm scent of spice and sandalwood washed over Minshom. "I didn't realize you were married. If I had, I would never have suggested . . ."

Minshom held up a finger. "I thought we agreed not to speak of that again?"

Thomas leaned forward until he captured the tip of Minshom's gloved finger between his teeth and drew it into his mouth. Despite the instant pulse of interest in his cock, Minshom kept still and made no attempt to either reciprocate or withdraw his finger. Eventually Thomas sighed and stepped back.

"I'm sorry."

"For what?"

"For being unable to let go of my stupid fantasy of us being together."

Minshom smiled slowly and forced himself to relax. This was a game he knew well, a game he excelled at. "Surely it is good to dream?"

"Not when it's unlikely to come true."

"There are hundreds of men in London who would be more than willing to oblige you."

Thomas met his gaze, his brown eyes far too honest, and his smile rueful. "But they wouldn't be you, would they?"

Minshom shrugged. "One man is much like another."

"That isn't true."

"In my considerable experience it is." He turned his head slightly so that he could still observe Jane and make sure that she didn't leave in a huff.

"But you aren't really drawn to men, are you?" Thomas persisted. "Using them and loving them are two very different things."

"My, you have been listening to gossip, haven't you?"

Thomas frowned. "I don't need to do that. I know why you crave sexual power. I used to be the same."

"And what changed you? The love of a good woman?"

Thomas's smile was breathtaking in its sincerity. "No, a man. He taught me that sex isn't about pain and domination, but about love."

Minshom forced a laugh. "And you believe that if I let you fuck me, I'll feel the same? Somehow I doubt it."

Thomas sighed. "I'm not stupid and I don't think I can perform miracles. You prefer women. If your father hadn't meddled, you wouldn't even question that."

Minshom frowned. Why did he feel as if all his certainties were being destroyed? And why did everyone he was acquainted with seem intent on undermining him? "Who gave you the right to decide my sexuality for me?"

"I'm not. I'm just asking you . . ."

"To let you fuck me so that you can feel better about yourself. I'm not interested."

Minshom moved past Thomas to pick up the wineglass he'd intended for Jane.

"Good evening, Major."

"Lord Minshom."

Minshom nodded and made his way quietly across the room to where Jane was sitting. She didn't acknowledge him when he slipped into his seat, her attention all on the music. For a moment he studied her and tried to forget the conversation with Thomas.

Damn it, he felt uncomfortable now. It was true that he'd never particularly enjoyed fucking men. He enjoyed the power of it, yes—the sense that he was better than everyone—but he certainly wasn't looking for tenderness or love out of a sexual encounter.

When had love ever had anything to do with sex? He glanced at Jane again and frowned. Love was a notion for women, a pretty wrapped parcel to conceal the necessity to procreate the species, body to body, mouth to mouth, sex to sex. Why make it more complicated than that?

Eventually the string quartet stopped playing and stood up to great applause. People began to move about again while the stage was prepared for Madame Catalani.

"Who was that you were talking to, my lord?"

Minshom blinked at Jane as she took the glass of ratafia out of his hand and sipped it. Despite her apparent lack of interest, she had been keeping an eye on him after all.

"An old acquaintance of mine, Major Lord Thomas Wesley, recently returned from India."

Jane frowned. "Do I know him? He looked quite familiar."

Unwillingly Minshom answered her. "There is a drawing of

us as young boys in the library at Minshom Abbey. Perhaps you have seen it."

Jane opened her fan and slowly plied it, her color slightly raised. "That might be it. I often take my sewing into the library—the light is excellent."

"Indeed." Minshom couldn't resist taking a look over his shoulder. Thomas was chatting to his host, his handsome face relaxed, his wide mouth smiling, much as he had looked in the pen and ink drawing Minshom's father had made. The likeness had been taken the summer he was twelve and Thomas was fourteen. The summer when his father had first introduced him into The Little Gentleman's Club. The summer when he'd lost his first fight to Thomas and suffered the brutal consequences.

Briefly Minshom closed his eyes as he fought the memories. He'd liked Thomas, hero-worshipped him even, and then had his dreams shoved down his throat in the most vicious manner possible. What was wrong with Thomas that he wanted to resurrect such awfulness? He was a soldier, not a romantic fool. He of all people should understand that all a man could do was bury the fear as deep as possible and move forward.

"All you all right, my lord?"

Jane touched his wrist and he fought a ridiculous urge to flinch away from her.

"I'm fine." He nodded in the general direction of the stage. "I believe Madame Catalani is going to sing now."

Jane immediately looked away from him, her excitement palpable as the diminutive soprano appeared, dressed in white, her dark hair piled on top of her head.

Jane grabbed his hand and squeezed it hard. "Oh, Blaize . . ."

He didn't pull away, let her fingers tangle with his as Catalani sung of places and emotions he had only dreamed of, emotions that tore at his soul, making him aware of what he lacked and even more aware that he had no ability to change. Encouraged by his mother and his teachers, he'd dreamed of becoming an accomplished musician. Unconsciously, he flexed his left hand. His father had managed to break three of his fingers for some imagined transgression, no doubt deliberately. And Minshom had simply stopped playing anything.

Beside him Jane swayed to the music, her lips slightly parted, her hazel eyes wide in the half darkness. Despite the press of her fingers, he'd never felt more conscious of being alone.

When the concert ended, he even endured Jane's meeting with the great soprano, added his own compliments to Jane's and restrained from making a single caustic remark. The grateful look she gave him as they entered their carriage unsettled him deeply, made him want to shout at her, to shake her, to tell her not to show him how vulnerable she was to his smallest kindness. With a jolt, he realized she was speaking.

"Thank you for a wonderful evening, my lord."

He inclined his head. "As I said, it was for my benefit but I'm glad you enjoyed it."

She smiled at him and launched herself into his arms. He caught her more by reflex than design, felt her arms close around his neck. Her lips descended over his and she kissed him. He opened his mouth and kissed her back, allowed her warmth to warm him, to fill the void within him with the thrill of sexual attraction. This he understood, this he could control. He took command of the kiss and pulled her astride him until the wet heat of her sex rode his satin-clad cock.

She pulled slightly away from him. "Let me touch you, let me suck you."

He opened his legs wide and lowered her between them, watched her soft green skirt spread around her as she knelt at his feet. He liked her on her knees. He opened his pantaloons and gripped his shaft around the base, brought it forward to rub against her soft waiting mouth.

"Suck me."

She opened her mouth and drew him inside and down her throat, taking him as deeply as he would've have wanted, would've have insisted. She sucked hard, curved her hand under his tight balls and caressed them too, as she worked his thick shaft. Minshom refused to succumb to the desire to close his eyes in order to appreciate the sensation more. He needed to watch her take him, to see her expression when he came.

He couldn't help his hips rocking into the motion, trying to take control, trying to force the pace. But she set her teeth on him and held him to her rhythm and he gloried in that even more. He came faster than he had anticipated, great waves of seed pumping into her, leaving him biting his lower lip to stop himself from shouting out.

He realized the carriage had stopped moving and carefully raised Jane to her feet before buttoning himself up again. She looked flushed with desire, her heavy-lidded eyes more green than brown in the new gown. With a muttered oath, he smoothed down his hair and opened the door, glared at the blank face of his footman as if daring him to comment.

Ignoring the footman's proffered arm, he turned to help Jane down himself and led her into the house and up the stairs to her bedchamber. He followed her inside and relieved her of her cloak. She glanced at him over her shoulder.

"Shall I send for my maid?"

"No."

He set his fingers to the task of unlacing her, enjoyed watching the fine curve of her back emerge from the constraints of her clothing. He bent to kiss the nape of her neck, felt her shiver in response and smiled. She was always so eager for his touch, so ready to do whatever he wanted—in bed. If only she was half as biddable out of it.

Minshom straightened and took an uncertain step back. He didn't want this, this softening toward her, this *need* . . .

"Good night, Jane."

She turned toward him, hands clasping the front of her dress to her breasts.

"You are leaving?"

He managed to shrug. "You're unlaced."

"But I thought . . ."

"Women shouldn't *think*, Jane. You know it isn't becoming."

Color rose on her cheeks. She walked away from him, sat down at her dressing table and began to rip the pins from her hair, her movements jerky, the pins going everywhere. "Good night, then."

Some devilish impulse made him pause, his fingers already on the door handle. "You aren't going to fight with me tonight?"

"No." She met his gaze in the mirror.

"Why not?"

"Because I've had a lovely evening and I'll be damned if I'll allow you to spoil it."

Minshom raised his eyebrows. "Such language, Jane. Ladies aren't supposed to swear."

"Then I'm obviously not feeling very ladylike tonight, am I?"

"Indeed." He bowed extravagantly and left, walked the short distance to his own bedchamber and opened the door. There was a warm fire in the grate and his night things were laid out over the back of a wing chair. The handle of a warming pan stuck out from the side of the bed.

"Good evening, sir."

Minshom frowned. "I thought you were off chasing Captain Gray?"

"I couldn't find him, sir." Robert came toward him and efficiently divested Minshom of his coat.

"Gone to ground, has he?"

"It appears so, sir." Robert continued to undress Minshom, his gaze steady on his task, his expression blank.

"I'm sure he'll turn up at some point."

"I'm sure he will, sir." Robert's mouth quirked up at the corner. "That is, if he doesn't do anything stupid."

"I don't think he's that kind of man, Robert. He's a sailor, for God's sake; he lacks imagination."

Minshom stretched out his arms and allowed Robert to pull his shirt over his head. The front was still damp from Jane's earlier ministrations. He pictured her mouth on his cock, her teeth . . . God damn her to hell, why couldn't he stop thinking about her?

"I intend to visit the pleasure house on Friday night."

"Yes, sir." Robert gathered up the discarded clothes and placed them in a bundle on a chair, took Minshom's dressing gown and handed it to him.

"I wish you to take a note to Madame Helene in the morning and one to Major Lord Thomas Wesley apprising them of my visit."

"Yes, sir."

Minshom caught Robert's chin in his fingers and held him still. "If you act like a cringing servant for one more minute, I will dismiss you."

Robert held his gaze. "I thought you already had."

"No, I simply threatened you. As it stands you are still mine."

"I understand that, my lord."

"Good." Minshom rubbed his thumb along Robert's lower lip, heard his servant catch his breath. God, another person wanting him. What was wrong with them all? "Good night, Robert."

Robert blinked at him. "You don't wish me to stay?"

"No." Inwardly Minshom groaned. Now Robert looked rather like Jane had earlier, all big puzzled eyes and quivering mouth. "I'll see you in the morning."

Robert was quick to pick up the bundle of clothes and retreat to the door. "Good night then, my lord."

Minshom removed the warming pan from his bed that Robert had forgotten in his haste to be gone and slid between the covers. There was one major difference between Jane and Robert's reaction to him; Jane had wanted him to stay and Robert had been glad to escape. Minshom shut his eyes. In truth, he wasn't sure anymore which reaction surprised and aroused him the most. And surely that was the most dangerous thing of all?

Jane had taken control in the carriage and he'd let her, and he'd enjoyed her attentions far too much. What was happening to him? If he wasn't careful he would become as weak as his father had always suspected. In some part of his soul, he felt like he was fighting for his life, for his very existence . . .

He opened his eyes. But he was good at fighting, that was one thing he was very sure of. Perhaps Jane and Thomas and Robert needed to remember that.

17

Lizzie cleared her throat. "His lordship says that when you are ready to get dressed, I should tell him."

"And why is that?" Jane asked, her fingers already busy removing her day dress in anticipation of the evening to come.

Lizzie shrugged, apparently unconcerned with the abrupt dismissal of her services. "I dunno, my lady. That's just what he said."

"It seems a trifle odd, but I suppose we should do what his lordship says." Jane sighed. "Why don't you unlace me and then go and inform Lord Minshom that I am at his disposal."

She hadn't seen Blaize all week; he'd been sequestered in his study with a series of visitors. For a man depicted in the scandalous cartoons as a wastrel and a libertine, he was incredibly busy. But she'd known that already, had watched him rebuild his family's fortunes from the ground up.

As Lizzie bustled about and then left to deliver Jane's message, Jane pressed a hand to her stomach and swallowed hard. There was a strange metallic taste in her mouth that tainted everything she ate. She grimaced at her reflection in the mirror.

Perhaps she needed a tonic or perhaps it was simply her body protesting living in a city, where the food was rarely fresh and sometimes definitely suspect.

Her distracted gaze settled on her clothes chest where the box about The Little Gentleman's Club was hidden. She'd looked for Thomas Wesley and had found not only his name, but some drawings of him fighting and bloodied, his smile gone, his face bruised and defeated. It wasn't surprising she'd thought she'd known him. She only hoped Blaize hadn't noticed her unguarded comment.

The door banged as Lizzie returned.

"My lady? His lordship will be here in a moment."

"Thank you, Lizzie." Jane smiled at her maid and took a sip of her now-tepid tea. "You may go."

Jane resumed her seat at the dressing table and smoothed some cream into her skin. London was wearing in more ways than one. She'd been here for only a couple of weeks. If she stayed much longer she'd have to resort to rouge to restore the color to her cheeks.

"Good evening, wife."

She looked over her shoulder to see Minshom coming through the door between their two suites. He wore his brown silk dressing gown and his black hair was still damp from his bath. His pale skin was slightly flushed and he smelled of sandalwood and citrus. He carried a large dress box in his hands, which he placed on Jane's bed.

"Good evening, my lord." She nodded at the box. "Is this another dress for me?"

"It is, but not from Madame Wallace's. I borrowed this one from Madame Helene."

"From the pleasure house? Will we be spending the evening there?"

Blaize didn't answer as he opened the box and took out something lacy. He seemed intent on keeping his distance from her, both emotionally and physically. It wasn't surprising when she had gotten far too close to him during their last sexual encounter. She'd sensed his conflict when she took control of his cock.

"That doesn't look like a dress," Jane said doubtfully.

"It isn't. It's a corset." Blaize advanced toward her, the garment held in his hands. "Stand up, Jane."

Jane didn't move. "But I have a perfectly decent corset of my own. Why would I want to wear that one?"

"Because it is necessary to wear this particular one under this particular dress." There was a hint of impatience in his voice, and when she met his gaze, his eyes were hard. "Stand up."

Jane sighed and rose to her feet and let her dressing gown fall from her shoulders. His heated gaze dropped to her breasts, to the curve of her waist, to her sex. "Turn around."

She turned back toward the mirror. His arms came around her, bringing the gray silk-covered corset into contact with her warm skin. Jane wiggled. "It is too short."

"It is what it is. Now keep still."

He molded the boned fabric to her chest and started lacing up the back. He kept one hand wedged between her breasts to hold the front up.

Jane drew an experimental breath. "It still feels wrong and my breasts aren't really covered at all."

Her nipples sat well above the lace, and the corset ended at her waist rather than her hips. She sucked in a breath as Blaize continued to tighten the laces until she could hardly breathe.

"It's too tight."

"It is how I want it to be. Now put on these stockings."

"You'll have to do it for me. I can't bend down now."

He raised his eyebrows at her and knelt at her feet, smoothed the first black stocking over her foot and up to her knee and tied the garter. She fixed her gaze on his long fingers as he tied a neat bow at the side of her knee.

"Give me your other foot."

She presented her left leg and he eased the stocking on, pausing to straighten the seam and make sure the garter was tightly secured. His hand lingered on her knee and then stole upward to slide between her thighs, pushing them slightly apart.

She shivered as he widened his fingers to cup her mound and stroke her clit.

"Wet for me already, I see." He leaned forward and she felt his hot breath on her skin, the flick of his tongue over her already-swollen bud. "I like that, Jane. I like your obedience and your readiness." His middle finger slipped lower, teased the entrance to her sex.

Jane shivered and slid her fingers into his still-damp hair, then moaned as he pushed away from her and stood up. He put his hand in his dressing gown pocket and brought out a jumble of jewelry, showed it to her.

"You'll wear these for me, tonight." He placed the jewels on her dressing table and plucked at her exposed nipples until they were tight and aching before loosely attaching two clamps. The black and red polished gemstones gleamed and trembled with every labored breath she took.

"And this." Blaize knelt again and set his mouth over her clit, sucked it until she was writhing in the chair and lifting her hips toward him. She gasped as the metal gripped her swollen bud, forcing herself to breathe through the constriction of the corset lacing and her own arousal.

"Don't move. I'll fetch the dress." Blaize got up and went behind her to the bed. When he reappeared he had a gown draped over his arm. "You'll wear this tonight."

"With no petticoats?"

His smile was full of lust and anticipation. "Petticoats would just get in the way. I want you to be . . . available."

"To you?"

He shrugged. "That's my concern, not yours."

Jane raised her chin. "Are you suggesting that I have no say in what happens to me tonight?"

He met her gaze, his pale eyes glittering. "You are my wife. You have never had any say."

Jane swallowed hard. He had obviously decided she needed to be put in her place again, preferably beneath him, servicing him or simply bowing down to his demands. She licked her lips. "I'm not sure I want to do that."

"I'm not giving you a choice. You agreed to our bargain, you agreed to take my cum—why pretend you don't like it?"

"*Your* seed, Blaize. Not someone else's. You told me you wouldn't countenance that when I first arrived, so how can you change your mind now?" She made as if to get up. "In truth if you find fucking me so distasteful, I'll simply go back to my original plan and find a lover."

She hardly had time to react before he pressed her back into the seat, his hand cupping her chin, his mouth slamming over hers in a deep possessive kiss. When he finally drew back she was panting and so was he. Her aching breasts were crushed against his hard chest and his erect cock, which had escaped his dressing gown, prodded her stomach.

"I like fucking you."

"But not enough to stop another man having me?"

"Damn you, Jane."

She saw the battle in his eyes, his need to possess her at war with his need to show her who was in control. Damn him for thinking he could share her and not regret it.

"You changed the rules, Blaize. You should abide by them."

He kissed her again, this time more savagely until she was clinging to him and trying to angle her body so that his cock would fit exactly where she needed it. She managed to get her hand between their bodies and grabbed for his slippery wet shaft. He cursed and moved off her, making her lose her grip.

"I'm not going to be passed around your acquaintances like

a whore, Blaize." He stared at her, his eyes narrowed, his cheeks flushed. "If you try and do that to me, I'll . . ."

"You'll what? Leave?"

"I'll make you sorry you ever lived."

He smiled. "You already do that quite admirably merely by existing." He rubbed his hand over his face as if rubbing her scent into his skin. "If you do what I say this evening, I'll stick to our bargain, Jane. I am, after all, a gentleman. Now put on the dress."

Jane scrambled to sit up and then jumped up from the chair. She poked him in the chest. "*You* are insufferable."

He caught her chin in his fingers and kissed her again. "And yet here you are, still wanting me despite yourself."

She stared at him, unable to deny the truth of his words or the excitement coursing through her. Could she walk away from him or was he banking on her stubbornness to make her stay and see it through to the bitter end? His thumb caressed her jaw line.

"Put the dress on."

She closed her eyes as he dropped the filmy fabric over her head and kept them closed as he deftly laced her into the gown. His soft murmur of approval stirred the fine hairs on the back of her exposed neck.

"Good lord, Jane, you look quite . . . exotic."

She opened her eyes and stared at her reflection. The tiny black silk-puffed sleeves were barely large enough to support the weight of the bodice, not that there was much of that either, settling as it did, just below the ruffles of her corset leaving her bejeweled nipples visible amongst the lace and the creamy swell of her breasts.

The rest of the bodice hugged her figure as did the narrow skirt, the long line of her thigh in evidence against the clinging silk. Black lace inserts in the skirt also offered glimpses of her legs and buttocks. It took her a long moment to find her voice.

"I can't go out wearing this." Jane sounded uncertain, breathless, yet he could feel the tension in her body, the barely contained excitement.

He cupped her breast and angled his thumb to stroke her already-tight nipple. "Yes, you can. It just depends where you are going." He came around and took her by the shoulders, urged her down to sit in the chair. He carefully folded up her skirts and placed her right foot on the arm of the chair, opening her wide for him. "In truth, you look so delicious, I need to fuck you just a little before we go."

He undid his dressing gown to fully reveal his cock. Leaning over her he fed the first two inches inside her and gently rocked back and forth. Bracing his hand on the back of the chair, he added another inch, making her moan.

"I want you to smell of me and taste of me so that all the other men know you are already taken." God, he sounded so possessive—felt it too. He couldn't share her cunt. It was for him alone, had always been for him.

He forced himself to withdraw and looked down at her. His pre-cum glistened on her skin and thighs. He liked it, wanted her always to look like that for him.

"Wait here. I'll be back in a moment." With a stifled groan, he retied his dressing gown and went to get ready. The pantaloons he intended to wear were tight at the best of times, but with the raging erection he now had, his state would be all too evident. At least the satin was black, which wouldn't show how wet he was as well. He fastened the placket, enjoyed the pressure of the fabric against his hot shaft.

He shrugged into his coat unaided, as Robert was out looking for Captain Gray again. He knew his valet would disapprove of his actions, so perhaps his absence was for the best. Minshom stared at his reflection as he carefully folded his cravat and secured the folds with a black pearl pin. Tonight it wouldn't matter who saw him. In truth, his aroused state would only enhance the experience.

He went back into Jane's bedchamber, saw she was still sitting where he had left her and felt a thrill of excitement. She frowned at him when he came into view.

"Why are you looking so smug?"

He picked up her cloak and held it out to her. He was already dressed to go out. "Because for once you did what you were told and stayed put."

"I stayed by the fire."

He threw the cloak around her shoulders and couldn't help but let his knuckles graze her nipples as he tied the strings. He drew the hood carefully over her hair and handed her a black mask. "Put this on when we get there."

"When we get where?"

"To the Cyprian's ball. What were you expecting, Almacks?"

Her mouth dropped open. "You are taking me to a whore's ball?"

"Yes. I thought you might enjoy it, and it is my turn to choose our entertainment."

"I thought we were going to Madame's, to a more private venue, not a public event . . ."

He took her arm and walked her to the door, kept her moving even as she kept talking and right into the carriage.

She sat opposite him, her hazel eyes huge in her face, a mixture of panic and arousal he found immensely stimulating. It was but a short ride to where the ball was being held. He wondered idly if she would try to bolt, knew he'd stop her before she got too far.

The carriage came to a halt and he jumped up to open the door and hand her out. Keeping her tightly against him, he tied on her mask and then his own and held out his hand.

"If you're too afraid, you can always go home."

"I'm not afraid."

Sheer bravado but he didn't care. He'd make sure she enjoyed herself whether she wanted to or not.

As she and Blaize proceeded into the crowded building, Jane couldn't help but stare avidly around. The circular floor of the old theater was empty of seats to provide a rudimentary dance floor, and the ground-level boxes were also occupied by people. Signs of neglect were everywhere, the plush blue velvet curtains tattered and faded, and the gilt paint flaked and scratched. A small orchestra on the upraised stage at the front of the theater attempted to be heard over the cacophony of shrieks and wails and the roar of conversation.

Some people were dancing, but not in a way Jane had ever seen before. Hanging around a gentleman's neck while he suckled your breasts wasn't exactly encouraged at a society ball. There were also other oddities—men dressed as women, women dressed as men and groups of people simultaneously engaged in sex wherever they seemed to find a spot to settle.

"What do you think?" Blaize murmured, his hand on her shoulder, fingers idly caressing her throat. He led her into one of the vacant boxes and shut the door, although Jane wondered why he bothered when they were still visible to all.

"It is extraordinary. Have you been here before?"

"Indeed, I have." He shrugged out of his cloak giving Jane her first view of the outrageously tightly cut front of his black pantaloons. She could see everything through the taut satin—the curve of his balls, his thick shaft, even the head of the metal piercing on his cock. "Robert and I have enjoyed many a tryst here."

"So you dress like this to impress men?"

His smile was intimate. "Women seem to like it too. You don't agree?"

She swallowed hard as he feathered a hand over his cock and cupped his balls. "It seems a little obvious, and thus unlike you."

He took her hand and drew her toward one of the empty chairs. "That is true, but here I don't have to worry about what anyone thinks of me. It's simply about the sex."

Jane just stopped herself from nodding in agreement. Blaize *would* like that, not having to bother with all the emotional responsibilities of love, the guilt and the complex sexual desires he struggled to conceal. She could well understand how sex at its most basic and anonymous would appeal to him.

"Good evening, sir, ma'am. Do you want company?"

Two women dressed in only their shifts, stockings and corsets leaned over the edge of the box and made eyes at Blaize. "We're quite willing to share."

Jane frowned at them. "Well, I'm not, so go away."

Giggling, the girls winked at Blaize and sauntered off arm in arm, looking for someone else to play with. Jane turned to her husband, who was watching the girls retreat.

"Is that what you did with Robert? Found some women to have sex with?"

Blaize shrugged and leaned up against the wall, long legs crossed at the ankle. "Not necessarily. Robert and I preferred to fuck men. Sometimes adding women offered some protection from those who might find such behavior offensive."

Jane shivered inside her cloak. She couldn't forget that Blaize's sexual activities with men were still subject to the most stringent strictures of the law and could result in public humiliation, flogging or death.

"Take your cloak off, Jane."

She blinked at the sudden order and drew the cloth more firmly around her. "I'm quite cold, my lord. I'll take it off later."

He straightened and held out his hand. "It's as hot as Hades in here; take it off."

She met his gaze, saw the determination in his and licked her lips. "What if I refuse?"

He shrugged. "I'll take it off for you and I won't be quite as careful of your dignity as perhaps I should."

She brought her fingers up to the ties. "I feel far too naked."

He smiled and gestured at the seething, swaying crowds around them. "Here? You are more decently covered than most. Take it off."

She complied and watched his eyes narrow as her skimpy bodice was revealed.

He held out his hand. "Now come here."

Jane swallowed hard, stood up and walked the three small steps toward him. If he was able to experience sexual freedom here, could she? No one knew her here either. He raised his hand and stroked her cheek, ran his fingers down her throat until he reached her breasts. She held her breath as his thumb nudged her oversensitive nipple.

"You look very nice. Come and dance with me."

"Dance?" Jane stuttered. "You know how I feel about dancing."

He took her hand, stepped out of the box and lifted her over the low barrier. He dragged her inexorably toward the crowded dance floor. She gasped as they were surrounded by the jostling throng, felt his strong arms close around her and hold her tight. There was no question of dancing in the approved manner here. She rested her cheek on his chest and heard the reassuring thump of his heart.

One of his hands drifted lower and caressed her buttocks, pressing her tightly against him, his cock thick and hot against the thin silk of her dress. He bent his head and nipped at her throat and she arched into the caress, jumping when his lips moved lower and his tongue licked a slow wet path around her nipple.

She didn't stop him, aware of nothing but the seductive pull of his mouth on her breast and the heat of his hand on her buttocks. She shoved her fingers into his hair and held him close, allowed him all the liberties he demanded and held nothing back.

The music faded, as did the crowd as he pushed his thigh between hers, stimulating her already wet and excited sex. She gasped as he crowded her against a wall, his hand now under her skirts, molding and shaping her right buttock, bringing her leg up and out to the side to accommodate his hips and the grinding, rocking pulse of his satin-covered cock.

Jane moaned as she came and Blaize laughed into her mouth. She bit down on his lip and he still laughed, his fingers stabbing into her soaking-wet sex from behind as she continued to shiver and pulse against him.

He tore his mouth an inch away from hers. "Do you want me, Jane? Right here when everyone can see? Do you want my cock?"

"God, yes." She didn't care anymore, just wanted him between her legs, pounding into her, filling her up with his cum. He didn't bother to reply, his fingers busy between them hiking up her skirts and freeing himself from the constraints of his pantaloons.

"Take it, Jane. Take my cock."

He grunted as he drove inside her, the piercing scraping against her flesh as he filled her, pumped in and out. She desperately tried to hold on, to experience every second with him, to come when he came and collapse against him, her face shielded by the breadth of his shoulder.

A smattering of applause and a few raucous comments on their performance reminded her that they were still at the ball and having sex in front of strangers. Blaize let go of her and her legs slid down to the floor. She kept her arms around his neck and was glad of it when her knees buckled.

He cupped her jaw and brought her head back up for another hot, deeply lascivious kiss. "We haven't finished yet, Jane."

"What?"

"We have another engagement this evening at the pleasure house."

"Right now?" Jane eased away from him, aware of her flushed cheeks, the wetness of his seed between her thighs. "Can't we go home and change first?"

"No." He looked up at her as he finished tucking his cock back into his pantaloons. "I want you to look just the way you do now."

"Like a well-bedded whore?"

His smile was devastatingly intimate. "If that is how you feel." He bowed and walked back toward the box, leaving Jane to follow him through the dancers, enduring the pinches and less subtle groping of her fellow guests. When she reached him, he was already wearing his cloak and holding out hers. She allowed him to place it around her shoulders and tie the ribbons.

"Isn't that why you brought me here, to make me feel like a whore?"

"Why would you think that?"

She shrugged. "Because you want me to feel bad about desiring you. You want to equate my feelings for you with any other basic sexual encounter. You want me to feel ashamed of myself."

"Do I? Perhaps I brought you here because I thought you might enjoy it." His rigid tone didn't invite a response, but he wasn't the only one who could play games. She swung around to face him.

"You fear intimacy. You wish sex was simply about power and dominance rather than about love and happiness."

His smile was supercilious. "You seem to enjoy being dominated."

"That's not the point, is it? I enjoy having sex with you because I find you incredibly arousing."

Something flickered in his cool blue eyes. Had she hurt him?

Had he really tried to share something immensely personal with her? "You would find any man just as arousing. I've seen the way you watch Robert being fucked."

She touched his arm. "Don't you understand? I enjoyed it because Robert was with *you*. I find the thought of anyone touching you arousing."

He stepped back and walked across to the door, flung it open. "Your brain must be addled. Now come along."

Jane held her ground, waited until he looked back at her. "Do you really believe I could find sexual satisfaction with any man?"

"I just said so, didn't I?"

"But you will not put that arrogant assumption to the test?"

He scowled at her. "You are not taking a lover, Jane."

She glowered right back at him. "Why not? Then at least I could conduct a proper experiment and confirm my suspicions that you are the only man I want in my bed. It seems I am convicted of being a slattern who loves sex with anyone without any proof."

Without replying, he marched off down the hallway. For a moment Jane bared her teeth at his retreating back. Getting him to understand that she wanted only him seemed impossible. Why did he repudiate the idea so vehemently? Did he truly think her amoral, or was it more complicated than that? Did he truly believe he was unlovable?

On that unsettling thought, Jane picked up her skirts and hurried after Blaize. Her evening wasn't over yet. She still had plenty of opportunities to both enjoy herself and irritate her husband.

18

"Can you slow down, my lord?"

"No, or we will be late."

"Late for what?"

Jane struggled to keep up as Blaize towed her along the hallway of the second floor of Madame Helene's pleasure house. White doors passed in a blur of numbers and suggestive titles until he stopped so suddenly, she almost cannoned into him. He opened a door and bowed to her.

"In here, my lady."

Jane lowered her voice as they entered the rear of darkened room. "What exactly are we doing here?"

"We've come to watch something."

"What?"

He took her hand again and marched her into the center of the room. "Actually, we've come to watch you."

"*What?*" she hissed, and tried to pull out of his grasp, although she knew he was far too strong.

"Kneel on the stool, my lady."

Jane licked her lips, aware that there were already about

twenty people sitting in the rows of chairs surrounding the small intimate stage. Petite candles set in a circle gently illuminated the central space. "Blaize, what is going on?"

Blaize maneuvered her over to the stool and stood in front of her, blocking her view of the audience. "It is part of our evening's entertainment. You've already let me fuck you in front of a theater full of people, why not here?"

"Because . . ." Jane stared up at him. "*You* are going to fuck me? I thought . . ."

He shrugged and removed his cloak, threw it toward the shadows beyond the circle of light illuminating them both. "Yes, of course it will be me. We have a bargain, don't we? I get to fuck you wherever and whenever I want."

Jane stared at him. Did she trust him not to exploit her? Was she any safer at the pleasure house than she had been at the ball? She'd loved him fucking her there, forgotten all about the need for caution, for restraint, and had simply been herself. He held her gaze, his blue eyes intent. He had discarded his mask, although she still wore hers. Was he expecting her to run? Would that finally prove to him that he was totally unlovable?

She swallowed slowly. "What do you want me to do?"

His mouth quirked up at the corner as if he wanted to smile, but he quickly repressed it. "I want you to do what I tell you to do. No arguing."

"That will be difficult for me."

"I know."

Still holding his gaze, Jane sank to her knees on the large red velvet stool. Blaize slowly exhaled and walked behind her to take off her cloak. A low whistle of approval came from the audience and Jane closed her eyes. She shivered as Blaize's long fingers settled on her shoulders and then drifted down to unlace the dress.

She was panting so fast that the jewels at her breasts shivered in the light and sent trembling rainbow shadows onto the floor below. The dress came over her head, leaving her in just the short corset, her stockings and the jeweled clamps. Another murmur came from the audience as Blaize reached his hands around and cupped her breasts, framed the nipple clamps with his finger and thumb and gently tugged.

Jane couldn't help gasping as her flesh throbbed and ached, the heat of arousal so strong that she wanted to sob. His hands slid lower to her hips and settled there for another long moment bringing her buttocks against his groin and the teasing thickness of his shaft.

She tried to look down as one hand went lower toward her sex to flick the jewel there and set off even more throbbing. He used his hand to widen her stance, let his fingers play in the thick wetness he'd created earlier, swirling around her clit, her pussy lips, the opening to her body.

"I need a volunteer."

Blaize's calm and totally unexpected request shocked her out of her slow slide down the treacherous path of desire.

"You, Major. If you would be so kind."

Jane opened her eyes to see a familiar figure walk into the center of the room. Major Lord Thomas Wesley looked as stunned as Jane felt. If Blaize had invited him, and that was doubtful seeing as how her husband tried to avoid the man, Major Wesley certainly hadn't expected to participate.

Blaize lowered his voice as the man drew nearer. "Major Wesley, you've often expressed an interest in fucking me—how about you show me exactly how serious you are?"

To Major Wesley's credit, he didn't look scared of Blaize, which was surely a good thing.

"What do you want me to do, my lord?"

"I want you to get down on your knees and lick my lady to a climax, Thomas."

Thomas shrugged. "If you wish." For a big man, he sank

quite gracefully to his knees and stared up at them both. "If your lady permits, of course."

Blaize laughed. "Nod if you agree, my dear. The major is a great stickler for the rules."

Jane managed to nod and Thomas anchored his big hands on her hips. She moaned as he delicately licked at her clit, the tip of his tongue caressing the jewel, the clamp, the hot needy flesh beneath.

"Lick her clean of my cum, Thomas, make her climax for me."

Jane leaned back against Blaize as Thomas increased the pace and length of his forays, licked her from front to back, his tongue probing her opening, his teeth grazing her swollen pussy lips. She forgot about the audience and came against his open mouth as Blaize squeezed her nipples.

"You haven't finished, yet, Thomas, so don't get up."

Jane felt Blaize undo his pantaloons and free his cock. He wrapped one strong arm around her waist and slightly bent his knees. His cock slid between her buttocks and rubbed against her soaking wet sex.

"Put my cock in her, Thomas." Jane heard Thomas exhale and curse under his breath as Blaize continued to talk. "Put your hand around the base and guide me inside her."

Jane couldn't see exactly what was going on, so the sudden fullness of Blaize's pierced cock entering her at such an extreme angle made her moan. Thomas groaned too as Blaize shoved deep and held still.

"Lick her again and lick me. Make us both come."

"God . . ." Thomas sounded almost as desperate as Jane felt, wanting Blaize to move, to let her come, knowing he would make her wait and make her crave him for as long as he could control his own desires.

*   *   *

Minshom stared down at Jane and then lower to Thomas as he felt the first tentative lick to his balls. God . . . this was so much more than he had anticipated, so much more than simply dominating the two people who had started to feature together in his most erotic dreams. Jane was straining against his hold, trying to move on his cock, trying to make him thrust into her as hard as he could.

But he held firm as Thomas drew one of his balls into his mouth and sucked. Despite Minshom's original resolve to remain aloof, the hand not holding Jane up came to rest on Thomas's head and urged him on.

He caught back a moan as Thomas released his balls and rimmed his arse hole with his wet tongue and gently probed it. Minshom froze. Did he want this? Did he want to order Thomas to slide his finger in there along with his tongue and pump it back and forth until Minshom climaxed? Thomas's mouth moved again, came to swirl and circle the place where Minshom and Jane were joined.

Jane mewled like a kitten when Thomas licked her clit and she came. Minshom gritted his teeth as she clenched around his shaft until he thought he would have to climax. His balls tightened against his body as Thomas mouthed and rubbed them with his chin, his teeth—Christ . . . Minshom groaned and spilled his seed deep, one hand buried in Thomas's thick hair, the other wrapped around Jane's ribs, squeezing the breath out of her.

The lights in the circle dimmed and most were completely extinguished by one of the footmen. There was some enthusiastic clapping from the audience, an audience Minshom had completely forgotten existed, and then it went quiet. The three of them remained frozen in place. Minshom's cock was still inside Jane; Thomas was still kneeling in front of her as she continued to shudder.

Slowly, Minshom unclenched his fingers and released his grip on Thomas's hair. Thomas looked up at him.

"Damn you, Blaize."

He surged to his feet and kissed Minshom hard on the mouth, almost crushing Jane between them. Minshom was so surprised that he fell backward, bringing Jane down with him. He managed to roll her to the side before Thomas crashed into him, his mouth punishing, nipping, demanding.

"Help me." Thomas groaned and grabbed Minshom's wrist, dragged his hand down to his groin where his cock was still painfully erect. Minshom couldn't help but close his fingers around Thomas's thick shaft and start rubbing. Within seconds Thomas climaxed, his hot cum soaking his breeches and Minshom's hand.

Thomas cried out and lay still, one hand covering his face, his chest heaving. Minshom couldn't bear to look at him and turned back to Jane as his cock thickened again. Jane's interested gaze flicked between him and Thomas. Damnation, he couldn't have her thinking he had *enjoyed* that, couldn't have her thinking anything at all.

He crawled over to her and straddled her, released the clamps from her nipples and her clit and let them fall to the floor. She was looking at him now, her gaze fixed on his, Thomas forgotten. He shoved his cock deep and pumped into her, his only desire to make her come, to forget himself in her arms, to forget Thomas.

But he couldn't. What if he turned his head and caught Thomas's eye. Would he end up begging to be fucked? Would he look as eager as he felt to have Thomas moving over him, his cock buried deep, fucking Minshom as Minshom fucked Jane?

Jane pulled his hair so hard he winced and opened his eyes. "If you want him, I don't mind."

He froze over her and struggled to breathe and contain the sudden pulse of excitement in his gut. When had he become so transparent, so needy, so . . .

Jane stroked his hair. "Blaize. It's all right."

He started thrusting again, the temptation to take her at her word and ask Thomas to join them terrified him. Didn't she know that? Of course she did, that's why she was being so accommodating. God, just Thomas's mouth on him at this moment would be enough to send him over the edge.

Jane wrenched her mouth away from his. "Thomas?"

"Yes, ma'am?"

"Will you touch him?"

Minshom went still again as he felt Thomas turn toward them.

"Christ, yes. Of course I will."

Minshom knew he should speak out, should stop Thomas from gently pulling down his pantaloons, and, God, kissing him, and licking him, sliding one finger in his arse and pumping it in and out. Minshom groaned and moved his hips, slid farther into Jane as Thomas added his second finger.

He forgot to protest then, as sexual pleasure escalated to heights he had never experienced before. He was trapped between two lovers, his cock deep in Jane, Thomas's fingers lodged in his arse, his mouth on his neck biting down. Their three bodies moving slickly, urgently together.

"Do you want his cock, Blaize?" Jane whispered. He opened his eyes to look at her, to say no, to deny he wanted anything of the sort, but the words stuck in his throat.

Yes, he wanted it. But he couldn't say it, had sworn he'd never beg for another man's cock.

"He wants you, Thomas, go ahead."

Jane took the decision away from him and Thomas responded. His thick wet cock replaced his fingers and he rocked slowly into Minshom, groaning with every thrust, making Minshom want to scream with the pleasure of it. When Thomas started to move on him, it was as if his own cock was doubled in length, the inches he slammed into Jane mirroring the inches

Thomas slammed into him, setting off an arc of ecstasy that he had never experienced before.

Jane climaxed, her fingernails digging deep into his shoulders, setting him off and then Thomas. God, he wanted to cry with the joy of it, cry with the horror of allowing himself to enjoy it. Thomas rolled off him and Minshom instantly struggled to his feet. He couldn't look at either of them, knew they'd think they'd mastered him, and knew it was true.

"Blaize?"

He ignored Jane and headed for the door, buttoning his pantaloons with shaking fingers as he went. He was wet, his arse dripping, his cock throbbing with overuse, and yet he wanted to go back and do it all again. He blinked hard and stared at his reflection in the mirror at the end of the hall; saw his younger bewildered self, his father's triumphant smile. Yes, he'd liked it, liked being fucked by Thomas while he fucked Jane. He truly was as perverted and weak as his father had always insisted. He smashed his palm into the glass and shattered his own face.

Now he truly was in hell.

19

"I don't know where Lord Minshom is, Robert. He disappeared almost ten days ago and he hasn't yet returned."

Robert halted in front of her, his expression startled. "He just disappeared?"

"So it would seem." Jane sighed and gestured for Robert to sit down at the table in the deserted breakfast room. Robert looked as if he had been having some adventures of his own; he was unshaven, his clothes were filthy and he was eyeing the food on Jane's plate like a ravenous dog.

"Have you eaten this morning?"

Robert swallowed hard. "Not yet, my lady."

Jane handed him a clean plate. "Then help yourself. There is plenty left. With Lord Minshom absent, most of the food is going to waste anyway."

"It doesn't go to waste, my lady. The kitchen staff will finish it up, don't you worry about that."

Jane waited as Robert loaded his plate with everything he could find and returned to his seat. He ate so fast, she couldn't believe he didn't choke. She poured him a cup of coffee from the full pot and returned to nibbling her toast. The smell of pork sausages drifted across the table and she swallowed hard as nausea hit her. Worrying about Blaize had taken its toll on both her appetite and her nerves. She'd barely been able to stomach anything in the last couple of weeks.

"I'm sorry I wasn't here to help you, my lady."

Jane cradled her chin in her hands. "Where exactly were you?"

A flush of red colored Robert's cheeks. "Lord Minshom gave me permission to look for Captain Gray. He's gone missing too."

"Ah, that's right; Lady Millhaven is very concerned about him. Did you find him?"

"No, my lady."

"Perhaps he is with Lord Minshom."

"I hope not, my lady, for both our sakes."

Jane sighed. "I frightened Lord Minshom away, Robert."

"I doubt it. His lordship doesn't scare easily. If he ran, it's far more likely that he scared himself."

Jane stared at him for a long moment. "I hadn't thought of that."

Robert cleared his throat and lowered his voice. "If there is something you want to share with me, my lady, I can promise you my complete discretion."

Jane reached out and patted his hand. "I know that. It's just hard for me to explain exactly what happened. I don't think any of us were prepared . . ."

"For what?"

Jane smiled. "For the sex to be so extraordinary."

Robert finished his coffee and poured himself another cup. "I'm still not quite sure I understand what happened."

"Lord Minshom and I went to a Cyprian's ball and then on to the pleasure house, where he had arranged for us to be the starring act in one of the rooms on the second floor. For some reason, Major Wesley was there, and Minshom invited him to help and somehow, after the lights went down we all ended up in a tangle on the floor and Major Wesley fucked Minshom while Minshom fucked me."

"Good God." Robert looked stunned. "His lordship let Major Wesley fuck him?"

"It was partly my fault. I could tell that he wanted him to, so I encouraged Major Wesley and . . ." Jane waved her hand in the air. "Oh my goodness, it was astonishing."

"And what happened afterward?"

Jane bit her lip. "My husband ran away."

Robert sat back and regarded her. "I'm not surprised. His lordship doesn't usually let anyone near his arse."

Jane nodded. "Because of what happened to him with The Little Gentleman's Club."

Robert paled. "You know about that?"

Jane winced. "I'm sorry, Robert."

"Lord Minshom *told you*?"

"Of course not. I found out accidentally when I was rear-ranging some of Lord Minshom's father's possessions in the Abbey library." She shivered. "What a diabolical scheme. I feel so sorry for you all."

"Does his lordship know you know?"

Jane shook her head. "Do you think I should tell him?"

"Good God, no."

There was silence as Robert finished his breakfast and Jane struggled with what to say next. "Do you think he will come back?"

"Captain Gray or Lord Minshom?"

"Both of them, I suppose."

"They have to return eventually, don't they, even if it is just to tell us they are leaving again?"

"That doesn't reassure me at all, Robert."

Robert's sigh was as loud as hers. "I know my lady."

"We are a pretty pair aren't we?"

"*You* are pretty, my lady." Robert grimaced and ran a hand over his jaw. "I need to shave and make myself presentable." He got to his feet and bowed. "I'll do my best to find them both, my lady, so don't you fret."

"I'll do my best not to, Robert, and thank you."

Jane watched him leave and then contemplated the emptiness of her day. Without Blaize to tease, there seemed little point in doing anything at all. She hoped he came back soon, even if it was just to fight with her . . .

She returned to her room to find Lizzie still fussing about with her clothes. Lizzie gave her a worried glance.

"Are you all right, my lady? You look a bit peculiar."

Jane slapped a hand over her mouth and looked desperately for a basin. Lizzie produced one with a flourish and Jane bent over it and began to retch. By the time the spasm ended she was exhausted and kneeling on the floor while Lizzie mopped her forehead with a wet cloth.

"Did you eat something peculiar, my lady, or do you think you're breeding?"

Jane slowly raised her head and contemplated her maid. "How would I know if I was breeding? I've only been here for five weeks. It's far too early."

"But you haven't had your monthly courses since I've been looking after you either."

"I don't always have them regularly, I never have." Jane licked her lips and then wished she hadn't. "I just feel sick all the time. It's nothing like my previous pregnancy at all. Good gracious, I can't possibly be pregnant." She tried to laugh. "God, my husband will never believe me if I tell him now. He'll think I've been . . ."

Remembering she wasn't alone, Jane stopped speaking, but

Lizzie was nodding wisely anyway. "He'll think it isn't his and that you'd been with someone else in the countryside before you got here."

"That's exactly what he'll think." Jane rose to her feet and sat at her dressing table. Her skin looked clammy, her mouth pinched and her hair was in disarray. She swallowed hard.

"I promised Lady Millhaven I'd go out with her today so I'd better hurry. Get me a fresh cup of hot sweet tea and then help me change out of this gown."

Lizzie looked doubtful. "Are you sure my lady? You still look a bit peaky."

"I'd prefer to be busy doing something rather than sitting here moping and worrying about what Lord Minshom is going to say when he gets back." Jane set about tidying her hair as Lizzie ran downstairs to get her some more tea. Her bedroom was in complete disarray but Lizzie could fix that after Jane had gone out. Unfortunately, fixing the rest of her problems wouldn't be quite so easy.

Minshom sprawled on the bed and stared up at the cracked beamed ceiling of his chamber at the Jugged Hare Inn. He'd already counted all the spiders and traced imaginary pictures between the crumbling plaster in the glow of his single candle. His fingers closed around a bottle of gut-rot gin and he brought it to his lips.

How long had he been here? From the rumpled state of his clothes and the smell, more than a few days. His hand had healed as well, tended to by a slatternly chambermaid who'd insisted the landlord didn't want him to die on the premises. Minshom drained the last of the cheap gin into his mouth and slowly swallowed. When he'd first arrived at the Hare, he'd intended to fornicate with everything and everyone he could find, but instead he'd requested a room, crawled up the stairs and concentrated on drinking himself into oblivion.

Below him, the inn still teemed with life and the heady sounds of people enjoying themselves, but he didn't want to go down and participate. He was still too busy licking his wounds and suffering the torments of hell to want to lick anything else. He'd let Thomas fuck him, and more to the point, he'd enjoyed it.

He groaned and let the bottle slip through his fingers and crash to the floor. And, of course, Jane had been there too, under him, encouraging him when Thomas climbed on top of them both and his whole world exploded into the most erotic experience of his life. Minshom sat up and winced as the room continued to spin around him. Jane would never let him forget this . . .

Damnation, he couldn't let her win. And he couldn't admit that his father had been right about his sexual tastes all along. There had to be a way for him to save face and come out on top. Thomas was going back to India, so that left only Jane . . . Minshom stiffened. And according to their bargain, Jane had only to get pregnant and she would be gone too.

Minshom struggled to find his boots and pull them on. All he had to do was keep fucking Jane until she was pregnant and that was scarcely a hardship, was it? She was always quiet when he filled her mouth with something. His cock twitched at the thought and he managed to stand upright. Somewhere deep inside, he knew he was still a coward and that his plan was that of a desperate man. He could hardly fuck her every time she opened her mouth, but what else could he do?

Three hours later, after bathing and changing with the help of one of his startled footmen, Minshom knocked on the connecting door between his and Jane's suites. To his immense surprise, he realized he was nervous. Would she berate him for running away from him or simply smile and accept him back as if he hadn't done a thing?

He hoped it was the latter, which worried him even more. He hesitated before turning the handle. Could he find peace with her after all? Believe that she could accept him just the way he was? It seemed impossible, but some part of him craved that, yearned to be loved . . .

"Ooh, my lord, you startled me!"

Minshom stopped short at the sight that met his eyes. His wife's room looked as if a herd of cows had run through it. Clothes lay everywhere as well as shoes and all the other garments apparently necessary to a lady's comfort.

"What exactly are you doing, and where is my wife?"

The maid blushed and bobbed him a curtsey. "I'm just spring cleaning, my lord, sorry for the mess." She dumped the load of dresses she was carrying on the bed and turned back to the clothes chest.

Minshom followed her across the room and waited until she turned back to him, her arms again full.

"Where is Lady Minshom?"

The clothes slipped from her arms. "Oh, I'm sorry, sir, I forgot to tell you, didn't I? She went out with Lady Millhaven, although I told her not to go, being as she looked so queasy-like . . ." The maid stopped speaking and went bright red.

Minshom frowned. "Her ladyship is unwell?"

"I couldn't say, sir, it could be any number of things. Who knows what's going about on those dirty London streets."

Something was wrong, Minshom could sense it. Was Jane really sick and concealing it from him? He decided to be blunt. "Is her ladyship coughing up blood or anything?"

"Oh no, my lord. She's just puking a lot." The maid returned to the chest and started throwing things out at random. "Not that that means anything, sir, she might just have a weak stomach, rather than . . ."

"Rather than carrying a child, perhaps?"

The maid straightened and clutched a flattened bonnet to her chest. "I didn't say that, sir."

"But you think it might be true."

"I . . ." The maid curtsied and ran for the door. "I have to get some new paper to wrap the winter furs in." She escaped through the door before Minshom could stop her.

He remained in the wrecked room and ran through the entire bizarre conversation. Was Jane pregnant? If so, she was obligated to tell him and she hadn't. His distracted gaze fell to the floor and a large box that the maid had tossed onto the fireside rug. Something about the box seemed all too familiar and made his blood freeze. He bent to pick it up, read the words "The Little Gentleman's Club."

He'd thought Jane finally knew the worst of him, but apparently she knew so much more. He sat down on the bed, his throat working convulsively as he opened the box and saw the written records of his torment, his pain and humiliation, of his victories . . .

God, she must despise him so much. So why had she come to him, let him make love to her, let him believe she wanted to be part of his life again? He slammed the lid shut and stood up. There was only one reason, and that had nothing to do with love.

He strode to the door and rang the bell. When his butler appeared instead of the maid, his suspicions were confirmed. He scowled at Broadman.

"Get that maid back up here and tell her to pack all her mistress's things, and then deposit them in the hall. Have my traveling coach brought out and kept in readiness for further orders."

"Yes, my lord." Broadman looked puzzled, but that wasn't unusual. "I'll go and find Lizzie immediately."

* * *

By the time Jane returned home, she was no longer capable of maintaining her bright smile. She was exhausted, sticky and ready for her bed. The ripe smells of the orphanage had almost been her undoing. For the first time she had struggled to stay and play with the children. She halted in the hallway which was filled with luggage. It took her a dazed moment to realize it belonged to her. She looked at Broadman who had opened the door for her.

"Am I going somewhere?"

Broadman bowed and avoided her gaze. "His lordship is in his study, my lady. Perhaps he can enlighten you."

"Lord Minshom is here?" Jane untied her bonnet as she walked toward the back of the house and the closed door of Blaize's study. Whatever her reception, at least he was home, at least she had a chance to see him again.

He was sitting at his desk, his dark head bent as he wrote something on a sheet of parchment. The room was half in shadow, the only illumination from the candelabra on his desk. He didn't stop writing when she walked around to face him. Jane waited patiently for a moment and then cleared her throat.

"Blaize?"

He looked up and there was no welcome in his gaze, no hint of anything but furious cold anger. Her hesitant smile died.

"I've arranged for a carriage to take you back to Minshom Abbey tonight."

Jane blinked at him. "Have you finally decided to come home with me? That is wonderful."

"I'm not going anywhere."

"I don't understand."

"You broke our bargain."

"I did what?"

He sat back, his hands folded together on the desk, his posture so relaxed she knew he was acting. "You agreed to tell me when you were pregnant."

"I don't know if I am pregnant, and how could I tell you anything when you haven't been here for almost two weeks?"

"Are you suggesting that you waited for my return to deliver your news in person?"

Jane took a step closer to the desk. "I don't *know* if I am pregnant."

"Your maid seems to think you are."

"My maid needs to learn to hold her tongue."

"So you *were* trying to keep the news from me."

"Blaize . . . why are you doing this? Why are you trying to tie me in knots?"

He shrugged. "Because you deserve it. I don't like being lied to, Jane. You should know that."

Despite her resolve to remain calm, her voice rose. "I didn't lie! Even if I am breeding, it takes several months to be sure and a lot can go wrong in the meantime."

"Which is why I just told you to leave."

Jane stared at him and tried to gather her thoughts. "When I can *confirm* that I am pregnant, and not merely overwhelmed by living in London, I promise you will be the first to know." She bobbed him a curtsey. "Now please, will you stop this? I'm tired and I want to go to bed."

He stood up and shook his head. "You're not staying, Jane. You're breeding, that's all you wanted from me, so now you can leave."

"That's not all I wanted, Blaize. Why won't you believe me?"

His smile was brittle. "Ah, that's right; you wanted sex as well, didn't you? Hopefully I gave you enough of that to last you for a while. And after you deliver my heir, you can fuck whoever you want."

Jane drew a deep careful breath. "Why are you doing this? Is it because of what happened with Thomas Wesley? I only thought to . . ."

"To confirm your suspicions about my sexual tastes?"

"I don't know what you mean."

"Yes, you do, don't lie." He pushed a familiar red box into the circle of light spread by the candelabra. "Thomas was the first person to fuck me—apart from my father, of course, did he mention that in his diaries?"

Jane's eyes filled with tears. "God, Blaize . . ."

He slammed his hand down on the desk. "Don't you ever feel sorry for me, wife. Don't you *ever* dare to presume you know what is best for me in bed or out of it."

"I don't feel sorry for you."

His laughter stung. "You're lying again. Now get out."

She fisted her hands in her skirts. "No, it's not like that, I want you to come home to me, I've always wanted you to come home . . ."

"For God's sake, be quiet!" Jane froze as he rounded the desk and came to stand toe-to-toe with her. She had never seen him like this before, so furious, so deadly. "You wanted another child and you didn't care how you achieved that aim." He pointed at the box on the desk. "Christ, Jane you even brought your own ammunition! If I hadn't given in and fucked you so quickly, would you have used my father's perverted diaries against me?"

"No!"

"Easy for you to say now, but hard for me to believe." He grabbed her by the elbow and started edging her toward the door. "You are leaving right now."

Jane dug her heels in and refused to budge. "I want to stay with you. I love you."

He went still, his pale eyes blazing down at her. "Don't say that; don't *lie*."

"I'm not. Yes, I wanted a child, but I wanted a child with you, I wanted us to be together."

"And you were prepared to do anything to get what you

wanted, weren't you? God, people think I am Machiavellian, but you . . ."

"No." She whispered. "I would never have used that information against you. I hoped that we would be able to sit down together and decide what to do with it. I didn't feel I had the right to destroy the box without consulting you."

"So you brought it all the way to London with you."

"Yes."

He met her gaze, his eyes full of skepticism. "It doesn't make any difference, you are still leaving."

"Why?"

"Because I have made other plans." He turned away from her and picked up the letter he'd been writing. "I've decided its time to get to know my eldest son."

Jane stared at him for a long moment and then tried to read the letter he'd held up for her perusal. "You can't do this to me."

"But it's not about you, is it? It's about what I want."

"No, it's just you thinking of the most horrible way to hurt me, to make me leave you." She raised her head, made him look at her. "It's about you running from the truth, using any excuse to stop me loving you or you daring to love me back."

His lip curled. "How melodramatic my dear and how utterly untrue." He marched toward the door and flung it open. "I don't love you and I don't need you, Jane. I don't require love in my life—I already have a son and you've reminded me that even Thomas Wesley has his uses, so why in God's name would I want you?"

She bit down on her lip and realized she couldn't look at him anymore. She swept past him to the door and headed for the hallway. Her baggage had disappeared, obviously preloaded into the carriage. Broadman leapt to open the front door for her and she kept going, even remembered to thank the coachman who held the carriage door open for her.

She picked up the fur rug draped across the seat and discovered a leather pouch full of money. It was the same pouch she had thrown at Blaize, the one containing all her savings. How typical of him to give it back to her now, as if to underline his victory and his lack of need for anything she could give him, even money. She drew the fur rug around her shoulders and huddled underneath it.

Her tears stopped as if her body finally realized what her mind already knew. There was nothing more to say and she refused to beg. She had her pride and if Blaize didn't want her, she would return to Minshom Abbey and make a life for herself and her child without him.

She'd survived losing him once, she would survive again. Within her, something precious crumbled and died. Robert had been right, bringing the box to London had been a mistake. It had finally given Blaize the excuse he needed to get rid of her. She rubbed at her eyes. Was he correct? Would she really have used it to get his attention?

God, she hoped she was pregnant. At least then she would have something to love, and to hell with Blaize Minshom. With a broken sigh, she closed her eyes and focused on the rocking motion of the carriage. She couldn't do this anymore, hold out hope for the unattainable. For the sake of her child, she had to look to the future and forget Blaize had ever existed.

Minshom sat down at his desk and waited until he heard the distant slam of the front door and the team of horses starting to move off. He stared down at the letter in front of him and methodically tore it into strips, his movements unsteady, his fingers shaking. As if he would ever contact his bastard son, as if he would ever burden the boy with the knowledge that his father was a weak, useless, bloody fool.

He picked up the gloves Jane had left on his desk and caught a hint of her familiar lavender scent. He'd managed it then.

He'd managed to destroy her faith in him and make her leave. The shock of finding her in possession of his father's diaries had goaded him to lose his temper, something he'd avoided for years. With a groan, he buried his face in the palm of the glove and slowly inhaled. At one point he'd thought he would have to resort to physically picking Jane up and throwing her in the carriage.

At least she'd gone quietly. And it was quiet now, just as he'd wanted. No one left to challenge his authority. No one left to feel sorry for him. He swallowed hard. No one left to care whether he lived or died.

He closed his eyes and pressed the glove to his lips. So why did he feel that watching the light die in Jane's eyes had completely annihilated him as well?

20

Jane hadn't bothered to write and tell him that she had arrived safely at Minshom Abbey or if she was pregnant. He only knew the former because his carriage had arrived back five days ago without incident. Minshom smiled thinly as one of his companions made a lewd joke about one of the dancers.

His planned evening at the theater with some of his male acquaintances had been passable. He'd even gone to the trouble of visiting the actresses in the green room afterward and pretended to seek a new mistress. But none of the women appealed to him, and for some reason, his companions seemed far too loud and vapid to amuse him either.

He could only hope that the rest of his night in the pleasure house would interest him. With a less than cordial smile at Christian Delornay, he bypassed the main salons and set off for the delights of the third floor. He hadn't had sex since Jane had left him, and he was determined to set that right. She couldn't be allowed to destroy his sex life; he needed the release and he refused to use Robert.

"Good evening, Lord Minshom."

Minshom stared at the three men who had gathered around him the moment he entered the room. He knew them all intimately, had catered to their perversions with a skill and expertise unrivaled by any other man.

"We've missed you, sir," Shaw mumbled, his eyes cast down as he knelt in front of Minshom.

"And why is that?"

"Because we couldn't find anyone else to punish us."

Minshom picked up a riding crop that lay abandoned on the chair beside him and tested it against his thigh. "No one at all?"

"No one as good as you, sir."

Minshom remembered how Shaw looked the last time he'd seen him, his mouth stuffed with Minshom's cock, his arse being attended to by Jane. His fingers tightened on the crop. God, he wanted to hurt someone, to make them feel the pain he carried inside him, to make them scream with it as he could not . . .

"My lord?"

Minshom put the crop back on the chair. "Not tonight, gentlemen."

"What?" Shaw looked devastated and tried to kiss Minshom's feet. "I'll do whatever you say, my lord, I'll do anything . . ."

Minshom turned on his heel and left the room, clattering down the stairs until he reached the ground floor as if the hounds of hell were after him. He forced himself to stop, heard only his shallow, panicked breathing echoing in the narrow space. What the hell was wrong with him? He'd wanted their pain, so why the devil had he walked away? He blinked hard and focused on the door in front of him. Perhaps he just needed more time to get over his wife's disruptive influence on his life. He'd stop thinking about her eventually. He'd done it once and he'd do it again.

He sank down onto the bottom step and cradled his head in

his hands. But last time he'd turned his rage and self-loathing outward and tried to dominate every man he met. If he could no longer bring himself to use others in this way, what was to become of him? He wanted to go home to Jane, to shove his cock deep inside her, to fuck her until he ran out of cum.

He raised his head and stared blindly at the closed door. What was she doing now? She was probably lying in her bed at Minshom Abbey, maybe crying herself to sleep over him. He swallowed hard, found himself smiling despite the pain. No, she wouldn't be crying. Jane was made of sterner stuff. She was probably wishing him in hell.

He wrenched open the back door and headed toward the stable yard to retrieve his horse. And perhaps she would have her wish. For some reason, he felt like he was in hell right now.

Jane sighed and stared out over the patchworked fields surrounding Minshom Abbey. It was very late but, used to town hours, she'd found herself unable to sleep. She focused on the full moon. Would Blaize be able to see it in London? Not that he would bother to look up—his sights were probably set far lower on some unfortunate woman or man he expected to slake his lusts.

She rested her hot cheek against the old diamond-paned glass and squinted at the now green-tinged moon. After her horrendous journey home, she'd taken to her bed for three days and allowed herself to weep. She'd also allowed herself to believe that she really did carry a child. The past week hadn't changed her opinion, but she was no longer weeping. She was determined to get on with her life and enjoy her friends again.

"Are you still awake, my lady?"

Jane turned to smile at her elderly maid, Becky, who had been with her for all the years of her marriage and had been a nurse to Blaize before he was sent away to school. "I am indeed."

Becky made a tutting sound. "You should be in bed, my chick, especially in your condition."

Jane cast one last look back at her writing desk, where several sheets of ruined paper littered the floor. "I was trying to write to his lordship."

"Whatever for?" Becky turned down the bed sheets and patted the pillows.

"To tell him that I got home safely and that I truly believe I am breeding."

Becky snorted. "That heathen should get himself on a horse and come back here to find out the answer to them questions. Don't you be making it easy for the young scoundrel, now."

Jane climbed into the massive bed, felt the feather quilts give and settle around her. "Perhaps you are right. It might be good for him to worry about me for a change."

Becky kissed her forehead. "Indeed. And if I catch sight of him before you do, after I've given him a clip around the ear, I'll tell him so myself."

Jane had to smile. At least she was among people who loved her. What did Blaize have? A group of friends who were afraid of him and a complicated relationship with Robert, who wanted to leave him. She was far better off where she was and so was her child. Her stomach rolled uneasily and she shut her eyes.

Was he missing her or had he managed to ignore everything they had done together and resume his old life? She knew he was stubborn enough to try, but with her departure and the looming rupture with Robert, would he be able to maintain his icy composure? She bit down hard on her lip. Goodness, she hoped not. She hoped he felt one tenth of the desolation she felt in her soul.

Two weeks later

"My lord . . ."

"What?" Lord Minshom stumbled over the threshold of

Madame's Helene's house and Robert held him steady. The hall was free of other guests; only a lone footman watched warily as Robert tried to prop his employer up against the nearest wall.

"Are you sure this is wise?"

Minshom shrugged. "I'm spending an evening at the pleasure house in the company of my peers. What could be wiser than that?" He lurched toward the staircase and grabbed the newel post at the bottom.

Robert sighed. "Sir, you are already drunk and we've only just arrived. What exactly are you intending to do with yourself?"

"Exactly what I want." Minshom scowled at Robert. "I don't remember asking for your opinion."

"You didn't, sir. I just decided to offer it anyway."

"Why? Because you are *concerned* for me, because you *love* me?" Minshom's smile was bitter, and yet Robert could see the pain in his eyes.

"All true, sir. Now are you sure that you don't want to go home?"

"Damn it, Robert. I'm not a child." Minshom staggered slightly and Robert had to grab his arm to stop him from falling back down the stairs. "I'm perfectly capable of making my own decisions."

"Indeed, my lord."

"Is everything all right, Mr. Brown?"

Robert looked up gratefully to see Madame Helene at the top of the stairs, her expression concerned. Her gaze fell on Lord Minshom and she frowned.

"My lord, are you unwell?"

"No, Madame, merely drunk." Minshom attempted a bow, which nearly knocked Robert over.

"Would you prefer us to leave, Madame?" Robert said. "I'm sure if I had some help I could get his lordship sobered up and back in his carriage."

Madame nodded. "Why don't you take Lord Minshom into the small salon at the end of the hallway? I'll send some coffee and brandy up to you."

Robert maneuvered Lord Minshom into the currently empty salon and guided him into a chair by the fireside.

"Where's the entertainment, Robert?"

Robert sighed. "I'm the entertainment, sir."

Minshom stared at him for a long moment. "You didn't find Captain Gray, did you?"

"Not yet, my lord."

"What a pair we are, eh, Robert?" Minshom's laughter was hollow. "Both deserted."

"I don't believe you were deserted, sir. By all accounts you threw her ladyship out."

"She still went though, didn't she?"

Robert glared at his master as anger overrode his normal caution. "What did you expect her to do when you treated her like that?"

A muscle twitched in Minshom's jaw. "I expected her to stay."

"God damn you, sir, we're not puppets created for your amusement!"

"She lied to me."

"Lady Minshom did?" Robert struggled to collect his thoughts. "Are you sure?"

"Oh, yes, I'm sure."

A footman appeared at the doorway carrying a tray of brandy and two coffeepots. Minshom scowled at him.

"What the devil are you doing here?"

"Compliments of Madame Helene, sir. She says that if you don't sober up, you will be escorted off the premises."

Robert winced as Lord Minshom's expression turned icy. "She said *what*?"

Robert cleared his throat. "Thank you for the coffee. I'll make sure Lord Minshom drinks it."

The footman took one look at Lord Minshom, dumped the tray by the door, and left as quickly as he could. Robert poured two cups of coffee and added a small dose of brandy to Lord Minshom's.

"Here you are, sir."

Minshom glared at the cup as if he had been offered poison. "I don't want that pig swill."

"It's got brandy in it, sir." Robert said. "At least give it a try."

Grumbling, Lord Minshom held out his hand and took the cup. He sniffed at the rising steam and then drank the whole thing. Robert immediately filled up the cup and gave it back to him.

"Don't you think you'd be better off at home, sir?"

Lord Minshom regarded him over the rim of his coffee cup. "Why are you so eager to leave?" He shifted restlessly in his chair. "There is nothing at home, nothing I want anyway."

Robert regarded his employer. "Might that be because you sent Lady Minshom packing?"

"Will you stop going on about that, Robert? Who made you my conscience?"

"I believe you did, sir." Robert picked up the coffee pot. "Will you stay here until I get more coffee?"

"As I'm obviously incapable of climbing the stairs without help, I expect I'll still be here."

Robert nodded and ran out of the room. He used the back stairs to reach the basement kitchen and refilled the coffeepot. His employer didn't realize just how oddly he was acting and seemed totally unable to link his current state to the departure of his wife three weeks previously. In truth, Robert had never seen Lord Minshom like this and was deeply worried.

He got the coffee and returned to Lord Minshom, pausing at

the doorway when he saw that his master was not alone. It took all his composure to set the silver pot down on the table rather than drop it to the floor. Captain Gray stood before Lord Minshom, his hands fisted at his sides, his blond hair disheveled and coming loose from its ribbon.

"My lord, Captain Gray?"

Both men turned to look at him. Robert advanced into the room and tried hard to keep his gaze away from Captain Gray's ravaged face. He found it impossible to keep quiet. Despite Lord Minshom's presence, Robert couldn't help his outburst. "Where the hell have you been?"

"I went down to Dover and tried to persuade my superiors to allow me to sail to India."

"So why aren't you on your way?"

David's smile was rueful. "Because I realized I couldn't go, and that I was behaving like a coward." He nodded at Lord Minshom. "I knew I had to come back and face Minshom."

Lord Minshom smiled. "Ah, Robert. You will enjoy this. David wants me to take him back."

A roaring sensation filled Robert's head. "I beg your pardon, sir?"

"Your Captain Gray has decided that he is so unworthy that the only suitable place for him is under me, being fucked, being abused, being . . . used."

Robert took a deep breath. "I won't let that happen, sir."

"And how do you think you are going to stop him?"

Robert turned to stare at David. "Why are you doing this?"

David shrugged. "Because I've realized that if I can't have you, I'd rather not have anything. And, as you refuse to leave Lord Minshom, that means I have to be where you are too."

"No. I won't allow it." Robert swung back to Lord Minshom. "He isn't thinking clearly, sir. He had some ridiculous notion that he is no longer worthy of respect."

"And why is that?"

David looked at Minshom. "Because I now understand why my 'father' chose me to compete in The Little Gentleman's Club, rather than one of my brothers." He swallowed hard. "He never loved me because I'm not his real son. I was fathered by one of the grooms."

Minshom frowned. "And that makes a difference because . . . ?"

"Because Captain Gray is a fool," Robert said angrily. "Doesn't he understand that he had created his own worth and that his birth is irrelevant?"

Something flickered in David's blue eyes as Robert confronted him, a sense of shame, of self-doubt that Robert had never seen before. "Don't let your father destroy who you are, David, and don't come groveling back to Lord Minshom for my sake."

"I haven't said I'd take him back yet."

Robert and David both turned to stare at Lord Minshom, who sat sprawled in his chair, his coffee cup still cradled in his hand. He nodded at David.

"If I ordered you to kneel at my feet now and suck my cock, would you do it?"

David shrugged. "If it meant I got to stay with Robert, then yes."

Robert stepped between the two men. "No." He faced Lord Minshom. "If you make him do that, I'll leave."

Minshom raised an eyebrow. "You'll leave *me*?"

"Aye."

"But you promised you'd never leave me."

Robert held Minshom's pale blue stare. "So did Lady Minshom."

"And I got rid of her, didn't I?" Minshom sat up and put his coffee cup on the table beside him. "You seem to be suggesting that I am somehow at fault."

Robert set his jaw. "I'm not suggesting anything, sir. I wouldn't dare. I'm just saying that I will leave your employ if you take Captain Gray back as a lover."

David touched his arm. "Robert . . ."

Robert shrugged his touch away, kept his attention all on his employer, his lover, his master. "I've spent my whole life trying to save you from yourself, and I find I'm no longer willing to do so."

"Really."

"Lady Minshom tried too, but you wouldn't let her, would you?"

Pain flashed across Minshom's face and was quickly concealed. "Don't presume to talk about my relationship with my wife, Robert."

"I respect Lady Minshom far too much to ever think of doing that, sir." Robert bowed. "I'm respectfully submitting my notice. Good-bye, my lord."

He made it through the door, blundered down the back staircase and into the kitchen before he could no longer see for the tears streaming down his face. He turned to face the brick wall under the stairwell leading down to the cellar, braced his face against his arm and let himself cry. He cried for his lost youth, for his friends, for his lovers . . .

Upstairs, Minshom regarded David Gray who was staring after Robert.

"I don't want you, David."

"What?"

"I don't want you back in my life." He nodded at the door. "Perhaps rather than standing here gaping at me, you should use your energies to persuade Robert to enter your employ. Seeing as he is now a free man."

"I don't understand."

"It's quite simple. Robert and I are done with each other, you are also done with me, so why not be happy? Why not take this chance and make it happen?"

David Gray frowned. "I understand that. What I don't understand is why you are doing this. You deliberately goaded him into leaving you. You forced him to make a choice."

Minshom opened his eyes wide. "Did I? In my opinion, I merely dismissed an insubordinate servant who dared to comment on my relationship with my wife."

"I'll never understand you, Minshom." David sighed. "But I'm not a fool. If Robert is prepared to listen to me, I'll do my best to persuade him to stay with me."

"Then do it." Minshom pretended to yawn. "This whole business is quite fatiguing." He tensed as David came forward and dropped down onto his knees. "Are you about to offer me a parting gift?"

David grabbed his hand and kissed his knuckles. "No, I'll save that for Robert. I just wanted to say thank you, and I know you always love me on my knees."

Minshom cupped David's chin and ran his thumb along his jaw. "Good-bye, David. Take care of Robert for me."

"I will." David rose to his feet and bowed. "I'm sure I'll see you again soon."

Minshom waved a languid hand. "I hope not. You'll probably be too busy fucking Robert to do anything for a long while."

David's smile flashed out. "If he lets me."

"He loves you. Now go."

David disappeared down the stairs, and Minshom sat back and contemplated both the empty space in front of him and the echoing space in his heart. He'd let Robert go, given him a chance to be happy. Could he survive the loss? It was almost as painful as giving up Jane.

He frowned into the stillness.

Exactly when had he realized that unpleasant truth? That Jane's departure had changed his life? Perhaps letting Robert go was a way to show Jane how much he now understood about love. Would she be proud of him, and why did it matter anyway?

"My lord, are you feeling any better?"

He looked up to find Madame Helene at the door, her expression somewhere between concern and determination. He'd always admired that about her, her ability to balance compassion with business.

"I'm feeling quite well, Madame, although it appears I've just lost my valet."

She tilted her blonde head to one side, came farther into the room and closed the door behind her. "Robert Brown has left your employ?"

"Indeed. I believe he will shortly take up employment with Captain David Gray."

Without asking for permission, she settled into the chair opposite his, her pale green silk skirts shimmering in the candlelight.

"And you allowed that?"

He shrugged. "Of course."

"There is no 'of course' about it, my lord. You are not known for being kind."

He glared at her. "And you are not known for your tact."

"That is true." She smiled. "But I still think you did a good thing."

He simply stared at her, realized he couldn't say anything that wouldn't sound remotely unconcerned, and he desperately needed to regain his detachment, to retreat behind the barriers that had protected him since he was a child. But those barriers were too thin tonight, ripped to shreds by Jane's defection and his decision to let Robert go.

Madame Helene stirred. "Did you bring your wife with you tonight?"

Ah, there was to be no respite then. "No, Madame. She has returned to Minshom Abbey."

"Was she unwell or did town life simply not agree with her?"

He smiled, realized he was too exhausted to contemplate disguising the truth, knew instinctively that Madame Helene would never betray him anyway. "You probably imagine she grew disgusted with the way I lived, don't you?"

"Not at all. From all reports, she seemed more than happy to participate in your sexual excesses, my lord. Why would I think that?"

"She left because I sent her away. We had a bargain that once she got what she wanted, she would leave."

"And what did she want?"

"Another baby." He winced at his own words.

"*Another baby*? You have children?"

Her complete disbelief made him blurt out the truth. "We had a son seven years ago who died."

Madame considered him, her blue eyes full of compassion. "That is very sad. I'm glad you will be blessed with another child."

He glared at her. "Glad? The thought terrifies me. Why do you think I've abandoned my wife in the countryside for seven years?"

"Because you were too afraid to create another child? It doesn't sound like you."

Minshom gritted his teeth. "I was the last person to see my son alive. He was discovered dead in my arms. My wife believed I smothered him in his sleep."

God, had he ever told anyone that before? And why the hell was he doing it now? It was a struggle to meet Madame's gaze. She reached out her hand and touched his knee.

"I'm sure she doesn't believe that anymore. She obviously loves you. Otherwise why would she have come all the way to London to find you and agree to make another child with you? Losing a baby must have been equally, if not more devastating, to her."

Minshom stared at the delicate hand resting on his knee as he contemplated her words. Was it really that simple? Was it all really about love and being brave enough to face your fears? He sighed.

"Madame, I wish it were that straightforward . . ."

"Ha! It is that straightforward." Madame snapped her fingers. "Why do men complicate things so badly?"

"I believe it is women who do that," he said dryly. "My wife is a master at it." He stumbled to his feet. "I think I will go home."

"Without visiting the third floor? I know some of our members are missing you up there."

"But I am not missing them." How extraordinary that he had just realized that. "For once I prefer my own bed."

Madame Helene smiled at him and he held out his hand to help her up. She stood on tiptoe and kissed his cheek.

"I will pray for you, my lord, and for your family."

"Thank you, I think." He turned toward the door. "Good night, Madame."

"Good night, my lord, and sleep well."

He smiled at her. "I'll try." Perhaps she expected him to thank her for listening to him or burst into noisy tears, but he hadn't quite sunk to those depths, yet.

There was no sign of Robert in the entrance hall so Minshom assumed all had gone well between him and David. He stepped into his carriage and closed his eyes, curiously at peace. For once in his life, he'd tried to do the right thing. He hoped Jane would be proud of him.

*　*　*

David ran down the back stairs of the pleasure house as if his life depended on it. He flung open the door to the deserted kitchen and paused, searching for signs of life. Under the stairwell he spotted a familiar figure pressed up against the wall.

"Robert?"

David pressed himself against the other man's back, kissed Robert's neck, his ear, any part of him he could get at. "Please don't go. Please stay with me. I don't want Minshom; I want you, only you."

Slowly Robert turned around and David saw the tear stains on his cheeks and used his mouth and tongue to lick them away. "Don't cry. God, please don't cry."

He put his palm against the side of Robert's face. "Stay with me."

"As your lover?"

"As whatever you want."

A small smile quivered on Robert's lips. "I'd probably better be your valet. It will cause less gossip."

"If that is what you want, if being in service does not make you feel obligated."

Robert touched David's lower lip with his tongue. "Obligated to what? Love you? That is an obligation I will gladly undertake for the rest of my life."

A sigh shuddered through David as Robert kissed him and he kissed Robert back. "Don't leave me."

"I won't." Robert whispered, one hand sliding down over David's back to cup his buttock and press him firmly against his hard erection. "Especially if you'll pay me more than that bastard Minshom did."

David started to laugh, which soon turned to a groan as Robert slid a hand between them and rubbed both of their cocks. "I want you, Robert. I want to fuck you right here."

"You think I'll stop you?"

Robert turned to face the wall and unbuttoned his breeches.

David undid his too, his fingers frantic and fumbling as Robert spread his feet wide and arched his back, offering himself. In too much of a hurry to go and look for oil, David spread his own pre-cum over the crown of his cock and drove deep. Robert didn't protest, he just welcomed him home with a sigh. David reached around to capture Robert's cock in his fist and worked him hard, knew he wouldn't last long, wanted Robert to come with him.

"God, David . . ." Robert groaned and tried to kiss David as he pumped into him harder and harder. "Make me come . . ."

David thrust forward one last time and felt his cum explode deep inside Robert's arse just as Robert came all over his hand. God, it was perfection, it was everything, it was enough to live his life on. He lowered his head until it rested in the curve of Robert's shoulder and sighed. He knew their life together wouldn't be easy, but he was going to try his hardest to make sure that Robert never regretted his choice for the rest of his days.

21

Minshom took great care folding his cravat and settling a diamond pin among the snowy folds to secure the whole. His waistcoat was black with silver embroidery, his coat and pantaloons black as well. It was odd getting ready to go out without Robert at his side. He still wasn't used to the hastily procured new valet Broadman had found to serve him.

"You look very nice, my lord."

"Thank you . . . um . . ." Minshom looked askance at the dark-haired man reflected in the mirror. "What is your name, again?"

"It is Smedley, sir."

"Smedley, I'm not sure when I'll return, so don't wait up for me."

"Yes, my lord." Smedley bowed and offered Minshom his cloak and hat. He then retreated discreetly into the dressing room and began tidying the discarded clothes. Minshom walked down the stairs, aware of the quietness settling around him. There was no Jane waiting for him in the hall, no Robert to remind him of his manners, just Broadman's lugubrious face and an empty carriage to climb into. For some reason, Minshom had no inclination to take up his old ways and invite his cronies to his house. He deserved the silence, he deserved to be alone.

When the carriage stopped, he stared out of the window at the grand mansion he'd visited four weeks previously with Jane at his side. This time he hadn't received an invitation, but he intended to join the party nonetheless.

No one prevented his entry into the house, and he ascended the grand staircase and headed for the ballroom. The receiving line was busy and he had to wait for quite a while before he was in front of his prey. To his credit, Lord Anthony Sokorvsky's smile didn't falter as he spotted Minshom.

"I don't recall inviting you, Lord Minshom."

"You didn't."

"Then might I ask why you are here?"

Minshom raised an eyebrow. "To wish you happy?"

"Ah, you heard about my engagement to Lady Justin, then."

"How could I not? It is the talk of the *ton*. And, if you remember, I promised that I would relinquish any claim I had on you if you ever got married."

Anthony Sokorvsky raised his eyebrows. "You have no claim on me anyway."

"Perhaps, but at least my sense of honor is satisfied."

"Your sense of honor . . ." Anthony regarded Minshom for a long moment and then held out his hand. "I heard what you did for Captain Gray."

Reluctantly, Minshom shook his hand. "Heard what? I did nothing."

Anthony stepped out of the receiving line, drawing Minshom with him. "You have an unfortunate habit of refusing to take responsibility for your kinder actions. Who would've imagined it?"

"I repeat, I did nothing except dismiss an impudent servant. If Captain Gray chose to employ him, surely that is at his own peril?"

Anthony Sokorvsky's smile was dazzling. "Would you like to offer your congratulations to Lady Justin? She is just over by the window."

"I . . ." Minshom found himself outmaneuvered and being led like a lamb toward the newly engaged Marguerite Lockwood, Lord Anthony at his side.

"Lord Minshom." Marguerite's greeting was not quite as welcoming as her fiancé's. She looked very beautiful in a pale blue silk dress with sapphires around her throat and in her dark hair. She glanced up at Anthony, a wary question in her fine eyes. In looks and stature, she resembled a darker version of her mother, Helene Delornay. In Minshom's experience, she had a lot of her mother's wit and intelligence as well.

Minshom bowed. "Lord Anthony insisted I come and offer my congratulations on your engagement."

"Thank you."

Anthony took her hand and kissed it. "You don't object if Lord Minshom joins the party, do you, my love?"

"Of course not. He is . . . welcome."

Minshom bowed low. "I will not stay long, and I promise not to make a scene."

Marguerite blushed and raised her chin at him. "I'm sure you won't. In truth, I suspect that in some strange way, you are partly responsible for Anthony and I falling in love, so perhaps it is fitting that you are here tonight to share our engagement ball."

"I doubt Lord Anthony would agree with you about that, my lady, but thank you all the same."

"Oh no, I agree," Anthony said quietly. "In truth you have given up quite a few things recently, haven't you? Is that because you have reconciled with your wife?"

Minshom's faint smile faded. "Lady Minshom is no longer in town."

"I'm sorry to hear that. I liked her." Anthony paused. "What did you do?"

"Why do you assume I did anything?"

"Because, as I said, you have a tendency to push anyone who gets too close to you away."

Minshom looked around to see if anyone else was listening to this extraordinarily intimate conversation between him and a man who should've hated him. "Sokorvsky, we are in a public place, and I hardly think my personal life is any of your damned business."

Anthony bowed. "You are right, it isn't and I apologize. Because I have found happiness, perhaps I am trying to arrange it for everyone else."

"Indeed." Minshom inclined his head a glacial inch. "Then perhaps I should leave you to wander off and interfere in the marital affairs of some of your other guests."

Lord Anthony grinned, took Marguerite's arm and moved away. Minshom looked around the crowded ballroom and spotted the card room beyond. He needed a drink, and if he had to stay at this damned ball, merely for politeness' sake and to reassure the *ton* that he and Anthony were at peace, he'd be damned if he'd do it without alcohol.

He made his way through the throng, nodded at his acquaintances, and found a footman to bring him a large glass of brandy to replace the champagne and wine being served. Anthony and Marguerite were dancing now, the joy in their faces almost too much to bear. Minshom pictured Jane's indignant expression when he'd made her dance with him and suddenly missed her so much it hurt to breathe.

"Lord Minshom?"

He looked up to see Thomas Wesley at his elbow and sighed. It seemed as if there would be no respite for him tonight and perhaps that was as it should be. If he was going to make a damned fool of himself, he might as well get it over with once and for all.

"Good evening, Thomas."

"May I speak with you in private?"

"Of course." Minshom kept hold of his brandy glass and led Thomas toward the card room, where he located one of the footmen. "Can you show me to a quieter room?"

"Of course, sir. The marquis's secretary has an office just beyond the card room."

Minshom thanked him and opened the door to a small stuffy book-lined office. Thomas knelt down to light the fire in the grate and then lit two candles to illuminate the cramped space. As Minshom sat on the edge of the desk and watched Thomas move around the room, he couldn't help but admire his grace and efficiency.

"Now what can I do for you, Thomas?"

Thomas sighed, took the chair from behind the desk and brought it over to the fire before sitting on it. "I'm wondering if I owe you an apology."

"For what?"

"For making love to you." Thomas shrugged. "For taking advantage of you when you were already sexually engaged with your wife."

"You didn't take advantage of me."

"I was so eager to fuck you that I let your wife answer for you; I didn't give you a chance to say no."

Minshom met his anguished gaze. "Sometimes my wife knows me better than I know myself. She was right to tell you to fuck me. She knew I was incapable of saying those words myself, even if I wanted to."

"I don't understand."

"You should. My father always swore that I liked being fucked by other men." Minshom tried to smile. "He wasn't quite correct about that—most men I despised, but I did like being fucked by you."

"Even back then?"

"Indeed. I hero-worshipped you, don't you remember? You could do no wrong in my eyes. But even after the shock of what happened, I couldn't tell you that, couldn't admit my father might've been right about me. So I chose to deny that side of me, to fight my inclinations and dominate everyone instead."

"And the other night at the pleasure house, you enjoyed that?"

"Yes."

"But you ran away."

"Yes."

"Because you enjoyed it."

Minshom sighed. "*Yes*, because realizing my father understood my desires better than I understood them myself made me think about what I've done to him."

God, why was he talking so much? It was as if Jane's departure had left so many holes in him that he could no longer stop all his secrets seeping out. And for Christ's sake, he was tired of it, tired of all the lying and the anger and the hate. Thomas was leaving soon, his confidences would be kept and the potential for exposure far away.

"What did you do to him?" Thomas frowned. "Surely he is the one who is at fault here, forcing us all to participate in The Little Gentleman's Club, forcing you."

"Did you know that my father had his first stroke when I refused to allow him to beat Robert half to death? I defied him, and while he was whipping me, he had a massive seizure. It kept him in bed for weeks. I hoped that the bastard would die, that he would never regain his strength or faculties and would never be able to hurt me or any of us again."

Minshom grimaced. "But he got better. He was never quite

the same after that, but he was perfectly capable of administering the estates and his little fighting club."

"He was a very difficult man, Blaize. I can understand why you must have hated him."

"I hated him because he lived and I had to watch him steal every last penny from the estate for his gambling, his horses, his women..." Minshom struggled to breathe. "And then one day, he caught me and Robert in bed together. Dammit, I wanted him to catch us; I wanted him to see us fucking, to know what kind of a man he'd created. He tried to shoot Robert. I stopped him."

Thomas sat forward. "You didn't kill him though, Blaize?"

"No, I simply fought him off, watched as he collapsed to the ground in convulsions, and left him there without calling for help. By the time he was discovered, there was very little anyone could do for him."

Abruptly Thomas got up, came across to Minshom and wrapped his arms around him. "He got what he deserved. I probably would've shot him in cold blood."

Minshom shrugged off Thomas's embrace. "But then you've always been a braver man than me."

"Blaize," Thomas cupped his chin and made him look into his eyes. "Your father was a monster."

"Was?" Minshom swallowed hard. "Don't you mean *is*?"

Thomas looked appalled. "Dear God, he's still alive, isn't he?"

"Barely. The last stroke totally incapacitated him, and he has been bedridden for years." Minshom sighed. "That's one of the reasons why my wife wants me to go back to Minshom Abbey. She's convinced he is finally dying and she wishes me to make my peace with him."

Thomas gripped him by the shoulders. "You must do it because you have to see him as he is; you have to forgive him for what he's done to you and move on." He winced. "I know it sounds ridiculous, but I returned too late to confront my father. I was never able to tell him how much I hated him for putting me in The Little Gentleman's Club. I left home the moment I was able to and never went back. God, I wish I'd had five minutes alone with him . . ."

Minshom stared at Thomas's grief-stricken face. Could he do it? Could he go home and make his peace not only with his father, but with Jane?

"I don't want to go home." Minshom tried to laugh. "God, I sound like a sniveling child, don't I? My father has been right about me all along. I'm a sexual deviant, a bad husband and a coward. Why the hell would I want to go home and admit that?"

"From what I saw of your wife, she certainly didn't consider you a bad husband, and as to your sexuality, personally, I have no problem with it at all." Thomas smiled. "And I'm sure you are not a coward. You'll go back. I know you will."

"How can you be so sure?"

Thomas leaned forward and kissed Blaize on the lips. "Because I know you."

"You used to know me, but I've changed, Thomas. I've done nothing to be proud of in the last ten years, ask Jane."

Thomas smiled, his kind brown eyes crinkling at the corners. "I have faith in you."

"But you're returning to India."

Thomas let out his breath, "Actually I'm not. There's too much work to do here on the estate for me to walk away from it now, and I need to settle my mother and sisters into the dower house." He hesitated. "I'll be here if you want me, if you need me."

Minshom studied Thomas's face and wanted to laugh. So much for easing his conscience and walking away. The thought of having Thomas, fucking him, being fucked in return stirred insidiously in his brain. Jane wouldn't mind either, he was quite sure of that.

"I don't know what I have to offer you, Thomas, but I'm glad you're not leaving." Minshom stood up. "I have to go home, don't I?"

"I suspect you do."

Minshom studied the toe of his shoe. "Jane's breeding."

"Congratulations."

"You don't mind?"

"Why should I mind?" Thomas shrugged. "She's your wife. And she gave us the opportunity to be together. I'll always be grateful to her for that."

"I didn't intend for that to happen, for you to fuck me. I set out to prove to you both that I was capable of bending you to my will."

"Well you certainly proved something."

Minshom halted by the door. "I don't get fucked, Thomas. The only person I've allowed to fuck me since I was seventeen is Robert."

"Robert Brown? Yet you let him leave you for Captain Gray."

Minshom winced. "Does everyone in town know about that?"

Thomas leaned back against the desk, his expression shrewd. "Not everyone. If Robert was so important to you, why did you let him go?"

"Because I've realized you can't force someone to stay with you." Minshom took an unsteady breath. "I think that's what Jane realized about me, why she left me."

"Even if you love them?"

"Love comes in many different shades, doesn't it? Jane said she loved me, and I threw it back in her face. And I used Robert. That's not love."

"Yet he loved you anyway."

Minshom gave Thomas an irritated look. "Have you been talking to Captain Gray as well?"

"I have, and he still can't believe his good fortune." Thomas paused. "I told him that he had nothing to worry about, that you were a man of your word and that I would make sure you never needed Robert again."

Minshom's faint smile died along with his hopes. God, this was hard—to share the depths of his depravity, to expose himself to his lover in more ways than one. How the hell had Jane managed it? Where had she found the courage to come back to him and open herself up to be hurt again? And he had hurt her badly, he knew that.

"You don't know what I made Robert do."

Thomas crossed his arms over his chest. "What do you mean?"

"As I said, I've changed from when you knew me." Minshom studied the door panel, unable to contemplate actually looking at Thomas. "Sometimes, when I felt as if I was no longer in control of a sexual situation, I would force Robert to hurt me, to fight me and then fuck me."

Thomas shrugged. "I'd do that for you."

Minshom had to look at him then. "Hurt me?"

"I don't think that's what you really need. Once you make your peace with your father, I suspect the desire to punish yourself will fade."

Minshom gripped the door handle and wrenched open the door. "You seem to think you have all the answers, don't you?"

Thomas smiled. "No, but I think you do."

"Good night, Major."

"Good night, my lord. I look forward to seeing you on your return."

"My return from where?"

"From Minshom Abbey, of course."

Minshom glared at him. "Damn you, Thomas."

The corner of Thomas's mouth kicked up in a smile. "Damn you, Lord Minshom, and you're welcome."

22

Minshom paused his horse on a slight rise before he came down into the valley that contained Minshom Abbey. It all looked remarkably the same. The passage of the last ten years was a tiny stitch in the rich tapestry of the land and the fate of the four-hundred-year-old house and grounds. Gray stone walls marked the boundaries of the ancient fields. Sheep grazed on the green grass, and in the distance he could plainly hear the lowing of the dairy herd and the raucous cry of the resident cockerel from the home farm.

Home.

He allowed his horse to amble slowly through the small village, nodded amiably at anyone who saw him, noting the surprise on their faces as they recognized him. In a place as tiny as this, news carried as fast as the wind. He reckoned by the time he reached the big house, Jane would know he was coming.

He didn't want to see her yet. He had more pressing business to attend to, so he took the back way around the side of the old cloisters, which led directly to the stable yard. His keen eye noted the new roof, the improved drainage, the rebuilt home farm on the horizon. Since he'd taken control of the family finances, he'd poured money back into the estate, and it was gratifying to see it bear fruit, to see his childhood home glowing like a well-polished jewel.

"Master Blaize?"

"Mr. Taylor. How are you?"

Minshom dismounted and turned to greet the elderly coachman who had first taught him to ride as a child. Taylor's hair was pure white now, his blue eyes dimmed, but the pleasure on his face couldn't be disguised. For the first time, Minshom considered the betrayal that his staying away from the abbey had been to all his tenants. Jane wasn't the only person he'd left behind.

"I'm fine, young master, apart from a gouty leg."

"Yet you still look as fit as a fiddle."

Taylor grinned to display several rotting teeth. "Get along with you. You always had a silver tongue and I see nothing has changed."

Minshom found himself smiling back at the old man. He had nothing to hide here. He was accepted just because he'd been born in the house and always had been part of the fabric of Taylor's life. Something inside him relaxed.

"Have you come to stay for a while this time, sir?"

"I hope so." Minshom loosened his horse's girth and buckled up his stirrups. "It depends."

"Well I can tell you that her ladyship will be pleased to see you." Taylor nudged Minshom in the ribs. "I believe she has some news for you."

"Really." Minshom handed the reins over to Taylor, who passed them on to a younger man who took the horse away. "I wonder what that can be?"

Taylor's face creased into a smile and then he winked elaborately. "I'm not telling, sir. It wouldn't be my place, but it's exciting, isn't it?"

Minshom took off his gloves and walked toward the side entrance of the house. "I'm sure it is." He paused at the door. "Is my father still in the earl's suite?"

"Aye, sir." Taylor's face sobered. "He's not looking so well these days. He'll be right glad to see you though."

Minshom doubted that, but he kept smiling and found his way through the maze of small crooked corridors and unexpected rooms into the more modern part of the house where the state apartments, once readied for Queen Elizabeth, were situated.

As he walked, stone flagstones changed to polished wood floors and Turkish rugs, ceilings lost their open beams and became molded plaster and gilded with gold. He stopped in the largest of the anterooms and took a deep steadying breath. Ahead of him was a set of double doors that led into the earl and countess of Swanford chambers. His parents' chambers, his father's living tomb.

He put down his hat, gloves and riding whip on one of the small gold tables and patted down his dusty clothing. He knew he was prevaricating, but it seemed almost impossible to move forward, to knock on the door and ask whoever had the dubious pleasure of looking after his father these days to let him in. It was one of those rare moments when he wished he truly believed in God and could pray for help. Instead, he pictured Jane's face and raised his hand to the door panel.

No one answered, so he opened the door and went inside. It was dark as a tomb and he immediately collided with a chair. After setting it to rights, the first thing that hit him was the stench of uncirculated air, of human waste, of old flesh. He instinctively recoiled as he tried to remember the layout of the rooms in front of him.

To his left, the door into the Earl's suite was open, and he could just make out the lines of the ornate four-poster bed with its gold and red silk hangings. He made his way forward, pausing in the doorway when he heard strenuous breathing coming from the bed.

Minshom frowned into the gloom. Where were the attendants he paid for? He couldn't believe that Jane would abandon the old man either. He walked carefully across to the windows and opened one of the sets of curtains a crack. A narrow stream of light patterned the faded carpet and illuminated the figure on the bed.

Holding his breath, Minshom forced himself to walk forward and peer at his father's face. Pale blue eyes that matched his own opened and he stared deep into them.

"Papa?" The boyhood name slipped past his lips before he realized it. "Do you recognize me?"

There was no response. He forced himself to hold his father's gaze, watched as recognition dawned and his father's mouth contorted with the effort to form a coherent sound.

"Son . . ."

"Yes. It's me. How are you?" God, what an inane thing to say to a man who was obviously bedridden and dying.

Blaize looked around for a chair. As his eyes grew accustomed to the lack of light he noticed other things about his father and the bedchamber. The bedclothes were spotless, the room clean and free of clutter. The taint of sickness overwhelming Minshom's senses came from his father, not his surroundings.

He'd always thought of his father as a big man, but the body beneath the covers barely raised them at all. He looked as if he had wasted away to almost nothing, his breathing so shallow Minshom could hardly hear it above the loud beating of his own heart. Gently, Minshom took hold of the gnarled hand on the counterpane. After the second stroke, the right side of his father's body had stiffened and petrified as if paralyzed by the Gods. He'd never regained full use of it.

Minshom cleared his throat and leaned closer to his father's ear. "I'm sorry I've been away for so long."

A muscle twitched in the earl's half-frozen face, but he didn't attempt to speak again. Minshom squeezed his hand. "I know we've had our differences in the past, but . . ." But what? What the devil was he supposed to say now? I love you, I'm sorry? But he didn't feel like saying those things; in truth, like a child, he desperately needed to hear them said to him.

With a sigh, he sat back and contemplated his father's face. But did he need to hear anything? He was an adult now, he had his whole life ahead of him to ruin or enjoy at will. His father had nothing, not even kind memories of his son to see him through to the end.

"My lord?"

A voice came from the doorway behind him and Minshom blinked. He turned around to see another familiar face from his past and forced a smile.

"Mistress Epsom, are you responsible for looking after my father?"

"I'm one of those responsible, my lord. He is cared for around the clock. I just went to get some fresh water for his wash."

She curtsied then set the jug and bowl she was carrying down on the sideboard and went to check on the earl. She laid her palm on the side of his face and frowned. "He is very warm, did you notice that?"

"Not really, but then I haven't seen him in so long, I wouldn't know."

"That's true, sir."

There was no reproach in the woman's voice and somehow that made Minshom feel even worse. He watched as Mistress Epsom dunked a cloth in the bowl, poured some water over it and wrung it out. She brought it back to the bed and began to gently wash the earl's face.

"Do you think he can recognize me?"

"It's possible, sir. Sometimes he seems to understand what is going on around him, but most of the time he just sleeps."

"He looks rather thin."

"That's because he finds it almost impossible to chew and swallow, sir. We mainly feed him gruel and soup, but it can be difficult to get anything down him."

Minshom sighed as she finished bathing the earl's face and returned the cloth to the wash basin. He leaned forward to stare into his father's eyes, realized he was being observed.

"I'm glad to be home, Father. I'll keep you safe."

It was little enough and still not easy to say. The idea of having to protect his own father seemed ridiculous, but what else could he do for this frail old man, this deflated monster from his childhood, but give him the dignity of dying comfortably in his own bed, cared for by his family?

The earl tried to speak, the sound trapped in his throat, his mouth working as he fought his paralysis. "Son . . ."

Minshom nodded, his own words almost as painful to utter as the earl's. "Yes, I'm here and I'll be staying for as long as you need me. Now rest and I'll come back and see you later."

"If you like, sir, I'll get one of the footman to call you when he's sitting up and is a bit more himself." Mistress Epsom frowned. "If that happens today; sometimes it doesn't."

"That would be much appreciated." Minshom stood up and studied Mistress Epsom's deft hands as she knitted some kind of sock or stocking. "Are you no longer presiding over the kitchens, then?"

"No, sir, my daughter Amy is in charge now." She looked up at him over her spectacles. "It became a bit much for me in my later years."

"I'll miss your delicate hand with an apple tart."

She smiled up at him. "My daughter's is even better, believe me, sir. Now why don't you run along and find Lady Minshom? I'm sure she'll be delighted to see you."

After one last look back at the now snoring figure on the bed, Minshom left the room, marveling at how Mistress Epsom made him feel simultaneously so at home and yet aged about ten. If he dared to be sarcastic or rude to her, he suspected, heir to an earldom or not, she'd still give him a clip around the ear.

His steps slowed as he reached the main hallway. He didn't share her certainty that Jane would be pleased to see him at all, but he was here now, so he might as well try his luck. He beckoned to the lone footman loitering in the hall.

"Where is her ladyship?"

"I beg you pardon, sir?"

Minshom sighed. Not only was the young man not familiar to him at all, but he obviously had no idea who Minshom was either.

"Where can I find Lady Minshom?"

"She's in the little sitting room, sir, but . . ."

Minshom made a dismissive gesture. "It's all right; I know where that is, I'll find her myself."

"Don't you want me to announce you, sir?"

Minshom glared at the blushing youth. "I hardly think I need announcing in my own house."

"Sir?"

Without bothering to explain, Minshom set off toward the back of the house, past the formal rooms and into the more homely part of the house where the family really lived. He didn't bother to knock on the sitting room door, just walked right in and found his wife sitting on the couch holding hands with another man.

"Good afternoon, my lady." Minshom looked down his nose at the other man until he let go of Jane's hands and rose to his feet. "Have we met before, sir? And regardless of that fact, may I suggest you stop mauling my wife?"

"He is scarcely mauling me, my lord."

Minshom barely spared a scorching glare for Jane, who

looked remarkably composed for a woman caught behaving scandalously with another man.

"Lord Minshom?" Minshom reckoned they were about the same age, although the other man was blond and bigger framed than him. "It is an honor to meet you, my lord. I'm Sir Derek Barrows; I recently bought the old Nash property adjoining your estates."

"How pleasant for you."

Sir Derek blanched at the chill in Minshom's voice and looked uncertainly at Jane. "Your wife has been most kind in welcoming me to the neighborhood."

"I'm sure she has." Minshom bowed. "But as of now perhaps you might consider you have *overstayed* your welcome and be on your way."

"Of course, my lord." Sir Derek smiled at Jane. "Thank you for being such an excellent listener, and I hope to see you again shortly." He glanced back at Minshom before returning his full attention to Jane. "And if you ever need my assistance, don't hesitate to call."

Minshom gritted his teeth. The man was obviously more courageous than he looked. As if Jane needed protecting from him. His fingers curled into fists. Mind you, sometimes the thought of strangling her was not far away . . .

"Good afternoon, Sir Derek." Minshom held open the door with a flourish.

"Good afternoon to you both." Sir Derek took his time kissing Jane's hands and then sauntered past Minshom with a big smile on his face. "A pleasure to meet you, my lord."

"Indeed." Minshom didn't smile back and closed the door behind the insolent pup. He leaned up against it and looked at Jane.

"Good afternoon, *wife*."

She tilted her head back to observe him and he drank in the

sight of her disapproval, the jutting angle of her chin, the fire and fear in her hazel eyes.

"And why exactly are you here? Did you get lost crawling between the beds of your lovers?"

"Hardly that, Jane; I keep all my lovers in Town, not in the wilds of Cheshire." He took a seat opposite her and crossed one booted foot over the other. "I came back to see my father." He waited for her reaction, was gratified to see the confusion in her gaze. "You wanted me to see him, didn't you?"

"Of course I did. It was one of the, I mean, it was the *main* reason I came to see you in Town."

"The main reason."

"Yes." She busied herself with pouring more tea. "Have you eaten? We keep country hours here, so dinner won't be much longer."

He studied her carefully. Was it too soon to discuss their marital predicament? She was probably expecting him to, but there were other matters to discuss as well—his father, Sir Derek. Perhaps he should make her wait, see how long her patience held out before she laid her own cards on the table.

"I'll wait for dinner. I need to change and wash the dust off." He smoothed his mud-streaked sleeve and stood up. "Perhaps you can find me someone to assist me?"

Jane frowned and rose to her feet. In her high-waisted gown there was no obvious sign that she was pregnant, and he was damned if he was going to ask. "You didn't bring Robert with you?"

"Robert is no longer in my employ." He walked to the door, held it open and waited for her to join him. "I believe he is now working for Captain Gray."

"You let him go?"

He inclined his head. "He resigned and I accepted his choice. There are always plenty of valets to be had in London." He frowned. "I have a new one. I believe his name is Smedley."

Jane was staring at him as if she'd never seen him before. God, he liked that, realized he felt more alive in her presence than he felt with anyone else. He turned on his heel and marched along the corridor, ducked his head to avoid a low beam and headed up the shallow worn main staircase toward the bedrooms.

Jane stared at the back of Blaize's head as he strode confidently up the stairs. How dare he appear in her house and act as if nothing had happened between them? That he hadn't trampled her heart and destroyed her dreams? Damn him. She wasn't going to make it easy for him this time, and she certainly wasn't going to fall into his arms and let him bed her. She panicked as he flung open a familiar door and went inside. His saddlebags sat on the hearth rug as if they had a right to be there.

"You aren't sleeping in here." Jane folded her arms across her chest and scowled at her husband. He picked up the dusty bags and deposited them on the bed, went across and pulled the bell rope.

"Do I have time for a bath before dinner?"

He stripped off his coat and threw it over a chair, started on his cravat.

"You are not sleeping in here."

"I am. It's my room."

"It's *my* room!"

"Exactly, and we are man and wife, are we not?"

Jane worried her bottom lip with her teeth. "I thought you came to see your father, not to spend time with me."

He stripped off his cravat and waistcoat, unbuttoned his breeches and drew his shirt over his head. He emerged with his black hair ruffled and his cheeks flushed with color. He tossed the shirt to her and she reflexively caught it, trying not to look at his muscled chest and fine shoulders.

"I did come to see my father. In fact, I've already seen him." He shrugged. "Not that he was able to acknowledge the fact."

Jane clutched the shirt to her bosom and tried to focus on his words. "I'm sure that he is far more aware of what is going on than we sometimes realize."

He met her gaze, all the teasing and the artifice gone from his pale blue eyes. "I told him I would always care for him."

"You did?" Jane swallowed hard. She was so emotional these days it was hard not to cry, and she did *so* not want to cry in front of Blaize at this moment. "That was very good of you, considering."

"Not really. I failed to tell him I forgave him." His mouth twisted. "In truth, I find myself quite unable to do so."

She nodded. "Perhaps that will come in time."

"I doubt it." He sat down and tugged at his boots. She resisted the impulse to help him, to kneel at his feet, to look up into his beautiful eyes. She focused on his elegant stockinged feet.

"How long do you intend to stay here?"

"How long do you think he has left to live?"

"Not long, by all accounts. He seems to be wasting away and there is nothing that we, or his doctors, can do about it."

"I guessed as much."

Jane headed for the door; cowardice seemed a far better alternative to valor at this moment. "I'll go and see what is keeping my maid. And I'll send a manservant to help you bathe and dress."

He looked up. "Thank you, Jane."

She nodded briefly. "Dinner will be at six in the small dining room." Still clutching his shirt, she made it to the door and turned the handle.

"Do we have any guests at dinner?"

"No, it will just be us, although I'm sure the food will be plentiful. Amy is an excellent cook."

"I know. You forget, I grew up with her and watched her learn at her mother's elbow."

Of course. Sometimes she forgot it was his home too, more his than hers, and he could evict her from it in a second if he chose to. She swallowed down her unease and the sensation that he was watching her like a cat. She would not sleep with him. While dinner was being served, she would have Molly remove some of her clothing and prepare one of the guest chambers for her use.

"Is Sir Derek a frequent visitor to my house?"

Jane glanced over her shoulder at Blaize and opened her eyes wide. "Oh yes. He has been such a comfort to me since my return from London. I don't know what I would do without him."

To her annoyance, Blaize's smile emerged, the one that said he was simply humoring her. "Laying it on a bit too thick, my dear?"

She stiffened and smiled right back at him, showing her teeth. "Didn't you tell me that I could fuck whoever I wanted once I got home? I'm simply reviewing my options and Sir Derek is not only a fine specimen of manhood, but remarkably convenient." She noted his suddenly blank face and let his shirt slip through her suddenly nerveless fingers. "I'll see you at dinner."

She sped off down the corridor, half hoping Blaize would come after her but also relieved when he didn't. She ran down the stairs and paused by the door to the kitchen wing, her heart thumping wildly. She wasn't ready to forgive him yet, just because he'd turned up and seen his father. She deserved more. So why was she so flustered? Perhaps seeing Blaize on his knees, begging, would be a good place to start though . . .

23

Dinner was excellent, not that Minshom was surprised. Word of his return had spread through the great house, and everyone who'd known him both as a boy and as a young married man had come to see him, congratulate him on his return and commiserate about his father. He found it difficult to understand the lack of animosity toward him and wondered if perhaps the servants had known more about the true nature of his relationship with his father than he dared to contemplate.

There was animosity present though, in the form of his wife who sat opposite him through the meal without smiling at him or answering any of his cordial questions with more than one-word answers. She looked tired, with dark circles beneath her eyes and her cheeks sallow. He was also concerned by her lack of appetite. She spent most of the meal pushing the succulent food around her plate and pretending to eat.

Minshom sipped at his wine and noticed Jane wasn't drinking either. He gestured at her glass. "Is the wine not to your liking?"

She wrinkled her nose at him. "It is fine, thank you, my lord."

"I hate to drink alone. You didn't poison this bottle, did you?"

"I didn't think to." She shrugged. "What a missed opportunity."

Minshom sighed and put down his glass. "What do you want from me, Jane? I did what you asked, I came back to see my father. It was one of the hardest things I've ever had to do in my life, and yet you are treating me with complete disdain."

"Which is exactly how you treat me, my lord."

"As I said, what do you want?"

She met his gaze in the candlelight, her hazel eyes clear. "I don't want anything from you." Her hand unconsciously settled over her stomach. "I have everything I need here at Minshom Abbey and your promise to leave me alone forever."

"I don't remember promising any such thing."

"You said you didn't want me, that you had everything you wanted in London."

He pretended to frown. "I don't recall that conversation at all."

Jane leaned across the table, one hand planted perilously close to the apple pie. "You are impossible."

"Am I?" He faced her. "Are you carrying my child?"

She sat back down and busied herself with her napkin.

"Jane . . ."

"Why would you care?"

"Because I would like to know if I am going to be a father again." He forced himself not to flinch away from her obvious distress, reached across the pie to hold her hand.

"I think I am." Her smile was wobbly. "If not, I am simply going into a decline and will soon be dead, so you can marry again at will." She tried to snatch her hand back but he resisted her efforts. "I'll write and tell you if things go awry."

"And what if things go well? Will you write and tell me then?"

"You said you didn't care."

"I lied." He struggled to find the right words to heal the world of hurt he sensed in her. He felt so inadequate because he'd never ever tried to comfort anyone before in his pitiful life.

"Then I will write and tell you."

He studied her shaking fingers, smoothed his endlessly over them. "Will you let me see the child?"

"Of course. Why would you think I would not?"

He swallowed hard. "Because of what happened before?"

"Blaize . . ." The hint of tears in her voice almost undid him. "I told you . . ."

"Because of Nicholas." He brought her fingers to his lips and kissed them, tried to force himself to be honest, to share part of himself that was still almost too painful to bear. "I could not live with myself if I hurt another child. I'd rather stay away."

Silence fell and eventually he was forced to look at her.

"Blaize, is that why you sent me away, because you were *afraid*?"

He let go of her fingers and sat back. "That wasn't the only reason, you know that."

"But . . ."

He shot to his feet. God, this was too hard. He simply couldn't bear it. "If you will excuse me?" He shoved back his chair and blundered his way out of the room and up the stairs. In his bedroom, Jane's maid was piling Jane's possessions on the bed.

"Excuse me, my lord, I was just carrying out her ladyships' orders. I wasn't expecting . . ."

He waved her apologies away and backed out of the room. Of course Jane didn't want to sleep with him. Who would? Only the scum who understood him, who craved the sexual oblivion he did. That's why he'd always been so fascinated and intrigued by Anthony Sokorvsky and David Gray, men who were able to set aside their pasts, who refused to be dominated by him and had found happiness.

He opened the door in front of him and found himself in the old nursery. Distantly he noticed that it had been cleaned and given a fresh coat of paint. Jane had obviously been busy. He walked slowly toward the fireplace and stared at the old wing chair that still stood there and sat down.

He'd sat there that last night with Nicholas, held him cradled against his chest and sung nonsense rhymes to him until he'd slept . . . and woken to find that Nicholas slept on and could not be roused.

His father hadn't helped, had accused him of deliberately killing his heir simply from spite, and for one horrified second, Minshom had looked at Jane and thought she agreed with his father. Had waited for her to fly to his defense and waited in vain.

"Blaize?"

He looked up. She was there, of course, had come after him. Had he wanted that all along? Jane to keep coming after him even when he was impossible? He supposed he had. She came around and knelt at his feet, tears falling down her cheeks. She wasn't beautiful when she cried, but he'd rather look at her than at any other person in England.

"After I thought you sided with my father and accused me of murdering Nicholas, I knew I had to leave you. But I also knew I had to get even with my father for his deliberate meddling in our marriage. I found Robert and took him into my father's bedchamber, let my father find us fucking. I wanted him to see what a monster he'd created."

Minshom shrugged. "Of course, my father was enraged and he tried to shoot Robert, shouting that I was unnatural, perverted, a disgrace to my name. And I shouted back, told him to go to hell and that he was the real pervert. Then I watched him fall to the floor in convulsions. I forced Robert to come away with me and left my father there writhing on the carpet."

"I didn't know that."

Minshom smiled at Jane. "Hardly anyone does. It's not exactly something to be proud of, is it? Destroying your father, alienating your wife and killing your son all in one night."

Jane put her hand on his knee. "You were distraught and that was my fault. I didn't stand up for you against your father. I let you down. You didn't kill Nicholas and you might have provoked your father, but he made his own choices too."

He took her hand, his fingers shaking so much he could barely manage it. "And you? Have I lost you, Jane? Because if I have, I have no idea why I should bother to continue my existence."

"I'm here."

He looked down at her and drew her up onto his knees, kissed her soft mouth until she kissed him back. "I'm sorry, love. Sorry for everything."

She drew back and stared at him. "Did you just apologize to me?"

"I believe I did."

She made as if to jump off his lap. "Mayhap I should get a pen and paper and make you write it down, for I doubt I shall ever hear you say those words again."

He held her close and kissed his way down the side of her neck. "Perhaps later, Jane. I would much prefer to be inside you now." He looked into her eyes.

"I would like that too. I've missed you."

"I've missed you too."

He kissed each tear away on her cheeks, ravaged her mouth so slowly and thoroughly that she moaned and pressed against him, her nipples tight, and the scent of her arousal driving him wild. Her hand drifted down to his buckskin breeches and released his straining cock, her fingers cool against his heated flesh as she wrapped them around his shaft.

"I want you, Jane," he whispered in between kisses, "I want you more than I can breathe and it scares me to death."

She kissed him back, murmured reassurances and coaxed him into bringing her down over his shaft and settling inside her. When she began to move on him, he groaned with every stroke, let her take him, let her control the pace and passion of his orgasm, let her love him.

He came in thick shuddering waves, one hand buried in her hair, the other on her hip holding her down on his pumping cock. She collapsed over him, her head nestled against his shoulder and he held her tight.

After a while, he kissed her cheek. "Do you want to go to bed?"

"In a moment."

He found himself smiling into the darkness at her sleepy tone and stayed still, content to listen to the sounds of the countryside, so different from those of the town. He felt more at peace with Jane in his arms than he had ever felt before in his life. But all the same—he would also like his bed.

"Thomas Wesley isn't going back to India. I thought we might invite him down for a visit. Perhaps we can fuck him together."

There was no response other than a drowsy murmur of assent. Minshom tried again.

"Did you know Anthony Sokorvsky is getting married?"

Jane stiffened and then raised her head. He could just see the indignant shine in her hazel eyes.

"Why did you say that?"

"To wake you up? To persuade you to move into a more comfortable spot for lovemaking."

"Oh." She sighed. "Did you wish him well?"

"Sokorvsky? I did. He and his intended see me as some kind of perverted cupid."

"You?"

He shrugged as he picked her up and headed for the door. "Indeed. Some nonsense about my devilish plans throwing them together or something."

"I suppose they are right."

He kicked open the door to their bedroom, appreciating the soft glow of the fire and the shadows of the large four-poster bed. He laid Jane gently in the center of the bed and stood over her, rapidly dispensing with his clothes.

"Apparently, I'm responsible for the happiness not only of Robert and Captain Gray, but Sokorvsky and Lady Justin."

"And us."

He stared down at her. "No, love. That's all due to you." He reached forward to unbutton her gown and froze when she brought her hands up and crossed them over her bodice. "You don't want me?"

Jane grimaced. "It's just that I'm a little plumper than I think I should be at this stage of a pregnancy. I don't want to shock you."

"Do you think I care about that? You could be the size of an elephant and I'd still want to look at you."

"Thank you, I think."

She hesitated again and he realized he was holding his breath. "Have you changed your mind about being with me?" He took an unsteady step back, felt more vulnerable than he had ever been in his life before. "I can sleep somewhere else . . ."

She sat up, pushed her long hair out of her face and held out her hand. "No, that's not what I want. It's just that I know you are as scared as I am about having another child . . ."

"I'm not scared."

"Blaize . . ."

"I'm terrified."

She nodded. "Which is why I'm reluctant to share what Mistress Goody told me yesterday."

He struggled to breathe. "Tell me."

"She said I was so big there might be more than one child."

"Good God." He blinked slowly and then slid down to his knees, still holding her hand. She crawled closer to the edge of the bed to look down at him.

"It's not certain, but Mistress Goody is very experienced."

"I know, she was at my birth." Was that his voice, that thin, reedy piping sound? He licked his lips. "How the hell are we going to manage, Jane?"

She yanked on his hand until he got back on his feet and then wrapped her arms around him. "I don't know." He looked down at her and realized he had the opportunity denied to his father—to make things right, to turn his life around and make Jane and his children proud of him.

"Jane, I know I don't deserve your trust, but will you trust me anyway?"

She studied him carefully and then nodded. "I'll try."

"Then I swear to you that I'll do everything in my power to protect you and our children from harm."

"I know that."

He climbed onto the bed with her and held her close. Things were far from perfect. He'd have to work hard to regain her trust and to sort out the complications that were bound to occur in their far-from-orthodox love life. But for the first time in his life, he truly believed they could be happy. If he allowed himself to be happy, if he allowed himself to love. He took a deep breath.

"I love you, Jane."

"I always knew that." She turned her head to look at him, her expression serious. "Now you just have to show me."

Something strange happened to his voice and he had to clear his throat several times. "That will be my pleasure."

"And mine too, I hope."

He rolled her over onto her back and leaned over her, took his time undressing her and told her she looked as beautiful as ever. He kissed her soft mouth until he'd mastered the absurd feeling that he might be about to cry. Minshoms never cried. Jane kissed him back and he positioned himself between her thighs and slid home.

He paused to blow out the candle beside the bed before he started to move inside her. If by chance his emotions did overwhelm him, and he feared they might, Jane would never notice in the darkness. And even if she did, she'd understand, and he'd deny it completely. He smiled as she walked her feet up the backs of his thighs to keep him close. And that was exactly why she was the only woman he had ever wanted.

Can't get enough of Kate Pearce and her
House of Pleasure series?
Then please turn the page for an exciting sneak peek of
the next sizzling installment,
SIMPLY FORBIDDEN!

1

Knowles House, England, 1822

"Why on earth did you invite him, Christian?" Lisette Delornay-Ross nudged her twin's arm and nodded at the corner of the sunny breakfast room where Major Lord Gabriel Swanfield read the newspaper and continued to ignore everyone around him.

"I didn't invite him." Christian poured himself more coffee. "Philip did."

Lisette leaned her elbows on the table and contemplated her brother. "But he's nowhere near Father's age, so how do they know each other?"

"I've no idea. Why don't you stop bothering me and go and ask Lord Swanfield?"

"Because he'll stare at me as if I'm a worm and then give me a one-word answer that tells me nothing."

"I take it you've already met him then?" Christian smiled. "Is he really that unforthcoming?"

"When I was introduced to him last night he barely bothered to say a word to me." Lisette stood up. "Perhaps I'll go and ask Father. He'll probably tell me the truth."

Christian leaned back in his chair to study her, his blond hair catching the light, his long elegant body shown to advantage in his brown coat and black breeches. "The real question is—why are you so interested in Lord Swanfield?"

"Because I hate being ignored?"

"That's certainly true, but there are plenty of other gentlemen here this week eager to flirt with you. Why not go and bother one of them?"

Lisette frowned. "Don't you like him, Christian?"

"As if you would pay any attention to me if I did." Christian shrugged. "He doesn't mix much in society. In truth, I know very little about him."

"But what you do know of him, you don't like?"

"Don't start, Lis." He sighed. "As I said, if you really want to be nosey, go and talk to the poor man."

"Perhaps I will."

Determined not to be shown up by her brother, Lisette marched across to where Lord Swanfield sat hidden behind his newspaper and cleared her throat. He lowered the paper the merest inch and studied her over the top of it.

"Yes?"

Lisette gave him her sweetest smile. "I just wanted to wish you good morning, my lord. We've scarcely had a chance to speak since your arrival."

The paper came down another three inches, allowing her to look into his eyes. Up close, they were a very dark blue and fringed with long lashes.

"And you are?"

Good lord, the man didn't even remember being introduced to her last night! Lisette kept smiling. "I'm Miss Ross, Lord Philip Knowles's eldest daughter. I'm acting as my father's hostess this weekend."

"Ah. A pleasure, ma'am." His fingers twitched on the newspaper as if he intended to flip it back up and dismiss her, but

Lisette was quicker. If he intended to be short with her, she could definitely be a little forward.

"I was wondering what brought you here on this particular weekend to Knowles House. I don't remember your name being on the guest list." She smiled graciously. "Not that you aren't welcome, of course."

His dark brows drew together. "I'm looking for some horses. Your father told me to come down anytime I liked. I didn't realize all this nonsense would be going on."

"Or else you wouldn't have come."

He met her gaze properly for the first time, a hint of wary surprise in his. "Exactly."

Beneath the careful upper-class cadences of his voice there was a slight northern burr which deepened his tone and made it rougher and far more interesting.

"Well, I'm sorry that we are spoiling your quiet weekend in the countryside."

"Thank you."

He was either incapable of detecting her sarcasm or really quite rude. She couldn't decide which, but both attitudes annoyed her. "You think us frivolous and unworthy of your interest, my lord?"

He started to fold the paper and she caught sight of the deep parallel scars on his left cheek that disappeared below his high collar. "I didn't say that."

"But you obviously think so. I don't believe you've spoken a single word to anyone since you walked into this room."

He raised in eyebrows. "I've spoken to you."

She stared at him for a long moment as she struggled to control her tongue. "I suppose you have. Are you going out with the shooting party this morning?"

A shudder of something that looked like revulsion passed over his face. "No, Miss Ross, I'm not."

"Then would you like to join me and some of the other

ladies in a walk around the estate?" She wasn't quite sure why she made the offer when he was being so objectionable, but she refused to be defeated by any man.

"Unfortunately, I'm already engaged. Your father has found someone to show me around the stables."

"Which is why you came here in the first place."

"Indeed."

He stood up and dropped the newspaper onto the table. She found she had to look up at him, which was unnerving. She'd only viewed him from above last night when her father brought him into the great hall. At five feet eight, she was tall for a woman, but he topped her by at least five inches. He was as lean and elegant as a greyhound, his shoulders accentuated by the confines of his black coat, his long thighs encased in clinging buckskin. He inclined his head the merest inch.

"Good morning, Miss Ross."

She dropped him a quick curtsey. "Good morning, my lord."

He nodded and strolled away, stopped to talk to one of the footmen positioned by the door and was directed on his way.

"Well." Lisette huffed as her half sister, Emily, and her friends came up beside her. "What an incredibly rude man."

"What did he say to you?" Emily inquired, her face flushed and her blue eyes eager.

"He said that he didn't want to be here, and that he'd only come to look at a horse."

"He didn't!"

Lisette smiled at her younger sister's indignant expression. "He most certainly did. I suspect he wishes us all to the devil."

Emily's two friends giggled and whispered at Lisette's language and she reminded herself to be more careful. At eighteen, Emily's prospects for an excellent marriage were much on her mind. Lisette didn't want to spoil anything for Emily by drawing the *ton*'s attention to her less than reputable half sister.

"I wonder if he will attend the ball on Friday."

Lisette sighed at the hopeful gleam in Emily's eyes. What was it about dark-haired brooding men that sent all the young girls into a flutter? In her experience, good-looking men did not make good husbands or lovers, being far too concerned with themselves to care about a woman's feelings.

"I'm not sure if he'll be staying the full week, Emily. Once he's decided on a horse, he'll probably be off."

"Oh." There was a wealth of regret in Emily's response that Lisette tried to ignore. She was very fond of her sister but also frequently amazed at the differences between them. Emily had been protected by her father all her life, whereas Lisette had only met him three years ago. Emily's safe romantic view of the world had never been Lisette's and never would.

"If he does stay, I'm sure he'll dance with you." Lisette patted Emily's shoulder. "He can hardly say no." She paused to consider her own words. "Well, he probably could, but I'm sure Father could persuade him to change his mind."

Emily pouted. "But I don't want him to ask me out of duty. I want him to ask me because he can't *bear* not to dance with me. He is an *earl*, Lisette!"

Lisette struggled not to smile. "Then make yourself pleasant to him over the next few days, and I'm sure he'll come around and ask you to dance. Why wouldn't he?"

"He'd probably rather ask you. What man wouldn't?" Emily looked glum.

Lisette chuckled remembering the complete lack of interest in Lord Swanfield's rather fine eyes. "After the way he just spoke to me, I doubt that."

Emily grabbed her hand. "Oh, shall we have a wager to see who can get him to ask us to dance first? Wouldn't that be fun, Lisette?"

"But I don't want him to dance with me."

"Then you'll let me win, won't you?" Emily smiled at her

companions and the three of them disappeared into the garden, still whispering and giggling.

Lisette smiled fondly at Emily and went to talk to the other guests. The house party wasn't large and was mainly for Emily's benefit as she was going up to London for the Season later in the year. Philip had decided to introduce Emily to some of the other girls who were making their curtsey to the Polite World so that she would feel more comfortable during her debut.

"Well?"

Lisette stopped at the table to look at Christian who was grinning up at her. "Well what?"

"Did Lord Swanfield tell you why he was here?"

"He did, thank you." She made as to go past him and he caught her hand.

"Don't tell me—he's looking for a wife."

"How amusing, Christian. However did you guess?"

His hazel eyes narrowed. "He's not after Emily, is he?"

Lisette disengaged herself from his grasp. "Of course not, although she seems to have developed quite a tendre for him."

"But he's only been here for a few hours!"

"That's all it takes, brother mine—think of Romeo and Juliet."

Christian laughed. "And think how happily that ended." He reclaimed Lisette's hand and walked with her to the door and into the shadowed hallway beyond. "You weren't as silly as Emily when you were eighteen."

"Thank goodness. But there was scarcely an opportunity for me to be silly in a convent-run orphanage was there?"

"That's true, but when we moved to live with *Maman* you certainly made up for it."

There was an edge to Christian's words that made Lisette pause. "What is that supposed to mean?"

"You've gained a reputation, sister mine, a reputation that won't help Emily at all."

Lisette stopped walking completely. "Are you suggesting I'm too 'fast' to associate with my own half sister?"

He regarded her steadily, his long body aligned with hers as he leaned in close. "Yes, I think I am."

"And since when did Emily's well-being and comfort become more important to you than my own?" Lisette was surprised at how much Christian's defection hurt. They'd always had each other. Were things about to change?

Christian sighed. "Lis, that's not what I meant and you know it. I'll always put you first."

"Obviously not and, for what it's worth, your reputation is far worse than mine."

He shrugged. "And I'm a man and so it doesn't matter as much. You might not like it, but that is the way of the world."

Lisette realized she was a snap away from losing her temper. Dealing with obstinate males one after the other was extremely trying. "What do you think I should do? Find a husband and make myself respectable enough to please everyone?"

His smile was wicked. "Well you could always start with Lord Swanfield. I believe you said he was looking for a wife."

Before Lisette could retaliate, Christian was gone, his laughter echoing down the long hallway to the back of the house. She stared after him, her lower lip caught between her teeth. How dare he suggest that she was somehow at fault? She'd been more than polite to Lord Swanfield, endlessly kind to Emily and was being the perfect hostess for her father. What more could she do to ensure the house party went off well—remove herself from it?

But that was what Christian had implied she should do, distance herself from Emily. Lisette set off to the kitchens, her thoughts in turmoil. Perhaps she shouldn't have volunteered to help out this week and would've been better off staying in London with her mother. Philip had already found an elderly relative to chaperone Emily through her first London Season as Helene, Lisette's mother, was hardly a suitable candidate for the job.

Lisette sighed as she fixed a smile on her face. It was too late to change anything now. She would make sure that Emily was protected from any hint of scandal, even if it meant staying in the background for once and behaving herself. Perhaps she should simply sit beside Lord Swanfield and be ignored. She could scarcely get into any trouble with him.

Gabriel Swanfield admired the twenty-stall stables and the large barn beside them and wished he had something half as grand at his property in Cheshire. Not that he ever went there, not that he cared whether the place thrived or rotted to the ground . . .

"My lord?"

He turned to attend to the head coachman who had been assigned to be his guide. "I do apologize, Mr. Green, what were you saying?"

"I was just mentioning that the current Lord Knowles has spent the last few years improving both the stables, the facilities and the breeding stock, sir. We have several very promising colts and youngsters to show you."

"Excellent. I'm also looking for at least one four-year-old and at least a couple more youngsters to bring on."

"Well, we'll be happy to help you, sir. Would you care to walk down to the main paddock?"

Gabriel followed behind the older man and admired the greenness of the fields spreading out around the mellow Elizabethan manor house, the wilderness areas and the maze. In the near-distance he could just see the colorful skirts of the young ladies on the terrace, no doubt getting ready to go for their walk.

He imagined Miss Ross taking charge of them, knew that, like a good sergeant-at-arms, she would have no trouble controlling her troops. She'd startled him that morning with her directness, the way she'd taken him on and left him in the dust. Despite himself, he'd also admired her hazel eyes and fair hair, the high arch of her eyebrow and the determined angle of her chin. For a chit not long out of the schoolroom she was indeed a formidable opponent.

He glanced back at the huddle of ladies and realized they were meandering down toward the stables. He quickened his step and caught up with Mr. Green and enjoyed the sight of the young colts kicking up their heels in the pasture. He pointed at a young black horse.

"That's the one I'd pick."

"You have a good eye, sir. That's Thunderbolt, his lordship's pride and joy."

"Then I doubt he'll be selling him." Gabriel searched the other horses. "What about the gray?"

"That's Shadow. He's a three-year-old and also very promising. I'm sure his lordship would be more than happy to tell you all about him."

"Good." With one eye on the rapidly approaching ladies, Gabriel gestured back at the stables. "Shall we go back and look at the older horses?"

"Yes, sir."

Gabriel managed to avoid the chattering women and took his time peering into all the stalls as Mr. Green told him about each horse. At the end of the second row, he found a horse he liked, a big chestnut-colored gelding. He nodded his approval at Mr. Green.

"Is it all right if I go into his stall and take a good look at him?"

"Of course, sir. That's Wellington. He's got a nice tempera-ment, that one; he's not scared of much." Mr. Green unlocked the door. "Take your time, sir, and if you want me to get him saddled up for you, just give me a shout." He gave a heavy sigh. "I need to go and be civil to the ladies and stop them scaring my horses with all that squeaking they do."

Gabriel went into the small stall and put one hand on Wellington's rump so that the horse knew he was there and hopefully wouldn't kick out. He walked around the side of the horse, noticed the way its ears flicked toward him with interest but without fear. He ran his hand along the horse's flank and up his long neck until he reached his face.

"You're a nice lad, Wellington, aren't you?" The horse whick-ered back and appeared to nod his head. Gabriel scratched under the horse's chin, produced a carrot top Mr. Green had given him and held it out on his palm. "Here you go, boy."

Nice manners, a soft mouth and an intelligent face. Gabriel slid his hand down the horse's front leg and checked his ten-dons, hock and finally his hoof. Then he repeated the process on the three other legs. As he crouched down in the straw, he heard girlish laughter and stayed where he was. Hopefully the ladies would pass him by without noticing him.

To his dismay, they seemed to stop right outside the stall door.

"I'm sure Mr. Green said that Lord Swanfield was around here somewhere. I wonder where he has gotten to?"

"If he has any sense, he's probably running back to the house as fast as he can. No man wishes to encounter a large group of ladies while he's talking horseflesh."

Ah, he recognized that second voice, the slight hint of a French accent, the intelligence behind every word. It was Miss Ross, but who was she talking to?

"Well, I'm disappointed. I wanted to begin my campaign to get him to ask me to dance at the ball."

"As I said, he probably won't be here by then. He doesn't strike me as a particularly social man."

"But I want to dance with him. He is an earl and he is so tall and handsome."

Gabriel grimaced as the unknown voice described him. She epitomized exactly what he disliked about the women of the *ton*; all she cared about was his title and his looks. And God knows, he had no illusions about his looks and his title was a sham.

"Lord Swanfield is also far too old for you."

"He's not. Father says he's only just turned thirty."

"And you are only eighteen, Emily." Miss Ross laughed, but there was no malice in it. "Think how old he'll be when you are twenty-five, positively ancient!"

There was a slight pause. "I hadn't thought of that."

"And five years after that, you'll have to push him around in a bath chair and take him to Bath for the waters."

Despite himself Gabriel grinned. How clever of Miss Ross to point out all his potential failings as a husband rather than outright forbid the younger girl to think of him.

The girl named Emily sighed. "Well, I suppose we should go back. The others will be waiting for us."

"Yes, indeed we should. Maybe you can capture Lord Swanfield's interest at the dinner table with your sparkling wit and conversation."

"What an excellent idea. I'm sure I can win our wager and get him to promise to dance with me before you can."

Gabriel's smile disappeared as the two women made their way back along the row of stalls to the exit. Miss Ross had entered into a wager, had she? He discounted the younger girl, knew he would have no problem disappointing her in short order. But Miss Ross? Watching her try to exert herself to win his favor might be amusing.

Gabriel stood up and brushed the hay from his breeches. Perhaps he would stay on until the Hunt Ball after all.